The Blue Ridge Resistance

The New Homefront,
Volume 3

By Steven C. Bird

D1125278

The Blue Ridge Resistance: The New Homefront, Volume 3

Written and published by Steven C. Bird at Homefront Books

Edited by Sara Jones at www.torchbeareredits.com
Final review by Carol Madding at
hopespringsediting@yahoo.com
Illustrated by Keri Knutson at www.alchemybookcovers.com

Print Edition (8.23.15)
ISBN-13: 978-1507806647
ISBN-10: 1507806647

www.stevencbird.com
www.homefrontbooks.com
scbird@homefrontbooks.com
www.facebook.com/homefrontbooks

Table of Contents

Table of Contents 3

Disclaimer 5

Dedication 6

Introduction 7

Chapter 1: The Taming of the Ewes 9

Chapter 2: The New Life 15

Chapter 3: Meeting of the Minds 19

Chapter 4: The Burden of Blessings 26

Chapter 5: Facing Reality 34

Chapter 6: The Unexpected Visitor 43

Chapter 7: News from the North 50

Chapter 8: Prepping for the Move 57

Chapter 9: A Community Venture 62

Chapter 10: Getting Underway 69

Chapter 11: Keeping Watch 79

Chapter 12: Beyond Del Rio 86

Chapter 13: The Mounted Patrol 90

Chapter 14: Pressing On... 95

Chapter 15: Daryl's Dilemma 101

Chapter 16: Rabbit Stew 106

Chapter 17: Helping Hands 115

Chapter 18: Return of the Guardians.................................. 120

Chapter 19: Moving On 125

Chapter 20: Living in Hell 135

Chapter 21: The Spider's Web... 138

Chapter 22: Killing the Spider 147

Chapter 23: Intensive Care..160

Chapter 24: A Fork in the Road 164

Chapter 25: Rendering Honors...170

Chapter 26: Keeping Watch 177

Chapter 27: The Encounter...183

Chapter 28: Rude Awakenings..191

Chapter 29: An Unbearable Loss 197

Chapter 30: The New Reality..201

Chapter 31: Insurgents 206

Chapter 32: A Tragedy Fulfilled 215

Chapter 33: Reprisals 217

Chapter 34: A Helping Heart..223

Chapter 35: Farmageddon 226

Chapter 36: The Pursuit..233

Chapter 37: Friendships through Fire 241

A Note from the Author 243

Disclaimer

The characters and events in this book are fictitious. Any similarities to real events or persons, past or present, living or dead, is purely coincidental and are not intended by the author. Although this book is based on real places and some real events and trends, it is a work of fiction for entertainment purposes only. None of the activities in this book are intended to replace legal activities and your own good judgment.

Some items in this series have been changed from their actual likenesses to avoid any accidental sharing of Sensitive Security Information (SSI). The replacement values serve the same narrative purpose without exposing any potential SSI.

Dedication

To my loving wife and children, and all of my friends and colleagues that inspire me and believe in me.

As I continue with this series, the support I have received from family and friends has motivated me to press on and continue to write, which has become a true passion in my life. To be honest, I was the last person I would have expected to be a "novelist." Although always a dreamer with a creative side, I've spent my life devoid of an outlet to channel my thoughts, love, fear, and imagination. When I first began writing *The Last Layover: The New Homefront, Volume 1* on my Android phone's word processing app, I didn't even take myself seriously as a potential author.

Along the way however, family, friends, coworkers, and now colleagues from within the industry, have motivated me to continue to improve and evolve as a writer, keeping sight of the real possibility that someday this could be my full-time career and not just a side project.

I thank each and every one of you who have supported me, constructively critiqued me, and cheered me on during this journey.

Continued from - The Guardians: The New Homefront, Volume 2

Introduction

It was now spring, and after the Guardians' victory over the Muncie gang, there had been relative peace for the confederacy of homesteads. Word of "The Guardians" and how they had dealt with criminal intruders in their area had spread throughout the surrounding region over the course of the winter. This had brought peace and stability to many of the surrounding counties as well. Due to the secret nature of the Guardians, with no one outside of the partnering homesteads ever having encountered them and lived to tell about it, their name grew into an urban legend. Any act of vigilante justice in the region was attributed to them, which, of course, kept the threat of swift and permanent justice on the mind of anyone who might have otherwise attempted to take advantage of the collapsed state of the nation, at least in East Tennessee.

During the winter, Mildred and her cattle were moved back to the Thomas Farm, along with Haley, who was now considered by all to be Mildred's adopted daughter. In addition, Nate, Luke, and Rachel had volunteered to move in with her to help her run the farm. Judith moved in, as well, to help Mildred run her growing household. This was also beneficial, as Evan and Molly's Homefront had already been running at its maximum capacity. In addition, Nate's experience on the Peterson farm in New Mexico, during his journey to find Luke, was a godsend for Mildred, as she was physically unable to tend to her cattle by herself after the loss of her dear husband, Ollie.

The political quagmire that had engulfed the nation after the initial attacks had festered into what seemed an inevitable civil war. The struggle for power between those loyal to the Constitution and those loyal to the president, grew increasingly tense as he attempted to use the state of collapse as an opportunity to remake the United States into his dream of a central-government controlled, socialist state.

The homesteaders had yet to be touched by this political struggle directly, with the exception, of course, of the absence of government and the shattered national infrastructure, but they feared it was only a matter of time before their beloved isolation in the hills of East Tennessee was disrupted by an outside force. They monitored the outside world closely via their HAM radio stations, and met regularly to discuss anything they felt might affect them in the future. In a sense, they had become their own local government.

Chapter 1: The Taming of the Ewes

After the dust had settled from the struggles of the previous fall, Evan acquired a small flock of Katahdin sheep from a man in Del Rio. The man could no longer care for them, as he was setting out on a journey to southern Alabama. He was heading out to link up with surviving family members who had been running a farm and had sent word that they needed his help to keep the place going. Without fuel and other resources, farming had returned to being a labor-intensive endeavor where a large family was once again an asset, as it had been throughout human history prior to the technological advances of the twentieth century.

Evan traded the man a bicycle, a lever action .30-30 rifle, and a box of two hundred rounds of ammunition for his journey, in exchange for twelve ewes and four rams. The flock was comprised of a fairly well mixed gene pool with unrelated rams and several families of ewes. This would give them a good start in regards to breeding, in order to grow the flock. They knew that at some point, however, they would need to find some outside blood to keep the flock genetically diverse enough for the long term.

Over the course of the winter, Evan was amazed at the lack of trust his sheep, especially the ewes, had for humans. "That's a healthy fear to have," he would often joke. He quickly learned that one does not simply put his hands on a ewe without confining her first. He hoped they would eventually warm up to him to make life a bit easier, but alas, they did not. The rams, on the other hand, being much bolder than the ewes, had no problem interfacing with humans. During his short tenure as a shepherd thus far, he learned how to work around their skittish behavior and began to feel quite comfortable with his flock.

He was also pleased that nine of his ewes were pregnant and that all of the pregnancies made it through the winter, and the ewes would be having their spring lambs any day. Considering this, he spent a lot of time watching the flock, trying to be ready when they started to give birth, so that the lambs could be immediately cared for in order to better ensure their survival. He saw this as worthy of his time, rather than having them hidden off in the bushes somewhere, unprotected from predators. The survival of his flock could one day mean the survival of his family in the world they now occupied.

Coyotes, feral dogs, and even the occasional mountain lion had become a big problem in the area. This meant that keeping livestock in a rural area near the woods and forests required a lot of attention. Evan didn't mind; he much preferred four-legged predators over the two-legged ones he used to have to contend with on a much too frequent basis.

Today, Evan was dutifully watching his flock from a hunting tree stand with an accurized DMR-style AR-15. With a Designated Marksman Rifle (DMR), as the military referred to an accurized twenty-inch-barreled M16 with a magnified optic, he could address any predator situations that might arise at long-range, as well as having the magazine capacity of an AR-type rifle in the event he had other problems to contend with.

He had been in that particular stand for several hours and was becoming restless, when he saw something dart through the tall grass, just beyond his flock, as he glassed the area with his binoculars.

He scanned the area, trying to find the target again, when out of the tall weeds, a large coyote sprinted for his flock. The sheep immediately began to panic and run in all directions as the coyote went for one of the pregnant ewes. Evan dropped his binoculars to their strap and quickly shouldered his rifle, zooming in on the altercation with his magnified riflescope. Just as the coyote jumped on the back of the pregnant ewe,

Evan focused on the rear hindquarter of the predator in order to avoid accidentally hitting his own sheep; he then let one of his hand-loaded, 69-grain boat-tail hollow-point rounds fly. The high-speed 5.56mm round instantly knocked the attacking coyote off the back of the panicking sheep.

Since the beginning of the collapse, they had been utilizing those very tree stands for security. It had become standard practice to be rigged up to a climbing rope, with a rappelling harness on, when anyone was in one of the stands. On this occasion, just like many that had come before, this practice proved itself to be immensely valuable. Evan quickly rappelled out of the tree, hit the ground running and sprinted for the downed animal. He knew he had hit the coyote and knocked it off the sheep, but a wounded predator could still be a threat to him or the other sheep if it was not put down hard. He came upon the tall grass where he had lost sight of it from a distance and found the offending coyote dragging its hind legs while whimpering and trying to escape. Evan did not have any personal ill will toward the coyote. They were indeed a threat to his livestock, but as he often joked, a coyote was just a dog being a dog, and he was just a shepherd being a shepherd. In an act of mercy, Evan pulled his .45ACP pistol from its holster and ended the coyote's suffering with a well-placed shot to the head.

He then turned and began to look for the sheep that had been in the grasp of the coyote. He walked the fence line in the direction he thought the sheep had traveled. He followed a faint blood trail to a peach tree that was consumed by vines and weeds, making the type of cover that his sheep generally loved to seek out for shade on a hot, sunny day. He found the young ewe hidden in the foliage, bleeding from several lacerations on her back made by the coyote's teeth and claws. After some wrangling, he managed to get a hold of her and pull her from the weeds. He threw her over his back with her front legs over his right shoulder and her hind legs over his left. He then hiked back to the house with the injured sheep continuously calling out a distress-filled *baah*.

As he approached the house, Molly, who had just been out in the chicken coup collecting eggs, heard the *baah* and saw Evan walking toward the house from a distance. She set down her basket of eggs and ran out to meet him. "What's wrong with the sheep?" she asked in a distressed voice.

"A coyote jumped her," he replied. "I popped it, but where there is one, there are more. I guess we need to stay extra-vigilant, with baby lambs on the way. If a coyote is watching when a ewe is giving birth, we will lose two at once."

"Bring her into the barn," Molly said. "We can confine her in one of the horse stalls that we're not using until she gives birth. I'll also give her some antibiotics for her wounds and try to stay on top of it. The last thing she needs is an infection with a lamb to bear and feed."

Evan and Molly had stocked up on livestock medication prior to the collapse as one of their preps. Drugs, such as antibiotics for livestock, are generally the same as those for humans, except without the inflated price and the need for a prescription.

"You know, maybe we need to put all of the pregnant ewes in the barn until after the lambs are born, just in case," Evan said, after thinking more about the threat his flock faced.

"Probably not a bad idea," she said. "We can always feed them hay and a little grain to get them by."

"Yep, let's do it then," he said as he picked the ewe up to carry her to the barn. "I'll take the livestock trailer out to the pasture with the tractor and round them up. This is one of the times I wish we had enough fencing to reach from there all the way to here. It sure would make moving them easier."

"Yes, in a perfect world," she said as she walked along to the barn with him.

As the two of them took the injured sheep into the barn, Griff came out of the house and flagged him down.

"What's up?" Evan asked.

"The group wants to have a meeting," said Griff. "They were asking if someone here could make it to the Murphy place tomorrow at noon."

"The Murphy place, huh?" Evan replied. "That's odd. I wonder what they have up their sleeves."

"I'm not sure," Griff said. "It does make one curious, though. Anyway, I'm on watch tomorrow. If you and Jason want to go, I'll hold down the fort."

"That sounds good. Is someone from the Thomas Farm going?" Evan asked.

"I'll find out. Judy is on the radio talking to Daryl Moses now," said Griff as he turned to go back inside.

"Okay, let me put this ewe in the barn for Molly and I'll be right in," Evan said as he turned and continued into the barn.

After getting the injured ewe set up in one of the stalls, Evan joined the others inside the house. He met them down in the basement where the CB radio base station and HAM radios were located. "So what's the deal?" Evan asked as they all gathered around the radio.

Judy, who had replaced Judith as the Homefront's communications person, replied, "Daryl didn't give much detail. He just asked that we bring someone from the Thomas Farm with us as well, so that all properties are represented. I've already contacted them. Nate said he would be able to go. He said just stop by on your way, and he will ride along."

"Hmmm, I wonder why the Murphy place," Evan thought aloud. "Well, we will find out tomorrow, I guess. Where is Jason?" he asked.

"He's in the woods teaching the boys a few things about hunting," answered Sarah.

Evan just smiled and said, "Do me a favor. When you see him, tell him about the meeting and that I'd like him to go along."

"Sure thing," Sarah replied.

As Evan walked back outside to finish dealing with his flock, he couldn't help but be concerned about the nature of Daryl's request. Life had been so peaceful over the past several months that he always felt as if the peace was too good to be true, and that it would all be shattered at any time. Was this it? Was something about to be brought to light that would interrupt their peaceful bliss?

Chapter 2: The New Life

Life on the Thomas Farm had been bustling with activity as of late. Nate and Lucas were busy making repairs to the home from the deterioration it had suffered from its temporary vacancy, in addition to their constant duties tending to the herd of cattle and Mildred's other farm animals.

Rachel had set up a small medical office in the basement so that an exterior exit could be used to see patients from the nearby homesteads if need be. Using the basement entrance not only added to patient privacy, but the sick would not have to pass through the main living quarters to see her, reducing the chances of spreading a communicable disease.

With all of the bustling activity, Mildred was happier than she had been in a long time. Ollie's untimely death had forever altered the course of her life, but now, with a new family that she loved dearly, and with young Haley in her care, she felt a renewed sense of purpose. On top of the day-to-day chores involved with running a household via mostly primitive means, Mildred and Judith were getting their things in order to plant their spring vegetable garden. They were excited to be using the opportunity to teach both Haley and Rachel the valuable life skills of growing their own food. Neither of the two had any previous exposure to self-sufficient food production, and Mildred insisted that everyone participate in order to pass those critical skills along to the younger generations.

As the evening drew near, Nate and Luke returned to the house after having spent a long, hard day mending fences and tending to the livestock. As they approached the house, they passed by the garden, where the ladies were hard at work, marking off the plots and planning where each of the vegetables would be planted, when Mildred shouted to them, "Come on over here, boys."

Nate and Luke altered their course and joined them at the garden as Nate said, "Yes, ma'am."

"Nate, do you think you boys would be able to plow and disc the garden for us tomorrow?" she asked. "We would like to get our early vegetables in the ground as soon as possible. It seems as if the threat of frost is past us now, and turning the soil is all we are waiting on."

"Yes, ma'am," Nate replied. "Well, after I get back from the meeting at the Murphy place, that is. I would put Luke on it while I'm gone, but he's never worked as a sod buster before, so he needs to do it with me the first time," Nate said, shooting his brother a crooked smile.

"Oh, yes, that's right," she replied. "Well, if you could just put that at the top of your to-do list, I would be grateful. What's that meeting about, anyway?"

"I'm not sure," he replied. "Judith got a call from the Homefront about it, and all they said was one of us needed to go, so I volunteered. You'll be in good hands with Luke while I'm away. If he gets bored, just put him to work doing laundry or something," Nate said, taking another stab at his brother.

"Ha," Luke replied sarcastically. "I've still got the roof work to do tomorrow, so I won't get bored. Don't you worry about that, brother. There probably isn't really a meeting, anyway; it's probably just an excuse to get out of work to sneak off and see Peggy for the day," he said in jest.

Rachel grinned at Luke. She loved the way the two picked at each other. She had noticed a big change in Luke's behavior, now that he was reunited with his family. Back in Texas, he was all business, only occasionally letting his true emotions shine through. Now that he was back with his mother and brother, he was lighthearted and carefree, taking each day as it came and simply enjoying every minute.

"I wish you were right," replied Nate. "That's surely where I would rather be right now."

Nate's mother, Judith, just smiled and asked, "So how are things going between the two of you, anyway? You keep too much to yourself, just like your father. I always had to pry something out of him if I wanted to know anything," she said, beaming with affection.

"It's all great, Mom," Nate replied. "I was actually going to ask Mildred if it would be okay if Peggy and Zack came over for a few days each week. They could stay in my room, and I'll take the couch. We need more time together, and little Zack needs more than just an occasional visit from me if we are ever going to get any closer. The poor kid is so distant, it takes the first day for him to warm up to me; at that point, I'm usually leaving to head back over here."

"Absolutely!" Mildred replied. "This is your home now, too, so treat it as such. Just honor that girl in my house the way God wants, and she can spend all the time here that she needs, day or night."

Nate smiled at Mildred's response and said, "Thank you, ma'am, and I will."

Judith beamed with pride. She had grown to love Peggy as a daughter, even before Nate was in the picture. The thought of her possibly, someday, being her daughter-in-law was a dream come true. How could a world so screwed up work out so perfectly, she often wondered.

Later that day, Mildred took her evening walk up on the hill and sat underneath her and Ollie's favorite magnolia tree, next to his grave. She had been visiting him there every evening since her return to their farm. As she watched the beautiful Tennessee sunset, she smiled and said aloud, "Ollie, you would be so happy to see how things have worked out. Our home is, once again, full of love and happiness. Little Haley is a godsend to what was my aching heart, and the love that the Hoskins family brings to our home fills it with warmth and happiness. I only wish you were here to feel it with me, but somehow, I know you are. Unless you or God gives me other guidance, I believe I will leave the farm and the care of Haley to the Hoskins family when I finally join you. I can't think of better hands for it to be in, and I know they will treat it with the love and respect that we always have."

She sat there for a few more minutes, enjoying the cool spring breeze as it flowed through the hills and said, "Well, my love, it's getting dark. I will talk to you again tomorrow. I love you." With a smile on her face, Mildred stood up and walked back down the hill toward her home. She could hear laughter from inside the house as she approached the back porch and was so happy to once again be living in a world surrounded by love everywhere she looked.

Chapter 3: Meeting of the Minds

Early the next morning, Evan and Jason prepared their daypacks, as had been their routine for each and every outing. Although the relative peace in the area gave them hope that someday soon, they may be able to stop preparing for the worst at all times, but for now, they felt it was still the prudent thing to do. With the reduced threat levels in the area, Jason had been leaving his Remington at home, and like Evan, carried a VZ58 carbine with the stock folded when off the property to cover most situations that might arise. In addition to their VZs and sidearms, they still carried their handheld radios, first aid kits, and flashlights as a minimum level of gear, even though it seemed to merely be extra weight to carry around, lately. After all they had been through, however, they just could not bring themselves to completely lower their guard.

After breakfast, they said their goodbyes, climbed aboard their bikes and headed out for the Thomas farm to join up with Nate. As the two men rode down the road toward the farm, Jason said, "Man, do you think we are going be riding bikes for the rest of our lives?"

"I would be okay with that," replied Evan. "So long as we have peace and quiet around here, I can live just fine without gas stations, traffic, and all the other crap that I've learned not to miss about our formerly civilized world."

"Yeah, good point," Jason replied. "We're gonna need some more fuel soon, though. Either we find some or we put together a moonshine still and start cooking up some alcohol to burn. Either way, without gas and diesel, we will be plowing with a donkey in no time, and the sheep will have to be our lawn mowers."

"Yeah, I've been thinking the same thing," Evan replied. "We may have to venture out beyond the local area for supplies, as I doubt they will simply come to us."

Jason replied with a silent nod as both men pedaled up the last hill leading to the Thomas Farm. When they reached the top, Jason looked down at the ground while catching his breath, and noticed some footprints that stood out to him in the dirt covering the road. "Ev...," he said as he stopped his bike and dismounted.

"What is it?" Evan said as he brought his bike to a halt alongside.

"Look at these tracks," Jason said, pointing at the ground as he knelt to get a closer look. "There are at least five or six different patterns of shoe soles here. There isn't anyone around here that walks in a group that large down this road. Everyone around here is pretty much on a bike, horse, or tractor when traveling this road."

"Well, let's get going," Evan replied. "The meeting that Daryl has called may have something to do with observed activity in the area."

"Roger Roger," Jason replied as he got back on his bike.

They rode on in to the Thomas Farm, where they found Nate ready and waiting. He had the Bushmaster AR-15 that he had recovered from the Muncie gang's attack on the Homefront last fall, as well as his old, faithful Beretta M9, which he retrieved shortly thereafter. Nate was starting to look more like a farm boy than the grizzled, road-worn soldier image he wore when he first arrived. His hair was getting shaggy and curled out from underneath his hat, and instead of government-issued camouflage pants, he wore old brown Carhartt work pants and a green, hooded sweatshirt over a thermal underwear top.

"Good morning, fellas," he said as Evan and Jason climbed off their bikes.

"Nate, you are starting to look and sound more like a good ol' Tennessee boy every day," Evan said with a laugh.

"Well, I'll take that as a compliment, sir," replied Nate as he tipped his hat. "I've never met people I've felt more comfortable with in my life, so I might as well assimilate, because as far as I am concerned, this place is home."

"Damn straight!" Jason said. "I'm a transplant myself, and I hear ya on that one."

"So what's this meeting about, Ev?" asked Nate.

"You know as much as I do," he replied. "Daryl didn't give any specifics over the radio, but that's to be expected considering COMSEC and all. Are you about ready to go?"

"Yes, sir; I've got that old mare Mildred traded the two cows for all saddled up. I figured I would get her out and stretch her legs. I kind of miss workin' horses from my days on the Peterson farm back in New Mexico. I might have only been there a few months, but that way of life sure sunk its teeth into me."

"Well, that's real livin' so that's understandable," Evan replied.

Jason added, "I have a feeling that's what the average person's lifestyle is gonna evolve back into in the future if this mess doesn't get sorted out soon. Once the hordes of the desperate, the looters, and the dependent die off or change, the self-sufficient will be all that's left."

Evan nodded and said, "We already get closer to that every day. That's one of the reasons this government hates the self-sufficient type. Those who are dependent on government are, by their very nature, under the government's control. We, on the other hand, resist that same control and just want to be left alone. If I were the president, I would prefer a country of self-sufficient citizens. They would be a piece of cake to govern. They would basically take care of themselves and leave me alone. But then again, those who seek such an office are seeking control in the first place, so I guess me, or someone like me, wouldn't be in such a position to begin with."

"Well, guys, let's get going," Jason said as he threw his leg over his bike. "I'm anxious to see what's going on."

"I'll get saddled up and meet you fellas out on the road," Nate said as he donned his pack and walked around behind the house to get his horse.

With that, Evan and Jason pedaled their bikes out to the main road. Jason came to a stop to wait on Nate, with Evan stopping alongside. Jason looked at Evan and in a very to-the-point manner, he said, "We need horses."

"I was thinking the same thing," Evan replied. "If things remain the way they are, we may even need to plow with one before long, once all the available liquid fuels dry up."

"That or find an old turn of the century steam tractor," Jason said with a chuckle.

"You laugh, but that would actually be a good thing to have. You would never run out of fuel as long as you had water and combustible material," replied Evan.

They heard the *clip-clop* of Nate's horse and turned to see him ride up alongside them. Nate pulled back on the reins, bringing his horse to a stop, and said, "All set?"

Evan put his foot up on his bike's pedal and said, "Yep, let's get going." He pushed forward, getting the journey underway.

~~~~

After an uneventful ride out to the Murphy place, Evan, Jason, and Nate arrived to find that most of the other homestead representatives had already made it. Daryl walked down off the front porch to meet them as they came up the driveway. Daryl, wearing his typical frontiersman attire, reached out and shook Evan and Jason's hands as Nate dismounted his horse. Daryl then tipped his hat to Nate as he was tying his horse to the railing. "Gentleman, glad you made it. Everyone is here now, so we might as well get started."

Evan, Jason, and Nate accompanied Daryl to the house, where everyone had gathered in the living room. Daryl had arrived early and opened all of the doors and windows to let the house air out, as it was a bit dusty and damp from being uninhabited for so long.

Daryl stood in front of the group and said, "Thank you all for coming. It's good to see everyone gathered together; we really need to make sure that happens more often. The reason I called this meeting is that we have been receiving word from over the airwaves, as well as word of mouth from folks down in Del Rio, that things aren't going so well out there. Many reports are coming in saying that the use of drones in our own skies has been increasing dramatically, and that the intel they collect is being used to develop a containment strategy to begin to put the squeeze on those who have not been living according to the president's edicts."

"There is also talk that the UN's so-called 'peacekeepers' have been arriving in large numbers and staging near the major population centers. Some folks have even reported that there have been drone and conventional airstrikes inside our own borders, but none of that has been confirmed. Jack Rouse of the Blue Ridge Militia says he believes that once they have their UN and other forces in place, they will begin to push out into the more rural areas to present an exhibition of force to those who may consider themselves to be living on their own terms. This, of course, will all be in the name of peace, stability, and the safety of the general public, as we've seen time and time again throughout history."

Evan raised his hand, spoke up, and said, "We have noticed that some of the HAM operators we used to get regular updates from have been off the air. If the administration is starting to tighten its grip, that would explain their silence."

"Good point," Daryl replied. "We've noticed the same thing."

"Those HAM operators have either figured out they had better lie low or they've been silenced. Either way, something is up," added Jason.

Everyone spoke amongst themselves for a few moments and then Daryl continued, "In addition to that news, now that spring has arrived, there seems to be a renewed wave of human migration taking place. People who survived the winter hunkered down are now on the move again in search of food and shelter. Most of the packaged foods will have been consumed or have gone bad by now; this leaves fresh foods, such as what we all raise and grow, as the only available resources. I fear that people, who will naturally head for the more rural areas like ours to avoid the horrors of the cities, will be looking at our resources and wanting them. We've had several sightings of groups of anywhere from five to ten people making their way through this area."

Jason interrupted. "That explains the tracks we saw back on the main road near the Homefront."

Daryl nodded and replied, "Most of the groups that have been observed passed through during the night. I guess even the average person is starting to think tactically."

"That, or those who don't, have been thinned from the herd by now," said Charlie Blanchard.

There were a few under-the-breath chuckles and comments from within the group as Daryl got back on point saying, "Either way, we think the lull of the winter may be over. This house, as well as the Muncie place, is ripe for the picking by squatters and vagrants. We only check on them from time to time, and even if you don't consider the threat of outsiders taking up residence here, they are deteriorating quickly from neglect and will be lost to the community if we don't do something."

"What do you propose?" Evan asked.

Daryl replied, "Well, we wanted to discuss it before we mentioned it to Jason and Griff, and we have already come to a unanimous consensus. We would like Jason and his family to take one of the homes, and Griff and his family to take the other. We would have more eyes on the area that way, and we would be ensuring who our neighbors are going to be, instead of having to deal with squatters. Besides, with all they have already done for the rest of us, they more than deserve to be permanent residents with their own homesteads."

Evan looked at Jason, who seemed a bit taken back by the gesture and said, "We would sure miss you at the Homefront, but he's right. That, and your family deserves a place of their very own. I think it's a great idea."

"Wow, I don't know what to say," replied Jason, who was caught off guard by the offer.

Daryl then said, "Just go back home and think it over, talk to Griff, and if you guys decide to take us up on the idea, you two work out who will be where and just let us know. We will all pitch in to help you make all of the repairs and cleanup necessary to get you moved in."

After a few more minutes of chatter and general discussion, the official side of the meeting began to draw to a close. The residents all shared stories of their recent projects and endeavors. They always learned a lot from each other, as the homesteading lifestyle without outside goods and services was still relatively new to most of them. Ever since Ollie's tragic death had united them as more than just trading partners, they gained wisdom and support from one another's failures and accomplishments, helping them to thrive in this new world they lived in, rather than merely surviving.

Chapter 4: The Burden of Blessings

Back on the Thomas Farm, Luke was on the roof of the house, repairing some damaged shingles that had been causing a leak. He was not experienced at such a repair, but did just as his brother said; which was to look at how the old shingles are installed, and do that. He was installing the replacement shingles and was quite proud of his self-taught accomplishment so far. He hoped to have the job completed before Nate returned home from the community meeting at the Murphy place. There were two reasons for this: to show his brother that he was capable of such a feat and to avoid the harassment that would surely come from needing Nate's help.

As he tacked down the last of the shingles, he saw a small group of people walking up the driveway toward the house. There appeared to be two women in their late twenties or early thirties with three children, ranging in ages from around five to ten. He immediately went over to the ladder and climbed down to meet them in the driveway before they could reach the house. He had his sidearm holstered on his right side, as he always did, but pulled his shirt to the side to make sure it was in plain view and readily accessible.

Once he reached the ground, he ran over to the front door and yelled inside, "Eyes open—visitors!" He then walked out to the women and said in a polite, but serious voice, "Can I help you?"

One of the women spoke up and said, "We've been on the road for a week now and are out of food for our children. Do you have anything you can spare?"

Nate looked around uneasily and replied, "Are you traveling with anyone else?"

"No, it's just us," the woman said.

"Are you armed?"

The woman replied, "I have a pistol in my backpack. I need it to protect my children, so please don't take it."

"I'm not going to take anything from you. I just need to figure out if you are a threat, and you did just come walking up our drive, not the other way around. You know as well as I do, you can't be too careful these days," Luke replied. "Where are you traveling to? And where did you come from?"

"We're coming from the Richmond, Virginia, area and are on our way to Indiana. We're trying to find some family we have up there, or used to, at least," the woman said.

One of the smaller children grabbed her mother's hand and said, "Mommy, my tummy hurts. When are we going to eat?"

The young mother just shushed the child, whispering to her to be quiet.

The look in the child's eyes was heartbreaking for Luke. He had seen and had been hardened by a lot of pain and misery, but it never gets any easier when it is children who are the ones suffering.

"Stay right here," Luke said in a serious tone. "Don't move. I'll get something for your children to eat."

As he turned to walk into the house, he heard Judith screaming from one of the back windows, "Get out of there! Get out! Luke! They are in the cellar!"

Realizing the women and children had been sent as a diversion, Luke quickly turned and saw that the woman who had been doing the talking was pulling a small revolver from her backpack. He immediately began to draw his pistol and screamed, "No! Drop it! Drop it!"

As she continued to raise the gun toward him, he fired a round at her as her gun simultaneously discharged. He felt as if a bee had stung him in the thigh while everything seemed to go silent and into slow motion. The woman fell backward with the jolt of the impact of the one hundred and eighty grain .40-

caliber bullet from his Glock 22. He stumbled back onto the porch, falling into the seated position while covering the other woman and the children with his pistol. They turned and began to run, leaving the downed woman behind. He couldn't shoot a woman or children in the back, so he lowered his gun and struggled back to his feet to check on the woman on the ground.

He stood over her with one hand on his wound while using the other to cover her with his pistol, just in case. He saw that the round had entered the center of her chest. There was no chance she could still be alive. He then began to limp around to the back of the house to check on the situation Judith warned him about. He found her standing on the back porch, shotgun in hand, pointing frantically at the cellar.

"They broke into the cellar. They were stealing our food," she shouted.

Just then, Rachel came running out of the house in a panic. "You've been shot!" she yelled as she ran over to Luke. He looked down at his leg and began to feel a throbbing, burning pain. He started to feel dizzy and reached over to grab the porch railing as Judith and Rachel, one under each arm, helped him up the steps and into the house. They sat him down on the sofa as Rachel frantically ripped his pants open to get a better look at the wound.

"There isn't much damage," she said, relieved. "The wound cavity is pretty small, and it doesn't look like it went too deep. What kind of gun did she have?" Rachel asked Luke.

"Some little stubby revolver," he said.

Mildred came running up the stairs from the basement. "Haley is downstairs in the basement," she said. She was carrying Ollie's old double-barreled twelve-gauge and had a fire in her eyes that the others had never before seen. "I'm sick of this! Sick of it! I'm sick and tired of having people come, take what is ours, and try to hurt us to get it. Enough!" she screamed as she walked over to the open door leading out to the back porch. "You filthy scoundrels had better keep running," she screamed as she fired both barrels sequentially into the woods in the general direction the men had run to escape. She quickly reloaded and said, "Judith, you watch the front of the house, I'll watch the back. Don't take your eyes off the road and the tree line until Nate is back with Evan and Jason. We don't know if those bastards are coming back for their woman or not, once they realize she is down. Rachel, you take him downstairs to your office and get him all fixed up. We can handle this," Mildred said as she nodded to Judith.

Following Mildred's direction, Rachel led Luke downstairs to her makeshift medical office. She cleaned the wound and removed the bullet from his leg. She wasn't sure what caliber it was, not being a gun aficionado herself, but she was thankful it was small and did not seem to carry much energy. After treating him as best she could with what she had, she closed and bandaged the wound and started him on an antibiotic to avoid infection. She was glad that in the farming environment, most farms had their own livestock antibiotics that could also be used on humans. This is something many preppers had caught on to before the collapse, but being that Ollie and Mildred raised cattle, they naturally had a supply on hand.

After she got Luke's wounds treated and wrapped, he said, "I'll stay down here with Haley. Why don't you go and see if Mildred or Judith needs anything."

She kissed him on the lips. "Okay, dear. Yell if you need anything," she said as she turned and walked up the stairs.

A few hours later, Nate, Evan, and Jason came into Judith's view as they rode up the driveway to the home. Nate was at a slow trot, trying to stay back with Evan and Jason, who were much slower on their bikes. Judith waved frantically to get their attention, as she was relieved they were finally home. As Nate saw her wave with one hand, he realized she had a shotgun in the other. He immediately nudged the horse in the ribs and raced to the house. Evan and Jason both jumped off their bikes and pulled their VZ58s around from their backs and into the ready position; they both scanned the surrounding areas of the house, not knowing what the threat was, or if it was still around. They then covered each other as they bounded toward the house.

As Nate rode up to the house, he saw the body of the woman lying on the ground with blood all over her chest. He quickly dismounted, checked her vitals, and picked up the small handgun that was on the ground, just out of her reach. He checked to see if it was loaded and found that it still held live rounds in four of its five cylinders. He stuck it in his waistband and ran on up to Judith to get debriefed on what had occurred in his absence.

"What happened?" he asked. "Is anyone else hurt?"

"They tried to rob us," Judith said, still under stress from the situation. "Luke shot her, but she hit him, too—"

"What? Oh, my God! Is he okay?" Nate interrupted in a panic.

"Yes, it wasn't bad. He's fine," Judith tried to explain as Rachel came out onto the front porch and gave Nate a hug.

Rachel said to Nate, "Oh, thank God you're home. Luke will be fine. I've got him all cleaned up, and he is downstairs watching over Haley. We've been watching the house from up here and have just been waiting for you to get home."

Evan and Jason joined them on the porch, keeping their eyes open and scanning the perimeter. "What happened?" Evan asked.

Rachel gathered her thoughts and said, "Two women and three children approached the house. Luke came down from the roof to confront them. They gave him some sob story about traveling alone with hungry children. Just as he decided to give them some food, Judith caught some men in the cellar around back and started yelling for Nate. The woman lying on the ground over there pulled her pistol and fired at Luke to keep him away from her men once they were discovered. He returned fire and she went down with one shot."

"What about the men and the other woman and the children?" Jason asked.

"The other woman and the children turned and ran toward the main road. Luke just let them go. The men around back in the cellar ran into the woods and got away," she replied.

"Cowards!" said Jason in disgust. "What kind of man puts women and children on the front lines when they are just going to run and hide to protect their own worthless asses if something goes down? I'm gonna go check out back," Jason said as he walked away, enraged by the situation.

Nate started to follow him and said, "Wait up; I'll cover you."

As Jason and Nate went around the house to check out the cellar and the surrounding woods, Evan went into the house to check on the women and Luke. He was glad to see that Luke appeared to be doing fine, and that the women had handled themselves admirably.

He then joined the other two out back. "Did you find anything?"

Jason replied, "Negative. It looks like they got away with some canned goods—well, jarred goods we call canning. They dropped and broke some of them during their cowardly retreat. We trailed them through the woods for a while, and from what we could see from their tracks, they doubled back to the main road, probably joining back up with their decoys. From there, it's anyone's guess where they went."

Evan looked around, gathering his thoughts and said, "Well, on the bright side, they seem to have been low-level thieves. Probably migrants desperate for food, but not an organized or skilled operation."

"So what now?" asked Nate.

"Well, we need to do something with the body, and we need to let the other homesteads know what happened here. They need to keep an eye out and never go outside without being armed. They also need to know the ruse that was used."

Jason added in disgust, "I guess Daryl was right; the winter lull is over."

"So what do we do with the body?" asked Nate.

"Hmmm," said Evan as he thought it over. "Well, we need to give her a burial... but not here. I think we need to find a place where bodies in this situation can be buried in a proper way, but not in a place where the victims are haunted, knowing their assailant is interned nearby." He paused for a moment and asked, "Nate, how many horses does Mildred have over here now?

"Three total. The one I rode today and the two in the stable."

Evan scratched his chin. "Well, Jason and I will deal with the body, but we will need to borrow your horses. All three. We'll use one for a packhorse for her, and we will ride the other two. That way we can make good time getting over to Daryl's place so we can talk things over with him. He seems to be the unofficial mayor around here these days."

Jason replied, "I guess that comes natural, as being a bachelor he has the time to get around to the other homesteads more than most."

"Good point," Evan replied. "That and the man who makes the bombs has some clout by default," he said with a chuckle.

"And the fur hat helps," added Jason. "It gives him that distinguished look."

The three men shared a stress-relieving laugh and began to get everything together to deal with the body. Once they had her wrapped up in some old bed sheets, they tied her securely to the packsaddle on the horse.

As Evan and Jason mounted up, Evan said, "We'll bring the horses back tomorrow and get our bikes. By the time we get this situation dealt with, it will be getting late and we'll need to get back to the Homefront. You keep an eye on them tonight," he said with a tip of his hat to Nate.

"Yes, sir," Nate replied.

Evan and Jason awkwardly got underway on the horses and began the trip over to Daryl's cabin. They both had learned the basics of horsemanship, but were far from being experienced and proficient.

As Nate chuckled under his breath, watching them ride away, he turned and began to walk back into the house, saying under his breath, "I'd rather fight off looters and thieves than the cartels any day."

Chapter 5: Facing Reality

As Evan and Jason rode toward Daryl's cabin with the packhorse in tow, they proceeded with great caution, not knowing where the dead woman's companions were, or if they still had nefarious intentions. They both scanned the road up ahead while simultaneously looking into the woods that lined both sides of the road. Jason finally broke the silence by asking the question, "What do you think the odds are that they are lying low to make another move?"

Evan replied, "Slim to none."

"How did you come to that conclusion so fast?" Jason asked.

"They have small children with them and the men ran off at the first sign of trouble," replied Evan. "If they were really bad news, like those that ran with Frank Muncie, Jr., they would have engaged when shots rang out. Also, the fact that they are caring for children, even if resorting to crime to make it happen, says they have other priorities than revenge or conquest. The true scumbags would have seen those little ones as liabilities a long time ago."

"That makes sense, I guess," replied Jason.

Evan continued, "My guess is that they were normal people—normal as in dependent on society, that is—who simply can't make it on their own now. Once you've got hungry children, you'll do whatever it takes to feed them. Now, you aren't the kind of man who would be dependent on others, but imagine if your lot in life was to live in an apartment you didn't own, without the resources to produce or procure your own food. You survived paycheck to paycheck, but somehow just barely got by getting anything you needed from within the system. Now imagine it all went away overnight. You and I had a game plan. You and I had skills and resources, and look how much we have still struggled, and how hard we have had to work in order to live as we do. That's just not something everyone is blessed with. If you were in the aforementioned situation and your paycheck stopped coming, your grocer stopped stocking the shelves, and the society you were so dependent on simply stopped functioning, how long would it take for you to realize your children would starve if you didn't take drastic measures?"

"About a week," Jason replied.

"Right," Evan responded. "Could you let your wife and boys ache from hunger because feeding them would mean you had to step away from your own values? I doubt you could, and neither could I. I just can't see a desperate family who has been changed by this world, as we all have, as evil just, because they steal to eat. But then again, maybe I'm just getting old and soft."

As Jason thought about what Evan said, they rounded the corner and saw a figure dart off into the woods. They immediately brought their horses to a stop, and looked and listened. They could hear the sound of rustling in the bushes as well as the muffled sound of a crying child. Evan got down from his horse and handed the reins to Jason. He whispered, "I hope I'm not about to eat my words." He turned and began to walk slowly up the road.

As he approached the area where he assumed them to be, the sounds of the crying child became more muffled. "Take your hand off of that poor child's mouth!" he yelled. "You aren't hiding from anyone, and nobody is gonna hurt you unless you pull some stupid move." He could hear the child sniffling, and could tell his mouth was no longer being covered. "Let me give you some advice," Evan continued to shout loud enough for them to hear him. "The people around here act as one. You hit one of us, and you will be hit by all of us. We've seen and done some things that you don't want us to repeat, trust me on that. The residents here are good people, though. If you are just passing through, do so in broad daylight, out in the open, and you will not be bothered. If you are desperate, especially to feed your children, speak up. Don't try to steal. If you do, you'll get caught, and I promise you, none of our family members' safety is worth risking while we try to determine your intentions. Now, whoever is with that child, I'm going to leave some bread and some jerky folded up in a towel on the side of the road. It's for the children, so give it to them and them only."

Evan then reached into his pack and pulled out some food that Molly had packed for him to take along. He placed it on the ground, just as he had said. As Evan turned to walk away, he stopped and said, "And if that was you that tried to rob my friends and got your woman killed, you had better look at yourselves as her killer. What kind of a man puts women and children in harm's way and then runs like a coward? You should truly be ashamed."

As Evan began to walk away, he heard a woman's voice say, while fighting back her own tears, "I'm sorry," followed by sniffling.

Evan paused and said, "Say a prayer and ask God for forgiveness. Ask God to show you the way. You're not going to make it without him on the road you've chosen."

He then turned and walked back toward Jason, who was in a state of shock at what Evan had just done. When Evan reached him, Jason said, "What in the world is the matter with you? You made yourself an easy target and could have gotten yourself killed!"

As Evan climbed back onto the horse, a woman crept out of the woods where he had laid the food. She picked it up and started to run back into the woods. Before she slipped away out of sight, she stopped and turned to face him and Jason. She looked weathered and beaten down. They could see the stories of tragedy and loss written into the lines of her face. She silently mouthed the words "thank you" and walked back into the woods.

Evan looked at Jason and said, "Some people need to be killed, and some people don't. They don't. Every now and then, we need to realize that we may have the opportunity to be the glimmer of hope for humanity for others who may have already given up. It doesn't do us much good, in the long run, to do nothing but protect our children from the world while doing nothing to leave them a better world to live in."

Jason smiled and understood completely what he meant. They both nudged their horses forward and continued down the road. As they approached the spot where they left the food, they heard a man's voice say, "Wait... please wait."

They brought their horses to a stop and looked over as a thin, disheveled man stepped out onto the road. "Is that her?" he asked, pointing to the body on the packhorse.

"Yes, it is," Evan replied.

"What are you going to do with her?" the man asked, unable to hold back his own tears.

"We are going to give her a proper burial," Evan said.

The man took a step toward the packhorse, stopped, and said, "Can I say goodbye? She was my wife. I've completely failed her in life. She didn't deserve this. It should have been me," he said, with tears running down his face. "Please, just let me say goodbye."

Evan motioned his horse forward, pulling the packhorse along, and brought it to the edge of the road. He tied the reins of the packhorse to a tree branch and said, "Take all the time you need." He then nudged his horse forward and motioned for Jason to follow. They rode to the next bend in the road and dismounted, tying their horses to a tree and sitting down on the hillside in the shade.

They watched as the man cried uncontrollably, holding onto her body, begging her for forgiveness. Two small children came out of the woods crying. He picked them both up as they shared the agonizingly painful moment together.

"Do you think they are her children?" Jason asked.

Evan poked a stick at the ground and said, "It sure seems that way."

The grieving lasted a few more moments, and then another man and the woman who had gotten the food, came down to the road with the third child to pay their last respects.

The other man nudged at his friend to come on. He sat his children back down on the ground, held both of them by the hand, and the group started walking down the middle of the road in plain view. As they approached Evan and Jason, they paused for just a moment, and the husband of the dead woman looked over to Evan and said, "You were right. You were right about everything." With that, the group continued down the road in broad daylight, no longer in hiding.

"Hopefully they'll stay out of the shadows from now on," Evan said.

"I have a feeling they will," replied Jason as he patted Evan on the shoulder and stood up. "Now let's get going."

With that, they mounted their horses, gathered the packhorse, and resumed their journey to Daryl's home.

~~~~

The rest of the ride was uneventful and quiet, with both men keeping a vigilant eye out for trouble while pondering the day's events. As they approached Daryl's place, they noticed a new and not so welcoming sign at the entrance to his property. It read, "Unannounced trespassers will be shot. Ring the bell to make yourself known."

Jason read the sign, chuckled, and said, "Looks like we had better ring the bell."

"I reckon so," replied Evan with a chuckle.

Jason pulled his horse alongside the sign, where Daryl had attached an old cowbell to a chain. He rang the bell, looked at Evan, and said, "Now what?"

Evan looked at the sign again. "I guess we wait."

It was only a moment later when Daryl yelled from the bushes, "I guess the sign works."

Evan shouted back to him, "Yep, as long as your visitors aren't up to no good, and as long as they can read English, I reckon it will."

Daryl came bounding down out of the woods and said, "Well, that's the idea. If I hear the bell ring, I have a chance to check out who it is before they see me. If I see someone poking around and never heard the bell, I assume they are up to no good. As a one-man show out here, I have to devise my own force multipliers."

The men shared a laugh until Daryl noticed their cargo on the packhorse, and the mood quickly got back to business. "Who is that?" he asked.

"A decoy for some thieves," Jason replied.

"What?" Daryl said, confused about what Jason had just said.

Evan and Jason then began to tell Daryl the story as it had been told to them, as well as their encounter with her family on the road. Once Daryl had all of the information, Evan asked, "So what do you think we should do with her?"

Daryl scratched his beard for a moment and said, "Well, I think you gentleman handled everything pretty well, and you are right about needing to give her a proper burial. There is a secluded patch of woods in between Blue Tick Road and Tackett's Creek Road. There isn't much that I could think of that we would need that land for in the future. I think that would be a suitable spot for these types of folks. Burn the hell out of the bodies of the true scumbag-types, though. Rapists and murders don't deserve to have a shovel lifted in their honor."

"Amen to that!" said Jason.

Daryl accompanied Evan and Jason to the burial site, bringing along several shovels. They fashioned a marker for her grave from a tree branch and whittled into it, "May she rest in peace," along with the date. They didn't know her name, unfortunately. They didn't think to ask her family when they crossed paths with them earlier.

Daryl placed his hat over his heart as they piled rocks on top of the freshly covered grave, and said, "It's a shame we didn't know more about her, or even her name."

"Yes, sir, it is," replied Evan with a heavy heart. "What's worse, though, is that her situation in life prior to the collapse didn't have her prepared to deal with the new world we all live in now, without having to turn to petty crime. It's a shame that the values that make self-sufficiency possible for people like us were lost in a single generation full of dependency. Whether it was dependency on government, society, or technology; in one generation, people left behind the ethics and skills it takes to survive in this cruel world. I'm sure before that society was taken away from her, she was probably a wonderful, typical American woman any of us would have been proud to call a friend."

"Amen to that," added Jason.

After a moment of silence, Jason said, "We should probably be getting back home. It's getting late and our wives are probably getting worried."

"Yes, I've got to get back home myself," said Daryl as he put his hat back on and turned to his horse. "I had some homemade soap cooking on the fire that I just remembered.

Jason, after you guys discuss the Muncie and Murphy properties, let us know what you decide."

Jason shook Daryl's hand and said, "Yes, sir, I will, and thanks.

With that, the men mounted up and went their respective ways. Daryl rode back to his place while Evan and Jason rode back toward the Homefront. After a few miles, Jason broke the silence of the somber evening by saying, "So what do you think? Should Griff and I move our families?"

Evan replied, "The selfish side of me wants you to stay onboard with us. We've gotten quite used to having the extra hands running the place and helping out with security. That, and you've become a part of our family. However, you deserve to have your own place. Your family left behind everything you had to join up with us. If everything settles down someday, you will need a place to pass on to your boys, and they will need a place to raise their families. That being said, barring some unforeseen event, I think you should do it. You and Griff can both take a portion of the animals at the Homefront to help get you started as well. The only reason we have as much as we do now is because you helped us raise and acquire it all."

Jason rode silently for a moment, taking it all in, and said, "Thanks, man, I really appreciate that. I can't imagine what this entire ordeal would have been like if we weren't in it together. Just imagining the escape from New York without another armed and like-minded friend is hard to comprehend. We made it out of there the way we did because we were together. My wife could have ended up exactly like the woman we just buried—desperate to feed our kids if I hadn't made it home to her."

"Same here, brother," Evan replied. "So are you going to do it?"

"I think so," said Jason. "Unless Sarah absolutely objects, but I'm sure she will feel the same."

"Well, good," Evan said. The two men quietly rode the rest of the way home, each silently reflecting on the events they had struggled through as a team, beginning that fateful day that started out as a routine layover in New York, when everything changed forever.

Chapter 6: The Unexpected Visitor

Just as Evan and Jason were nearing the Homefront, they heard an aircraft overhead. Both men were caught off guard, as the skies in their area had been silent for quite some time. The aircraft was flying low, barely above treetop level, and the unfamiliar sound startled the horses.

Looking frantically to try to get a view of the aircraft, Jason said, "What the heck? Do you see it?" he asked.

It was hard to spot the aircraft right away due to Evan and Jason's position in a heavily wooded area, surrounded by hilly terrain. Just as Evan started to reply, the single-engine airplane came into view over a ridge and flew directly overhead. Evan exclaimed, "Holy crap! Was that the Maule?"

"Our... I mean... Judith's Maule?" Jason asked.

"I think so," replied Evan as the aircraft flew out of sight.

"No way. Is that Ed?" Jason asked in disbelief.

"It has to be," replied Evan, hoping his assumption was right. "We did leave him a map of our location and told him he was welcome to join us if things got too bad for him in Ohio. He's probably looking for a place to land. This is some rough country compared to Ohio; he may have a hard time, especially with it getting dark."

"Well, we can't follow him on horseback with this terrain. Let's hurry home and get on the CB. We can see if the other homesteads can get a visual on him and get us a position," Jason said as he nudged his horse and rode hard for the Homefront with Evan in trail.

Upon reaching the Homefront, Evan and Jason rushed into the house where the women were gathered around the radios in the basement. "Thank God you're home," Molly said. "Several of the other homesteads have reported a low-flying aircraft in the area, and they are a bit concerned, to say the least."

"Get the Thomas Farm on the radio right away," Evan said to Judy, who was sitting at the radio operator's desk.

"Okay, but what's going on?" she asked.

"It's Ed Savio... Just get them on the line quick before he runs out of gas or daylight."

Judy hailed the Thomas Farm and received a quick reply from Judith. Evan reached for the microphone as Judy quickly handed it to him. "Judith, this is Evan. Ed Savio—from Ohio—is in your plane and may be looking for a place to land. Get Luke or Nate to go outside and keep an eye and an ear out. When they see him, pop one of the flares that are in the basement down by that old water heater. Ed is probably looking for a friendly place to land, and your back pasture may be the flattest clearing we have around here."

"What... my plane? I don't... Oh! Of course!" Judith replied, as it dawned on her what Evan was saying. She had all but forgotten about trading the *Little Angel* for the Maule, as she felt it was more a symbolic gesture than an actual transaction. At that time, she was just happy to be a part of a group and saw the trade as merely her finally being able to contribute. She quickly ran down to the basement and began to look for the flares. Finding them exactly where Evan had said, she grabbed several and ran back up to the porch, calling for both of her sons.

Nate came running from the barn to see what she was shouting about, fearing that they might again have intruders. "What? What is it, mom?" he asked frantically.

She tossed him the flares and said, "I'll explain later. Run out to the back pasture and stand in the middle. If you see a white and red airplane, a little one, pop one of the flares to get his attention. If he sees you, try and wave him into the pasture.

He's a friend. That's the plane I was telling you about that we left in Ohio!"

Nate turned and ran out to the back pasture as his mother had requested. As he quickly made a turn through one of the fence gates to get to the open pasture, he lost his footing with his prosthetic lower leg, slipped and fell, dropping the flares into a puddle of mud and water. As he struggled to get back to his feet, he cussed under his breath at his clumsiness and heard the low RPM hum of a small single-engine aircraft as it neared the farm. "Crap!" Nate said, realizing that he might miss his window of opportunity.

He grabbed the flares, got back on his feet, and ran for the pasture. As he saw the plane come over the trees, he attempted to pop one of the flares, to no avail. "Damn it!" he said, knowing that dropping them in the mud and water was the likely cause. The aircraft was now directly overhead as he attempted to light the second flare, and again nothing. He tossed it to the ground and attempted to light the last remaining flare; with a *poof*, it was ablaze with smoke and a bright red torch-like flame. He began to wave the flare frantically with his arms while chasing the plane. Just as it was about to clear the next tree line, he thought that he had missed the opportunity. The plane then made a gentle turn to the left and began to circle overhead. Nate continued to wave the flare to the pilot as if to say, "Come on in." After another circle overhead, the aircraft began to fly away to Nate's dismay.

As the aircraft flew over the tree line and the sounds began to fade, Nate tossed his flare onto the ground in frustration. As he stared at the ground and kicked the flare, he could hear the sounds of the aircraft's engine grow louder once again. He looked up to see the airplane coming back toward the field with its main wheels just barely dragging the tree tops as it made an approach to the pasture. Once the airplane cleared the treetops, the pilot cut the power and slipped the aircraft in for a bouncy touchdown on the rough old cow pasture, sliding to a stop in the wet grass.

As Nate began to walk over to the airplane, his mother, Judith came running up to him. "Oh, thank God! Yes, that's him," she said with a smile on her face. She grabbed Nate by the hand and ran toward the Maule as she saw Ed Savio climb out of the pilot's seat.

As he stepped out of the plane, Judith ran up, gave him a hug, and said, "Welcome to Tennessee, Ed."

"It's Judith, right?" he said.

"Yes, Judith Hoskins," she replied.

"I'm sorry, but our meeting back in Ohio was so quick and frantic that I didn't really get a chance to commit everyone's name to memory. But I sure do remember you," he said.

"What are you doing down here?" she asked.

"Things aren't going so good up north, or in a lot of places, for that matter. I'll explain more in detail later, but my options were getting limited, so I thought I had better take Evan and Jason up on their offer to meet up with you all down here, before things got any worse. I also needed to get your plane back to you," he said with a smile.

Nate just stood there scratching his chin, trying to soak it all in. His mom had clearly been on quite the adventure to be the owner of an airplane, when she used to be afraid of flying.

"Is Evan or Jason around? Is this Evan's place?" Ed asked.

"No, this is a dear friend's farm. I live here now with my two sons and a few other people you haven't met," she replied.

"You found your sons? What? How? Oh, my God. How in the world did you do that? I thought they were out west somewhere with no contact," Ed said, confused by the situation.

"It's an extremely long story," she said. "We'll catch up this evening. I'll tell you everything."

"But wait, now that I'm thinking about it, weren't you going to Newport with that young mother and her child?" Ed asked, confused by his cloudy memories.

"Yes, Peggy and little Zack are down here with us as well. Newport wasn't what we had hoped it would be," she replied with a solemn look on her face.

"Oh," he said. "Sorry."

"It's okay," she replied.

Nate then stuck out his hand and said, "I'm her son, Nate Hoskins. Pleased to meet you, sir. I don't remember all of the details of the story, but I do know you helped my mom and the others make it down here to safety, and for that I will forever be in your debt."

"Well, son, if it wasn't for your mother and her Maule here, I would have been stuck in Ohio with no way out, so I guess we can call it even," Ed said with a smile as he returned Nate's handshake. "And if you hadn't flagged me down, I would probably be in the trees in a few minutes. My fuel tanks were on fumes and I only knew the general area where everyone might be, not the specific location, at least as it is seen from the air. It's gonna be dark in just a few more minutes, and I would have had a hard time finding a friendly place to put this thing down. I would have had to just put it down on someone's property and hope for the best."

"Let's get you up to the house," Judith said. "We were just about to sit down for dinner, and I'm sure you are starved after your long flight down. While we are getting dinner ready, I'll set you up on the radio so you can contact Evan and Jason over at the Homefront. I'm sure they are dying to hear from you. They saw you fly overhead and called us on the radio, telling us to try and flag you down."

"That sounds perfect," Ed replied. "And I can't wait for you to catch me up on everything."

~~~~

Back at the Homefront, after having contacted Judith, Evan made contact with the other homesteads as well, asking for reports of any sightings of the plane. At this point, all they could do was wait and hope for some news. Evan and Jason were sitting in the basement near the radio station, monitoring the common homestead frequency while discussing what might be going on up north to make Ed pack up and leave his beloved property.

"I hate being in the dark about what's going on out there," said Evan, as he got up to pace back and forth to work off the stress of waiting. "Ever since our HAM guys have been dropping off of the air, I've had a bad feeling. I've tried to ignore it and hope it's nothing, but I just can't shake it."

"I know exactly what you mean," Jason replied.

Just then, Griff came into the basement and said, "Hey, guys, how did the meeting go? I've been out on the perimeter and didn't realize you got back. Judy mentioned something about an altercation at the Thomas Farm and something about an airplane."

"Heck, I don't even know where to begin," Evan said as he sat back down. "It's been an eventful day, to say the least.

Before Evan could continue, a radio transmission came through the CB with that old, familiar New York accent that Ed just couldn't shake after "immigrating to America," as he liked to call his move from New York to Ohio. "Hello, Homefront," he said.

Evan grabbed the microphone and replied, "Well, hello there! Where the heck are you, and what's going on?"

Ed replied, "I'm with Judith and her group at the farm. They flagged me in just as I was about to give up hope of finding you before I ran out of gas or daylight. Anyway, they tell me you guys are bringing their horses back tomorrow. I'll just see you then, and we will catch up on everything, which I'm sure is a lot from both sides."

"We are so glad to have you," Evan replied. "Rest up from your trip and we will see you tomorrow."

"Roger that," Ed replied, and was off the air.

"Well, it's a good thing we just acquired more housing," Jason said with excitement in his voice from having their old friend join up with them in Tennessee.

"More housing?" Griff said with a confused look on his face.

"Oh, yeah, we both get our own place if we want," Jason said. He then explained the day's meeting with Daryl and the other homesteads.

Griff didn't know what to think. He was excited about the prospect of having a place for his family—and for Greg's potential future family—in their new and uncertain world. At the same time, he was apprehensive about the security concerns that spreading the group over such a large area would bring. The men discussed the pros and cons for themselves, as well as for the community of homesteads as a whole, for the next hour. They carefully thought things out from every angle and finally decided to give it a try.

Once they had come to a consensus, Evan said, "If conditions dictate, you guys can always fall back here, to the Homefront, for mutual security. We're all set up for the numbers, can easily revert back if need be, and I think we should always continue to work as a team in that regard. I think the community and your families, will be better off in the long run, and you have both earned your place around here."

"Well, let's go talk to the women about it, and as long as they are game, let's do it," Griff said.

Chapter 7: News from the North

The next morning seemed to come early for the Homefront, as the adults stayed up a good portion of the night, catching up on the events of the day, as well as the long discussion concerning the ramifications of their potential change in living arrangements. They also caught Griff, Molly, and Judy up on Ed's involvement during Evan, Jason, Peggy, and Judith's harrowing journey from New York to Tennessee, and how they likely would not have made it without his help and generosity. The old Ford truck he loaned them to get to Jason's family, along with the intelligence he provided about the situation throughout the state, especially the Cincinnati area, had been a key to their success. Ed was one of those pieces of the puzzle that seemed to just fall perfectly into place, and now here he was in Tennessee.

After breakfast, Evan and Jason saddled up Mildred's horses and grabbed their daypacks and rifles for the outing to the farm to deliver the horses and retrieve Ed. They got Jake's mountain bike, removed both wheels, and secured the frame and wheels to the packhorse's saddle so Ed could ride back with them.

As they got underway, Jason jokingly said, "Man, I'm spoiled by this horse after just one day. I hate the thought of going back to a bicycle."

Evan chuckled and said, "Yeah, I know what you mean. I've been thinking more and more about the need to possibly venture outside of the area on a supply run for fuel and other things we've burned through—most of which we can't replace with what is available for barter amongst the homesteads. If the situation is getting worse out there, we should consider getting something planned sooner, rather than later before it gets too risky to travel. Maybe we should put horses on our shopping list, especially with the distance we'll be apart after you and Griff get settled in at your new homes."

"Things sure are getting busy around here in a hurry," replied Jason. "Our to-do list is getting pretty long. We are busy enough with food production and security, and now we have moves to make, homes to repair, supply runs, and who knows what else is just around the corner."

"Yes, they are," Evan said. "But at least Ed will be an extra set of hands and an extra gun when need be."

As they reached the Thomas farm, Evan and Jason approached with caution, as usual, but with a little extra care, considering the encounter with strangers the previous day. Once Nate waved them on up the driveway to the house, Mildred met them on the porch with her customary offer of fresh, hot coffee. As they proceeded into the house, Ed stood up from his seat on the couch and joined Evan and Jason in a group hug.

"Damn, it's good to see some familiar faces," Ed said.

"We're glad to have you, man!" Jason added, patting him on the back. "Did you ever make it to my place to get your truck back?" he asked.

"Na, man, I wrote that thing off," Ed replied. "It wasn't worth risking my neck to get it back. No big deal, though. I would have had to leave it behind, anyway, as all I could bring was what fit in the Maule. I'm just glad it's the 235HP model," he said jokingly. "About six months ago, my position with the state dissolved when the governor was arrested by the feds on some sort of subversion charges. It's all a bunch of crap. Once they got him out of the way, they installed an interim puppet governor, which goes completely against the state constitution, but then again, since when do constitutions matter to this administration? Once their Marxist puppet was in place, the entire chain of command was dismantled; state officials loyal to the lawfully elected governor were either arrested as accessories to the crime or they simply disappeared. Whether they disappeared of their own accord or were simply taken out, remains to be seen. The sad fact of the matter is, Ohio is now securely in the hands of the administration. Even though a lot of the guardsmen deserted when the feds basically seized the state, they now have their hands firmly on the guards' assets and facilities. The last word I received before my contacts completely dissolved was that they were setting up for the arrival of United Nations peacekeeping forces. Ohio is rumored to be a staging area for their expansion into the Midwest. New York, New Jersey, Massachusetts, and the Philadelphia and Washington, D.C. areas are already said to have blue helmets patrolling the streets."

Evan and Jason just stood there silently, shaking their heads, trying to take it all in. Jason looked at Ed and said, "Damn. It's hard to imagine just how this will all shake out. It's not like we can just vote things back to the way they were. The country is so fragmented and disconnected now, just getting the states together to discuss things seems impossible. Especially considering the fact that some of the states, like Ohio, don't have legitimate governments in place, anyway."

"I know, man," replied Ed. "That's why I bugged out of Ohio and came looking for you guys. I didn't want to just keep sitting there, waiting for it to get worse. The new governor banned the private ownership of all firearms, ammunition, body armor, and night-vision equipment throughout the state. There was no chance I was going to comply with that, and rather than end up in prison or worse, I packed some gear into the Maule and left."

"I swear, I think a zombie apocalypse would be easier to deal with," Jason remarked.

Evan chuckled and said, "You and zombies; it always comes back to that."

"That's because it's the only way I see a reset happening," Jason replied, only half-joking. "At least that way, you would have clear-cut good versus... uh, living versus dead, and once you killed off the zombies, you could just pick up the pieces and try to resume life as it was before. In this case, though, the zombies are among us. They are our fellow Americans who are taking advantage of the collapse, subverting the Constitution and our way of life in order to turn this country into just another socialist state. So many bad deeds have been committed by our own at this point, how do you even tell who is on our side?"

"They aren't just taking advantage of the collapse, they are part of it," Ed interjected. "Remember how many of the attacks were initially reported as jihadist activities by first responders, whose reports were later scrubbed and re-written as homegrown tea party terrorists or the like?"

"Yeah, that crap pissed me off," replied Jason.

"Well, after the initial attacks, there was no attempt at tracking down those responsible. Sure, there were some empty speeches and rhetoric, but no action was ever taken," added Ed. "After the dust settled, the president quickly forgot about his promises of bringing those responsible to justice. He immediately seized upon the situation to begin implementing his ideology of centralized government control, and never again mentioned the attacks. The governor's office received numerous reports of high-ranking officials within the DHS and DOD being replaced with individuals who had close ties with known Middle Eastern terrorist organizations. It's almost as if the attacks were planned, with people involved in the coordination of those attacks being rewarded with promised leadership roles, waiting on the sidelines ready to be plugged right in. Sharia law is being practiced in some areas with no government intervention of any kind. Christians, Jews, and other groups have been run out of those areas, or worse, just like we've seen play out overseas time and time again."

Evan spoke up and said, "I just don't get it, though. Why would a communist or Marxist-minded individual, which many clearly are, team up with Islamic radicals? That makes about as much sense as a rabbit helping a wolf catch a deer. Sure, he's on the wolf's good side... up until the point the deer has been eaten, but what keeps the wolf from eating the rabbit next?"

"Nothing. Nothing at all. You see, I guess they are thinking in the short term," Ed explained. "'The enemy of my enemy is my friend,' as the old adage goes. Initially, they both want the same thing. They both dislike the Judeo-Christian ethic the country was founded upon, they both hate capitalism and free markets, and they both hate individual liberty, to name just a few. The only problem is that Communism/Marxism/Progressivism, whatever you want to call it, is completely incompatible with any religion, not just Christianity. That's why communist states throughout history have always eradicated religion and become atheist states. You see, you can't get a man to give up control of his life to another man when he believes his god guides his way, above all others. That's why our nation was founded on the basic principles of Judeo-Christian ethics, where certain rights are bestowed upon us by our creator, and are governed by no man or system of collectivism, where the majority controls the minority. How those two strange bedfellows go their separate ways in the end, of course, is an interesting question. I would guess that they both have plans for that in place already."

"Damn, Ed," replied Evan. "You sure know how to kill a good mood."

"Tell me about it. Sometimes I wish I wasn't in a position to be in the know. It would be a whole lot easier to just be ignorant and go with the flow," Ed jokingly replied.

"That's what got us in this problem in the first place," Jason quickly added. "Everyone was so wrapped up in the political correctness scandal of the day or their reality shows, that not enough people were paying attention."

"Amen to that," Ed said in agreement.

"Well, guys, as much as I love a good doom-and-gloom conversation, we should probably get going," Evan said, changing the subject. "I guess we should put the Maule in the barn. There are a bunch of tarps out there we can cover it up with. That'll make sure it doesn't get too filthy to fly without a wash. You never know when we may need some close air support, and we want to keep it ready to scramble," Evan said with a chuckle. "Then we just need to put the third bike back together and start our trip back to the Homefront to get Ed settled in. We've got a lot on our plates these days, Ed. We could sure use an extra set of eyes and hands around here. I'll catch you up on everything else over the next few days as you get settled."

With that, the men spent the next few hours getting Mildred's horses taken care of, the airplane hidden securely in the barn, and their things ready for the ride back to the Homefront. Ed packed his most important items in his backpack for the ride, along with his Springfield Armory M1A rifle slung over his pack and his Smith & Wesson M&P 40 pistol on his side. They planned to retrieve the rest of his things from the Maule over the next few trips to the Thomas farm and as time permitted.

Before they left, insisting that they begin their ride on a full stomach, Mildred fixed them all a nice lunch to send them on their way. After they had eaten, as they began to climb onto their bikes, Ed looked at Evan and Jason and said, "Guys, I think I'm gonna be a diehard country boy in no time. I've not eaten this good or been treated this well since it all started to go down."

"We'll see if you still feel that way after we put you to work," joked Evan in reply.

Chapter 8: Prepping for the Move

Over the next few weeks, Ed settled in to the daily routines of the Homefront with ease. After having been mostly alone in Ohio after the collapse, and with no family to turn to, his spirits were higher than they had been in as long as he could remember. In addition to helping them work the land and the livestock, Ed was filling in with the security duties at the Homefront. With Jason, Griff, and often times, Evan, away on a regular basis working on community-wide projects, preparing the Murphy and Muncie homes for Jason's and Griff's families, the extra manpower was a true blessing. If they were going to have time to get crops in the ground that season at their new homes, in preparation for the following winter, the moves needed to be accomplished as soon as possible.

Jason and Griff both agreed that Jason's family would take the Murphy home and the Vandergriffs would take the Muncie home. Both were similar in size, acreage, and condition, so it was a relatively easy consensus to reach. Both men were just happy to have the opportunity to provide a home for their families and their potential future generations.

Virtually everyone from the neighboring homesteads contributed to the effort. Those who were physically able, helped with the laborious duties involved in repairing the damage and neglect to the properties. Others donated supplies and materials, as well as items to help get their households up and running. Both were extremely generous contributions, as the homesteading lifestyle didn't leave much free time to give, and supplies had been running thin for virtually everyone.

The need for additional supplies and resources for two new households made it clearer than ever that the men needed to venture out beyond their community in search of what they needed. They also hoped this would lead to a broader coalition of trading partners, connecting them with other homesteads in the region. The men decided that once the families were squared away in their new homes, they would put together a plan to do just that.

One day, while Jason and Griff were both away, working on their homes, Molly was going through the canned goods with Sarah and Judy, dividing things up equitably to help get their households running. "I feel like we are robbing you blind," said Sarah, feeling guilty for leaving Molly's pantry so bare.

"Nonsense," Molly replied. "Where do you think these canned beans, tomatoes, and everything else came from? They came from the garden that you and your families put a lot of work into. Just because the seeds weren't sown into your own soil doesn't mean you don't have rights to it. The same goes for everything else that we have all chipped in and raised around here."

"Well, thank you, anyway," said Sarah as she placed a jar of canned goods into her box. "You know, it's funny," she continued, "when we first got here, it felt strange living in such close quarters with other families, doing everything as a team, from the laundry, to preparing meals, to cleaning. But now, the thought of moving on to our own home seems strange. Like, how can I possibly get everything done without you two in it with me?" she said as her eyes became watery, and she wiped a tear from her cheek.

"I know," said Judy. "I guess we are going to be living like our great grandmothers. They did everything themselves the old-fashioned way and somehow got by. Of course, it was the norm for them. They didn't come from the generation of dishwashers and microwavable meals."

Each of the ladies laughed and shed a tear together. During their many struggles since the collapse, they had become more like sisters than friends. The hardships they had endured brought them closer than they could have ever imagined.

~~~~

That evening around dinnertime, Jason and Griff returned from a long day of work at their new homes. Their routine was that Griff would ride from the Vandergriff home to the Jones home, as it was a bit further away, and then the two would travel together for safety back to the Homefront. They had both already set up CB radio stations at their new homes in order to stay in contact with each other, as well as the Homefront, if a situation should arise while they were away working.

"You're just in time for dinner," Molly said as they walked through the door.

"That was the plan," replied Griff as he rubbed his belly. "I'm starved."

Jason asked, "Where is Evan?"

"Oh, he's out checking on the ewes and their lambs," Molly replied. "He should be back any minute. How did everything go today?"

"Great," replied Jason. "We are pretty much ready to go, except, of course, for a few supplies. Griff and I had a long talk on the way back, and we both think we need to venture outside of the area for supplies before we move our families. We don't want to leave them alone while we are gone, just in case it takes longer than we expect. After we return, we can all make the move and get settled without having to worry about leaving home anytime soon."

"I so hate the thought of you guys going on an extended run like that," Molly replied. "I know it's necessary, but the way things are out there... I mean, look at what it was like for you guys to get here, and for Nate, Luke, and Rachel to get here. There is no such thing as an uneventful trip."

As Griff took off his hat to have a seat, he added, "Yes, but there are a lot of things we all need. If we can make alliances with other like-minded folks out there, possibly even some sort of communications relay, we will be a lot safer in the long run."

Molly nodded her head in agreement as the door opened and in walked Evan. "Hey, guys, how are things lookin' over there?" he asked.

"Great," Jason again replied. "We were just talking to Molly and the girls about something we want to run by you."

"Go right ahead," Evan said as he took off his rubber muck boots and tossed them outside on the back porch.

For the next half hour, the men and the women discussed Jason and Griff's proposal, and with a unanimous consensus, everyone agreed that the extended supply run should be made prior to the moves. After dinner, Evan asked Judy to get on the CB and relay a message to all of the homesteads that they would like to hold a meeting, with at least one representative from each, the following day at the Vandergriff family's new place. With the neighboring homesteaders notified and the kids put to bed, the adults of the Homefront all met at the backyard fire pit for a relaxing evening together.

As Jason lit the fire, Ed spoke up and said, "Hey, guys, I know I just got here and all and need to pay my dues around here, and considering that I don't have a family here to be worried while I'm away, I would like to go on the run. Then maybe one of you guys with a family can stay behind to keep an eye on them while we are away."

"Thanks, Ed, that's not a bad idea," replied Evan as he took a sip of a new homemade tea recipe Molly had been working on. She called it Forest Tea because the ingredients all came from the neighboring woods.

"Damn, that's good," he said as he held his cup up in a solitary toast to Molly.

"Who should stay then?" asked Jason.

Griff spoke up and said, "I can hold the fort down here with Greg and Jake to help me with the outer perimeter, and the women can handle the watches on the inner perimeter. I hate to miss out on the trip, but the security around here, with everyone else away, is kind of a big deal."

"Are we sure we want three of us to go?" asked Evan.

"We can't send a group out too thin," Jason responded. "We want the group to be able to handle anything that comes up, especially considering everything we've heard on the HAM as of late. I think three is good. We can also draw from other homesteads while our supply party is away. We can even discuss with the other homesteads the prospect of establishing a quick reaction team of sorts, since they will most likely send a few warm bodies along as well. That quick reaction team can then be called upon if a security situation arises at any of the homesteads that are understaffed."

"That's an outstanding idea, Jason," Evan replied. "I sure am glad I rescued you from New York and brought you along," he added with a sneaky grin.

"Yeah, right," Jason replied with a sarcastic tone. "You just go ahead and remember things however you need to boost your self-esteem."

"I'm gonna miss having you around all the time to mess with when you guys move out," Evan said in a somber tone.

"Me, too, brother. Me, too," replied Jason.

Chapter 9: A Community Venture

The next day, Evan, Jason, and Ed left the Homefront for the Vandergriff's new home, which had been the requested meeting place due to its central location among the confederacy of homesteads. They arrived early in order to scan the home and the surrounding area to make sure no threats were in the vicinity before the representatives from the other homesteads arrived. Once they cleared the area, Jason climbed onto the roof to survey the area from a distance with the Nightforce scope on his Remington 700 while they awaited the arrival of the others.

"You're gonna like these folks, Ed," Evan said as he and Ed sat on the front porch. "They all have a lot of character, and we are truly blessed to have them as neighbors. You can put your life in their hands any time without fail. We wouldn't be here today if it weren't for each and every one of them."

Just then, Daryl Moses rounded the corner at the end of the driveway on horseback, holding the reins of his horse with his left hand, while he held his trusty lever-action rifle at the ready with the other.

"Here comes Daryl," Evan said. "He's like a character straight out of an old frontiersman movie. This place wouldn't be the same without him." Evan stepped out from underneath the porch roof and looked up at Jason, who was giving him the thumbs up to let him know the way was clear for Daryl. Evan then waved Daryl on up the driveway, letting him know the coast was clear.

"Howdy, Mayor Moses," Evan said as Daryl approached.

Daryl climbed down from the saddle, and while tying his horse to the railing of the porch, he said, "I don't know why you keep saying that."

"Because you're the glue that binds this place together, and if we ever vote for a leader, I'm nominating you for mayor," Evan replied.

Daryl just grinned, looked at Ed, and said, "So this must be your Yankee aviator. Glad to meet you, sir. We've heard a lot about you."

"Likewise, Mr. Moses," Ed said as he shook Daryl's hand.

"My father was Mr. Moses. Just call me Daryl," he replied as he returned the handshake.

The men chatted a few more minutes and then heard Jason whistle from the roof. Evan looked up and said, "Well, here comes Nate, who you met at the Thomas farm, of course."

"Who's that with him?" Daryl asked as he squinted to see.

"Oh, Judith must have come along with him," replied Evan. "Luke must have stayed behind to keep a lookout. It's smart not traveling alone."

One by one, the others continued to straggle in. Robert Brooks, Lloyd Smith, Charlie Blanchard, Jimmy Lewis, Linda Cox, Bill Duncan, and of course, Daryl, Evan, Jason, Ed, Judith, and Nate had all arrived and gathered outside the home. Once it appeared that everyone who was going to attend had arrived and Ed had gotten acquainted with them, Evan invited everyone inside. He then flagged Jason down from the roof and the meeting got underway.

"The reason we asked everyone to come, is that we think it's time to get our scouting trip put together to look for possible supply opportunities outside of our little comfort zone here. We, as a community, have done remarkably well providing for ourselves. From our gardens, to our livestock, to our barter of labor and skills, and our defense, one would be hard-pressed to want for more from their friends and neighbors. However, we do fall short when it comes to fuel, medicine, and a few luxury items such as coffee, salt, and other spices. We are also running short on a few raw materials. We are all well aware of the state of things out there. The reports coming in over the radio are that the political situation may be getting much worse, with outside influences such as the UN's so-called peacekeepers being brought into the mix. There is also the matter of the renewed migration of people that such things trigger. Some people will be running away from the encroachment of global government, and some will be running toward them with their hands out, in search of support. Either way, people are on the move and supplies will likely continue to dwindle before any sort of recovery begins, if it begins at all."

"What do you propose, exactly?" asked Charlie Blanchard.

"Jason, Ed, Nate, and I are going to make a supply run outside of the area, as we now have four households to support," Evan replied. "We would like to make the offer that if any of the other homesteads would like to go along to procure supplies, we would welcome the additional manpower. We can all work together while we are out there to search for whatever it is that each of us needs. We will work as a team, both in procurement and protection, at all times. If there is something you need, but you can't make the trip, we understand, but we ask that you at least contribute to the expedition in terms of food or fuel, and we will do our best to find what you need." Evan then looked at Linda Cox and said, "Like you, Linda, we all know you live alone, so leaving your house and your animals unattended isn't something you would be advised to do. We understand that."

"What about security while you... uh, or we... are gone?" asked Lloyd Smith.

Evan replied, "Griff has volunteered to stay behind at the Homefront to provide security with the help of Greg and Jake, who have both grown into more than capable young men. Luke will be at the Thomas farm, and we will delay the move of the Vandergriff and Jones families until after we return. I would like to ask that Daryl stay behind, as well, to set up and lead a quick reaction force for the homesteads that have members who are away on the trip, compromising their own security."

Daryl looked at Evan with a puzzled expression, paused, and said, "That makes sense. I was sure looking forward to getting out and about, but I can get around the area pretty quick on horseback. I would be glad to head that up. If I can get a few other folks who stay behind to join in, we can be the CB radio version of 911 until you return."

"Outstanding," Evan replied with a smile.

Jimmy Lewis then motioned for the room's attention with his hand and asked, "How do you plan on traveling? By car? Horse? ATV? Tractor?"

"Once we know who all is going and what sort of supplies we are looking for, we can hammer out a solid plan then. Right now, we are in the brainstorming stages, but we do need to consider fuel economy and pulling power. I imagine we will take a large livestock trailer or the like to haul what we find."

Robert Brooks looked around the room and then reluctantly stood up and said, "I've not been doing so well lately. My blood pressure is through the roof without my medication. I have headaches every day, and I just have no energy at all. I can barely keep up with the work I have to do around the house to keep us going. I was hoping going back to a natural diet, like all of us have, would help, but it hasn't. If you guys can keep an eye out for something that could help me, you are more than welcome to use my John Deere 2155 tractor. She's a tough old beast, diesel, four-wheel drive, and even has a loader. I could take the loader off if you think it would be in the way, but if you think it would come in handy, it will lift quite a bit. No offense, Evan, but it will pull a heck of a lot more than your little two-wheel drive Ford."

"No offense taken," Evan said with a grin. "Yes, that little Ford was supposed to be our starter tractor. We were gonna move up later, but, well... you know. Anyway, unless anyone else has any other ideas, we will probably take you up on that. We could pull Ollie's... um, I mean Mildred's twenty-foot livestock trailer with Ollie's homemade three-point hitch trailer ball set-up. Then maybe have a couple of guys follow along with ATVs or something."

Jason spoke up and said, "That would probably be way better than taking a street vehicle. Those big agriculture tires will go through a heck of a lot of crap if need be, compared to pickup truck tires. Who knows what kinds of obstacles we will come across... or the road conditions?"

"Yep, you'll be truly having a bad day if you get her stuck," Robert replied.

"Well, I think we are well on our way to a plan, then," Evan stated. "At this point, I think everyone should go home and think things through with your families, make a list of things you really need, and let's meet back here the day after tomorrow at the same time. We can hammer everything out then, and get going as soon as the next day."

After a little more social chat and catching up, everyone returned to their homes, discussed the tentative plans with their families, and began to prepare for what roles they could or should play in the upcoming supply run.

Back at the Homefront, the Vandergriff and Jones families put together a list of what they needed to complete the repairs on their new homes, as well as what it would take to adequately stock them with the things they would need for the foreseeable future. Evan and Molly also put a list together of things they needed, as well as things they thought would be valuable for the community as a whole, such as schoolbooks and other reference materials. The long-term nature of the crisis meant homeschooling for the children and medical supplies for Rachel, whom they all now looked to as their community physician, were things that had to be considered.

When the meeting finally came, everyone gathered at the Vandergriff home as planned. This time, several of the men brought their wives along, as they wanted to hear exactly what their husbands were getting themselves into. Everyone brought along their lists of needs, as well as lists of needs from the folks who were unable to attend the meeting and could not participate in the journey.

At the conclusion of the meeting, they compiled the lists and Evan read the results aloud. "Here is what we have, folks; other than the obvious need for gasoline, diesel, kerosene, etc., we seem to have several folks who need roofing materials of some sort. We need salt and spices of any kind available, coffee, and ammunition of various calibers. A few folks have some specific mechanical parts they need in order to fix tools and equipment they already have, and several of the guys are looking for scrap metal of any kind, as well as welding supplies. Molly wants us to keep an eye out for school or reference books to help with homeschooling the children. Rachel gave us a list of medications, in addition to yours, Robert, as well as some other medical and health-related supplies. Aside from that, I'm sure a lot of what we bring back will be stuff we come across along the way that we just can't bring ourselves to leave behind, so we will just adapt our list as we go."

Jimmy asked, "What do you think the chances are of us even finding that sort of stuff?"

At this point, Ed spoke up and said, "I know I'm new here, but I'm also the most recent one to have been out in the rest of the world. As far as medications and stuff go, the odds aren't good. Most pharmacies that I have seen that aren't heavily guarded government facilities, were looted and ransacked early on. Medicine cabinets in abandoned houses and things of that nature may be our only hope in that regard, but as far as building supplies and random resources go, you can find that stuff everywhere. You may have to tear apart an abandoned building to get it, so I recommend we take plenty of tools along, but it's there."

"The same goes for the school materials," he continued. "Not too many people bothered carrying that stuff along when they bugged out. Food supplies, though, have pretty much all been spoken for. I suggest we take some things along as barter for those. There may be a group out there with a cache of salt, for example, that would gladly trade it for some of the canned goods that some of you folks have put away from last season's garden surpluses. It's really all a big unknown, but all we can do is try."

After a little more chatter around the room, the plan was finalized and the group planned to set out in two days, in order to give everyone a chance to prepare for the journey. Going on the journey would be Evan, Jason, Ed, Nate, Charlie, and Jimmy.

Chapter 10: Getting Underway

The morning of the supply run had finally arrived, and over the past several days, everyone involved had been making their preparations. Evan and Jason had traveled to Robert Brooks' homestead to acquire his tractor for the journey, and had collected contributions of diesel fuel from everyone who could spare it. They had also collected thirty jars of canned green beans, ten jars of canned tomatoes, and a few random items like canned peppers and radishes from the previous season's harvest for barter. They also got a few bottles of whiskey that some of the residents had squirreled away. Jimmy Lewis brought along twenty jars of his very own moonshine for barter, which could be used, not only as alcohol to imbibe, but also as a cleaner or disinfectant, as well as for medical or hygiene purposes, due to its pure alcohol content.

To conserve fuel, the men decided to put the ATVs belonging to Charlie and Jimmy inside the livestock trailer, to be pulled out only when needed, or if they needed the room inside the trailer for the goods acquired along the way.

After everyone had said their goodbyes to family members who had accompanied them to the Homefront for their send off, Evan climbed up onto the tractor to take the first shift behind the wheel. Jason climbed up alongside him and sat on the toolbox that Robert had bolted to the rear fender, giving him a good position to ride shotgun with his Remington 700. Ed, Charlie, Nate, and Jimmy then climbed inside the trailer, taking up positions in the front, middle, and rear. Being a livestock trailer, there were plenty of viewing and shooting positions, allowing them to spread out to cover all angles while they drove.

While they were to be away, Griff and Daryl were planning on heading up security for all of the participating homesteads, as had been previously discussed. The two were to stay in regular communication with one another, and were to make rounds to the homesteads that were left vulnerable by the absence of the men on the supply run. It was also understood by the other remaining homesteaders that they were to assist Griff and Daryl in the event they were called upon during an emergency or a security situation.

Once they got underway, the plan for the first leg of the journey was to stop in Del Rio to visit Pastor Wallace of the Del Rio Baptist Church. Pastor Wallace had helped them out when Nate, Luke, and Rachel made their way to Tennessee to find Judith.

As they drove away and lost sight of their family members, everyone was silent at first. The unknowns of what could happen to them, as well as their families back home, were ever present on their minds. After several miles, Jimmy broke the conversational ice in the trailer by asking Nate, "So... how are things going with you and Peggy? Rumor around here is that we may be having a wedding sometime soon."

Nate just blushed, looked out the window, and said, "If I can be so blessed. Things are going great. Things have been so busy lately around the farm, getting everything ready for spring calves and planting, we haven't been able to spend as much time together as we would like. Once everything settles down a little, though, I plan on making her and Zack my number one priority."

"She sure seems like a keeper to me," said Charlie with a smile.

Just then, the tractor slowed abruptly and over Nate's handheld radio, the men heard Jason's voice say, "Movement... left side... at least two went into the woods."

"Armed?" Nate asked in reply.

"Unsure," responded Jason.

Nate signaled to Charlie and Jimmy to cover the rear and the opposite side while he and Ed watched for Jason's contacts and responded, "On it."

After a few hundred more yards, the tractor sped back up and things seemed to return to normal. "Negative contact," added Jason, noting that they had passed the potential threat.

Once the tensions eased and the men in the trailer returned to their conversation, Nate said, "And speaking of me and Peggy, one of the things I'm hoping to come across out here is a ring. I want to propose, and I want to do it right—the traditional way, but it's not like you can just run down to the local jewelry store these days. So if you guys could help me keep an eye out... I mean, I have no idea what we are going to encounter out here, but if we were to find a swap meet or something like that, I would be grateful if you let me know if you see something along those lines."

"Anything for love, man, anything for love," Jimmy replied with a teasing chuckle.

As the men rolled into Del Rio on Route 107, they came across a roadblock, positioned in plain view, and guarded by several armed men. Evan stopped the tractor, giving Jason a chance to check the situation out from a distance with his magnified riflescope.

"What do we have?" asked Evan.

"It doesn't look like a trap. They aren't hiding a thing. It looks like possibly some townspeople controlling entrance to the town. One has a shotgun, another has a hunting rifle, and the third has some sort of black rifle, probably a CETME or an FAL. They are checking us out with binoculars, too."

"Can we get through? If they will let us, that is," asked Evan.

"Probably. They just need to drag that flatbed trailer out of the way that they are using to block the road," Jason replied.

Evan looked at Jason as he lowered his rifle and asked, "What do you think?"

"I don't blame them for guarding the place. They're probably okay guys, just doing what we would do."

"Well, let's mosey on up there to them and check it out then, but let's drop off our backup first—just in case. We can't get ourselves into a bind this early on," Evan said as he nodded toward the trailer.

"Roger Roger," responded Jason as he got on his handheld radio and updated the guys in the back on the plan.

Evan eased out the clutch and got the tractor rolling again. As Evan drove the big John Deere tractor and trailer combination toward the roadblock, Jason laid his rifle across his lap with the barrel pointed off to the side in a non-threatening manner. Evan had his VZ58 rifle, with the stock folded, slung over his shoulder, with both hands across the steering wheel in plain sight.

As they reached the roadblock, the men on guard tightened their grips on their guns while one of them motioned for Evan to come to a complete stop. "Hello, there," shouted Evan over the noise of the tractor's diesel engine.

The man then gave him the signal of a slice across his throat, indicating to Evan to shut off or "kill" the tractor's engine. Evan complied and then the man shouted, "State your business."

"Hello, there," Evan said again. "We are just here to see Pastor Wallace. You guys probably know Charlie Blanchard in the back, as well. He ran the little hardware store here before the attacks."

As the men guarding the road looked back at the livestock trailer, Charlie opened the side door and said. "I think we've met before."

The man holding the FAL said, "Yes, sir. I've been in your store a time or two."

Evan then got their attention and said, "We are going on a supply run from our homesteads, and we sort of owe Pastor Wallace a favor. We just wanted to stop in and see if he needed us to keep an eye out for anything while we're out."

"Are you guys from the homesteads in the hills just south of town?" the man asked.

"Yes, sir, we are. I'm Evan Baird and this is Jason Jones."

"Are you guys associated with The Guardians, per chance?" he then asked.

Evan just looked at Jason and said, "We've heard of them."

The man stood there for a moment and then turned to the others and signaled for them to unblock the road to allow them to proceed. He said, "Sorry, fellas, we don't mean to seem unfriendly, but you can't be too careful these days. A lot more people have been passing through lately, and some of them ain't no good."

"We know exactly how you feel," Evan replied as he nodded to Jason. Jason got on the handheld radio and called Jimmy and Nate out of the tree line, rifles in hand. The men guarding the road looked surprised as Evan said, "See? We know exactly how you feel. We had to check you out first, as well."

The man shook his head as if he couldn't believe they could have been taken so easily. "Give the Pastor our regards."

"Will do, sir," Evan said, with a tip of his hat. Charlie, Jimmy, and Nate climbed back into the trailer and they were, once again, underway.

As they proceeded up Route 107 through town, Jason kept a watchful eye, even though they felt at ease in the small, unincorporated town of Del Rio, knowing the remaining locals had pulled together to secure their community just as they had. Although Del Rio was in a fairly isolated part of the country, waves of migrants had passed through, trying to find safe haven and opportunity. Through both charity and theft, they had depleted most of the resources of the town, leaving the remaining residents with a very low tolerance for outsiders.

On their way to the church, Charlie Blanchard called Jason on the radio from the trailer and asked him to have Evan stop by his old hardware store to see if anything was left. During the initial phases of the collapse, he had the presence of mind to pack up a lot of his remaining inventory and take it with him to his home, which he had been using for barter with the other homesteads over the past year. He wasn't able to move all of his stock, however, so he hoped at least something of use would be left.

As they pulled up to what was left of his store, Charlie was horrified to see that not even the door remained on its hinges. The windows had all been busted out and the building appeared to be completely gutted. Evan brought them to a stop in front of the store. As he and Jason climbed down from the tractor, Charlie, Jimmy, Ed, and Nate got out of the trailer to survey the damage.

"Damn!" Charlie said in disgust. "Hell . . . I guess this is what I expected. With me being holed up on my property, away from here all this time, I guess the people just took what they needed."

"The migrants probably had their pick of the place as well," added Jason. "You know how the mob mentality works. As soon as the first brick goes through the window, everything inside is fair game."

The men entered the building to find that even his cash register had been stolen. "Now what the hell could anyone need that for right now?" shouted Charlie. He walked to the back storeroom to find signs that someone had been staying in the building relatively recently. There was human waste in one of the corners of the room, with flies buzzing all around. He then walked back out to the front of the store and said, "That's enough. Let's go," as he stormed out the front door and back to the street.

Without saying a word, the men got back aboard and continued toward the church, as planned. Once they got underway, Jimmy looked at Charlie and said, "I'm sorry about your store."

"Oh, we didn't lose much. It's more the principle of the thing," Charlie replied. "The wife and I were nearing retirement anyway, so we had been letting our inventory get down to bare-bones levels in preparation to shut her down. We knew there wasn't a future in the small Mom-and-Pop hardware store business, with the big chain stores moving into Newport. It was only a matter of time before we went under, anyway."

"And now they're gone, too," said Nate with a chuckle.

"Yep, so I guess none of it mattered, anyway," replied Charlie.

As they pulled up to the church, two men stepped out of the front door, armed with shotguns, which caught Evan and Jason off guard. Following closely behind them, was Pastor Wallace.

"The church has stepped up their game a bit since the last time we've been here," said Jason.

Evan nodded in agreement and said, "Yep, that's not a good sign."

"Well, hello, gentlemen," Pastor Wallace said with a smile as Jason and Evan climbed down from the tractor. "To what do I owe this honor?" He then saw Nate step out of the trailer and said, "Mr. Hoskins, you sure look better than when I saw you last. It looks like these gentlemen have been treating you well."

"Better than I deserve, sir," Nate replied. "I'm staying and working on the Thomas farm, currently, with my brother, Luke, and his fiancé, Rachel, whom you also met."

"Oh yes, that was a shame what happened to Oliver," Pastor Wallace replied in a somber tone. "It sure is nice of you to stay on and help his widow like that, though."

"I'm just blessed that she'll have me, sir," Nate replied.

"So what's with the tractor and trailer?" Pastor Wallace asked.

Evan replied, "We're running a little low on supplies and thought we'd go out on a run to do some scavenging and bartering. We thought we would come by here and see if you needed anything—since we sort of owe you one."

"Oh, you don't owe me a thing," he replied. "Getting Mr. Hoskins here reunited with his family was all a part of God's plan, and I was just honored to be a part of it. But since you are offering, we are running a little low on food, and we could use some clothing and blankets. As you know, we've been opening our doors to give shelter to women and children who don't have anyone to help protect and provide for them. It's an ugly world out there right now, and it's an especially ugly place if you're a woman or child with no place to go. The sheer number of people we have reached out to help has depleted our resources to the point of desperation. The good people of Del Rio have given until it hurts, and many of those who remain have taken some of our refugees in, but there isn't much more to give. We've had a few people stay with us while passing through, only to move on and return again later because of the state of things. Things are tough all over and just aren't getting better," the Pastor said with a concerned voice. "Hence the shotguns," he added.

Charlie Blanchard replied, "We were wondering about that. What happened?"

Pastor Wallace paused for a moment and then said, "We had a group of migrant men find out we were sheltering women here. They snuck into the church in the middle of the night and abducted two young girls. The girls weren't found until a few days later. They had both been raped repeatedly and severely beaten. One of the girls—God rest her soul—died of her injuries before we found them. The other survived and has recovered, but is now pregnant and carrying the child of one of the rapists. We vowed to never let that happen again. Some of the members of the congregation were upset, initially, about my decision to protect our guests with firearms, saying that we must trust in God. I explained to them, it's like the joke about the man of faith during a flood."

"What joke is that?" Jason asked.

"It goes like this," said the pastor as he began to tell the story. "Heavy rains were coming down and there was a flood warning. The authorities sent a truck out to the man's house to tell him a flood was coming and that he needed to evacuate. He refused and said that God would save him. The flood then came, and the man was on his roof trying to stay out of the rapidly rising waters when a boat came to rescue him. He told them no, that God would save him. He prayed and prayed, but the waters continued to rise and the man was now standing on his chimney, with water up to his neck, when a helicopter came to rescue him. He refused help from the helicopter and said that he had faith that God would save him. Soon after, he drowned, and being a good Christian, he went to Heaven. At his first opportunity, he asked God why he did not help him. He explained to God that he had tremendous faith that he would be saved by him, but was left to drown. God looked at the man and said, 'I sent a truck, a boat, and a helicopter. What more did you want?'"

The men couldn't help but chuckle at Pastor Wallace's joke. Pastor Wallace said, "You see, sometimes you have to take the blinders off and realize that God has already provided you with what you need. And these good men here, who are willing to help us protect the church, may be just what he intended us to have. If I'm wrong, then I'll have some explaining to do when I meet him, but until then, I vow to never let a young woman under my care to go through such a thing again."

Chapter 11: Keeping Watch

Back at the Homefront, Daryl and Griff had just finished going over their strategies for how they planned on handling their patrols while the others were away, when Griff's wife, Judy, came around the corner and said, "Oh, there you are. Dinner is ready. Are you staying for dinner, Daryl?"

"No, ma'am. I need to be heading back before dark, although that is a tempting offer," he replied, wishing he were able to accept.

With a look of disappointment on her face, she said, "That's too bad. Well, I'll run and make you a to-go basket. You're not leaving empty-handed," she said in an insistent tone.

"Yes, ma'am. I'd love that," he replied with a smile.

Judy hurried back to the kitchen and started getting a meal together for him to take home, while he and Griff continued wrapping up their conversation. "So we're gonna get started tomorrow, right?" Griff verified with Daryl.

"Yep; how about we meet at the Thomas farm at nine in the morning, and then we will hit Charlie's and Jimmy's places and check in on their families together as we do our loop?" suggested Daryl. "You can just ride your bike over there, and we'll get Mildred to lend you a horse for the next day or so, until the guys get back."

Griff nodded in agreement and said, "That'll work."

Just then, Judy came out of the kitchen with a basket of food for Daryl, with Molly and Peggy in tow. As Judy handed Daryl his basket, Molly said, "If you are just trying to avoid traveling in the dark, you are more than welcome to stay here."

Daryl took the basket with a smile and said, "I really appreciate the hospitality, ma'am, but I've got to tend to my animals and stuff before tomorrow, as I imagine Griff and I will be out for most of the day."

"Well, okay, then. Travel safe," Molly replied.

He then said goodbye to everyone, including the kids, and climbed onto his horse for the ride back. As they all waved goodbye, Judy said, "We've gotta find that man a good woman."

Peggy replied, "Don't look at me; I'm taken."

"Oh, really?" said Judy with her hands on her hips, giving her the eye.

"Yeah, I don't see a ring on that finger," added Molly.

"Okay, that's my cue to leave," Griff said with a chuckle as he went inside.

In a stern voice, Judy then asked, "You'd better fess up about how things are going with you and Nate, or we're gonna put it in Daryl's head that you're available."

"Oh, stop it," Peggy said while blushing. "He's too old for me. Besides, things are going quite well with Nate. I have a feeling he's up to something. That's why I am so nervous about the trip they're on. I just have this horrible feeling that the one good man to come along for me and Zack is going to be taken away from me, like it's all just a big tease. It's dangerous out there, and I just want him to come back to me and never leave again," she said as her eyes welled up with tears.

Molly gave her a big hug while Judy patted her on the back and said, "Oh, stop putting bad thoughts into your own head. Just remember what the guys have been through already. They can make it through anything this screwed up world throws at them."

"God, I hope so," Peggy replied, wiping away the tears.

"Let's go see what Sarah is working on for dinner," Judy said to change the subject.

"I think it's rabbit," Molly said with a smile as they took Peggy back inside.

~ ~ ~ ~

Early the next morning, Daryl and Griff met at Mildred's as planned. Daryl had arrived early, which was his norm. Griff parked his bike and joined Daryl and Luke, who were sitting on the porch enjoying a cup of hot morning tea, catching each other up on the goings-on as each of them saw it. As Griff walked up the steps to the porch, Mildred came outside with a hot cup of tea for him and said, "Here you go, Mike."

"Thank you, ma'am," he said, thankful for the luxury of tea.

"The coffee is all gone, so I hope tea will do," she added. "Hopefully the boys will find us some coffee during their travels."

"Yes, ma'am, that would be nice," he said as he took a sip of her delicious homemade herbal tea.

She turned and went back inside as Daryl asked, "How was your ride in?"

"Uneventful, which means great these days," replied Griff.

Daryl then said, "Luke here has you a horse saddled up and ready to go."

"Great. I've got to warn you, though, I'm not the best horseman," said Griff as he took a sip of tea.

"Well, consider it a training day, then," Daryl said with a chuckle. "If this world doesn't get itself back together soon, we may all be reverting back to horsemen just to get around. Cars won't run without a civilized and functional society to supply them."

"Speaking of that," Griff said. "Have you guys ever heard of or seen a wood gasifier?"

"I've heard of them, but not anything specific," Daryl replied.

"A what?" asked Luke with a confused expression.

"A wood gasifier," Griff replied. "Also known as a wood gas generator. I used to be an admin on a prepper-minded Facebook page before the world took a dump, and I posted a few articles I stumbled across on the subject. It's something that's actually been around for a long time. After World War II, in many places where fuel rations were scarce, some people, especially in Europe, built them and added them to their existing vehicles in order to run their cars on wood."

"On wood? As in burning wood?" asked Luke.

"Yep, as in burning wood. I thought about it on the way over here, pedaling my butt off just to get around. It works by converting wood or charcoal into wood gas. Syngas, they call it. Syngas consists of nitrogen, carbon monoxide, hydrogen, methane, and other gasses. After syngas is cooled and filtered in the gasifier, you can run a regular internal combustion engine on the stuff. All you really need is some random scrap metal parts and some welding skills," explained Griff.

Luke replied, "Between everyone around here, we should have all the stuff necessary to make one, or two, or three of those things. We should give it a shot one of these days."

"When the others get back, let's see what we can come up with. I can't believe I haven't thought about building one until this morning," replied Griff.

"Well, I guess we had better get going," said Daryl as he stood up and stretched. "Being waited on and given luxuries like hot tea will spoil me and make me soft, if I don't get up and moving soon."

Luke chuckled and said, "Mildred will wait on you hand and foot, but in return you've gotta work your butt off to earn your keep."

"As it should be," Daryl said with a nod.

Daryl and Griff went around back to the barn where their saddled horses awaited. Daryl hopped right up onto his trusty steed while Griff took a more cautious and contemplative approach. After a moment getting acclimated to the feel of a horse again, Griff said, "Okay, I guess I'm ready."

With a nudge to the horses' sides, they were off. The first stop on their loop was Jason and Sarah's new homestead. The two approached cautiously from a distance, as they had seen signs that people had been in the area on the way over. There was a discarded plastic water bottle on the side of the road that Daryl was certain had not been there on his way through that morning. Griff dismounted and tied his horse to a small tree. He then crept around the fence line, which was overgrown with kudzu vines and other foliage, in order to get up close to take a look. Once he was confident nothing looked out of place, he motioned for Daryl to approach as he continued toward the home. He entered the home from the back door, and as Daryl arrived at the front of the house, he opened the front door from the inside and called it clear. Daryl then took a quick ride around the property's perimeter, as the final sweep, before moving on.

As Daryl completed his perimeter lap, he arrived back at the front porch where Griff was waiting and said, "Looks good to me."

"Excellent. I was thinking about starting a smoldering fire in the fireplace to make it look like someone is home, but with my luck, the place would burn down while I was gone."

Daryl grinned and said, "I sure as hell wouldn't want to be the one to tell Jason I'd burned his new home down by accident."

"Same here. I guess we'll just have to take our chances with the passersby," said Griff as he turned to walk back to his horse.

Once mounted back up, he and Daryl continued their rounds, stopping by Griff's new homestead, and then on to Linda Cox's place. While observing Linda's home from a distance, they saw smoke coming from the chimney. "That's a good sign," said Griff as they continued closer.

"Yep, a dirtbag that stopped by to rob the place probably wouldn't be taking the time to get all cozy," added Daryl.

As they continued toward the driveway, Daryl stopped his horse and said, "Look, another plastic bottle."

"Where in the world are people getting bottled water these days?" Griff remarked. "I thought stuff like that got used up or hoarded up during the beginning stages of the collapse, with the poisoned water supplies and all."

Daryl pivoted his horse toward Griff and replied, "Yes, well, either they looted someone who was well prepared or they were using refuse bottles to carry water during their trek through these parts."

"Let's get on up to Linda's," Griff replied quickly, as he was getting nervous about bands of unknowns traveling so close to a single woman's home.

They approached her house with caution, but with a quickened pace, compared to the others. As they approached her driveway, they saw movement around the side of the house as Linda opened the front door. Griff clutched his AR-15 and began to pull it up to the fire position as he heard the loud, angry bray of Linda's donkey, Jack, as he ran toward them, slowing his pace once he recognized Daryl.

Daryl laughed at Griff's reaction and said, "He's a guard donkey, not an attack donkey. Relax there, sergeant. He probably won't bite you."

Griff lowered his weapon as Jack, the donkey, trotted up to Daryl and began to sniff him and his horse, followed by the demand to be scratched behind the ears. Daryl and Griff then proceeded slowly to Linda's home with Jack trotting along behind.

"Sorry about that, guys," Linda said. "I let Jack have the run of the place now that my dogs are gone. He's a territorial fellow, so he makes for a great early-warning system. He's hell on the coyotes that come after my chickens, too. They've learned not to mess with him. He will chase them down and stomp the life out of them."

"I had no idea donkeys were good guard animals," replied Griff.

"Oh, they're great," added Daryl. "You don't have to feed 'em like a dog, either, since they eat the grass."

"Well, you two tie up your horses and come on in," Linda said as she pointed to her porch railing that she herself used for a hitching post. I just heated up some soup beans and cornbread on the wood stove. You need to take a break and eat."

Daryl just looked at Griff and said, "Oh, heck, yes."

Chapter 12: Beyond Del Rio

As Evan and the men on the supply run were just getting ready to leave the church to press on with the mission at hand, Pastor Wallace asked, "So where are you headed from here? What's your plan?"

Evan responded, "We were kind of hoping you could help us with that. Being a stopover point for migrants, we figured you might have heard a few things and could give us some advice on the subject."

"Well," the pastor said as he scratched his chin, "you've heard of the UN troops that are on the ground in places, I assume?"

Evan nodded and said, "One of our regular HAM stations that recently dropped off of the air made a few reports about them before he went silent."

"Yeah, that's the problem with transmitting stuff the powers-that-be might not be wanting put out. It doesn't take much technology or skill to track a radio transmission, especially a regular broadcaster. Anyway, from what the people passing through these parts have been saying, there are UN troops in the northeastern states that are said to be there as peacekeepers for a recovery, but they are behaving more like a pillaging occupying force. Without the worldwide media to report on them, it's like they are dogs, turned loose on the people. It's like they are enjoying the spoils of war the old-fashioned way, without, of course, having fought a war."

"At least not directly," Ed interjected.

"Exactly," replied Pastor Wallace with a look of mutual understanding. "Anyway, the closest I've heard of them to us is Atlanta. Atlanta is said to be a staging ground. They've been bringing transport planes into what was the Hartsfield-Jackson

International Airport, and are said to have converted many of the hangars into barracks."

Ed spoke up and said, "The same thing was going on in Ohio before I left, which is one of the reasons I finally decided to bug out."

"Son of—" began Jason in disbelief.

Evan interrupted with, "I can't imagine the militias in the south are gonna just roll over for that sort of thing."

"No, I'd imagine not," Pastor Wallace said in agreement. "One of the ladies who passed through with some of her family said her husband was killed by them while on an intel-gathering mission with a group of militias that banded together, known as the 'Southern States Defensive Alliance,' or 'Southern Alliance' for short. She said just having your name associated with the Alliance is dangerous these days. As the UN troops get dug in, just as in any similar occupation, they begin to root out any possible insurgencies or resistance movements, which, of course, would be any flag-waving American patriot these days."

Evan looked at Jason and the others as they each thought for a moment about what they had heard. Pastor Wallace broke the silence. "And don't you guys go getting yourselves all wrapped up in that fight, either. You've got families depending on you to get home to them, to provide for and protect them. Don't leave them in this broken world alone too soon. There are plenty of other able-bodied men out there rallying for the cause. You need to continue to protect this area like you've been doing. That's why you're here; I'm sure of it. Help those kids of yours grow up to be the next generation of patriots. We need that more than anything."

"You're right," Evan said, "but if—"

"If!" Pastor Wallace interrupted. "If they come this way and mess with the people around here, then you give 'em hell. Make them scared of these hills. Make them regret ever leaving their own homeland to mess with ours. But until then, do what God put you here for and protect your families and neighbors."

Evan just looked him in the eye and said, "Yes, sir."

"Now, considering all of that, I recommend you head over into North Carolina through U.S. Highway 70, or maybe follow the French Broad River," Pastor Wallace added. "If you go west, you'll have more of a chance of bumping into the occupiers, as they are probably using the I-75 corridor as a way to link up with their forces up north."

"That's some pretty sound tactical thinking, Pastor," Nate said, impressed with his grasp of the situation.

"Marine Corps, son," he replied. "I had another life before I got my calling."

The men looked at each other and smiled, as it was just so obvious now. "So, why North Carolina?" Jason asked.

Pastor Wallace continued to explain, "If you follow the French Broad or U.S. Highway 70 long enough, you eventually come across Hot Springs. Many of the migrants we've had come through have come in via 70 to avoid the troubles of the population centers. In the cities not actively held by the remnants of the state governments, the non-state-controlled governmental forces have taken over, like in Atlanta, and if not them, the gangs or other shady elements have. I've heard some talk of cartels, but I don't know the extent of that.

"Oh, great," said Nate under his breath in disgust. The last thing he, of all people, wanted was more encroachment by the cartels, considering his previous struggles.

"Just as God told Abraham to stay out in the wilderness and avoid Sodom and Gomorrah, that's still good advice here. Anyway," Pastor Wallace continued, "some of the folks passing through mentioned that there were actually a few swap meets and trading posts in the area. The Blue Ridge Militia, who just happen to be a key part of the Southern Alliance, has everything pretty well squared away for now, so it's a fairly stable place. Between here and there is anybody's guess, of course, but that's the best advice I've got for you."

"Well, sir, we greatly appreciate it," Evan said as he reached out to shake Pastor Wallace's hand in thanks. "We will do our best to bring back some supplies for you as well."

As the men all thanked Pastor Wallace for his help and prepared to get back on the road, Charlie Blanchard said, "Oh, by the way, Pastor, can you do me—or us, rather—a favor and call my wife on the CB and, somehow, discreetly let her know we are okay, without giving it away that we are gone?"

"Absolutely," the Pastor replied as he shook Charlie's hand.

With that, the men boarded the tractor and the trailer and got back on Route 107, headed for U.S. Highway 70. As they rolled through Del Rio, the empty homes, some burned to the ground by who knows what, were a sobering sight. If a small rural town like this can look so devastated by the collapse, just how could the rest of the country, and the world for that matter, possibly look? Considering that the world's economies were so interdependent before the collapse, they imagined the same could be found all over. Except, of course, in Russia and China, the two seeming to be the only true survivors of the resulting global financial collapse.

On the east end of town, they found Route 107 to again be blocked and guarded by several of the local men. This time, though, as the tractor approached, they pushed the old pickup truck that they were using as a barricade out of the way, allowing the tractor to pass unimpeded. As they rolled through, they all gave them a wave as one of the men shouted, "Good luck," to them as they passed.

"Time to put our game faces back on," said Jason, over the handheld, to the men in the back. Nate replied with a double click of the mic and off they went.

Chapter 13: The Mounted Patrol

After Daryl and Griff got their fill of Linda's delicious soup beans and cornbread, Griff said, "Linda, thank you so much for the meal. We thought we would be living on deer jerky today. That was a pleasant surprise."

"Anytime, guys," she replied with a smile. "I'm just glad to have the company. I won't keep you any longer; I know you've got a long day ahead of you."

"We'll be back by tomorrow, or the next day at the latest," added Daryl with a tip of his hat. "If anything out of the ordinary comes up or you need anything, just put the word out and we'll come running."

She replied with a smile, "You're such a gentleman, Daryl, as always. You two ride carefully."

With that, Daryl and Griff mounted their horses and headed on to the next property. As the day went on, they stopped at each of the homesteads and found everything to be secure. With the exception of the absence of the men who were away, it was mostly business as usual. As they approached Jimmy Lewis' home, however, their casual chat was interrupted by a gunshot that sounded like it was coming from directly in front of them, in the direction of the Lewis family's barn. Jimmy's wife, Beth, came running out of the barn screaming and yelling, with an old pump shotgun in her hands. As she racked another shell into the chamber, a shot rang out from the woods, whipping her backward, and knocking her to the ground, where she lay still and lifeless. Daryl and Griff kicked their horses into action and ran them at a full gallop to reach Beth.

As they approached her, Daryl could see there was nothing they could do; she had been struck on the left side of her head and died instantly. He yelled to Griff, "I've got the woods!" He altered his course in pursuit of the assailants.

Griff leapt off his horse as it came to a stop and checked her vitals, even though the cold hard truth was obvious, due to the severity of her wound. He then climbed back aboard his horse and rode off to join Daryl in the pursuit. Although he was feeling more comfortable on horseback as the day progressed, he felt barely in control of the horse as it ran at full speed through the tight confines of the surrounding woods. He ducked and dodged limbs and branches that the horse easily fit under, but which left little room for a rider in the saddle. Small limbs would smack him in the face while he focused on dodging larger ones. One small branch managed to catch him in the eye, stunning him, causing him to lose focus for a moment. He looked up with his good eye open just in time to see a dark object... and then there was darkness.

While in pursuit and closing in on the assailant fleeing on foot, Daryl narrowly avoided hitting a hog that had apparently been turned loose by the attacker. "Damn thieves," he said under his breath as he adjusted his course. He saw the man dive behind a root cluster of a fallen tree, armed with some sort of bolt-action rifle. Daryl brought his horse to a stop and dismounted while pulling his .45-70 lever-action rifle from its scabbard. He chambered a round as he took cover behind a tree and smacked his horse to get it to run away and out of the line of fire.

"You can't get away!" he yelled. "There are a lot more of us in these woods than just me."

"You're not the only one with friends out here," a man's raspy voice replied. "You had better get back there and tend to your woman before you get yourself killed."

"You're gonna die today," yelled Daryl in a cold and dark voice.

Just then, the bark of the tree Daryl was using for cover exploded just above his head as a shot came out of the woods from his right flank. Stunned by the impact, he instinctively dove to another tree just behind him while he aimed in the direction of the shot. He saw a man in old style woodland camo BDUs take aim in preparation to fire another shot. Daryl fired as a second shot rang out. As he heard a bullet whiz by his head, narrowly missing him, he cycled the lever of his rifle, chambered another round, and fired again, striking the man in the lower abdomen, dropping him to the ground where he writhed in pain like a wounded animal.

Daryl turned his attention back to the location of the man hiding behind the fallen tree and yelled, "I just met your friend. He's not doing too well at the moment, though. Give it up!"

Except for the ringing in his ears from the gunshots, all Daryl heard was silence. He pulled the signaling mirror that he always carried from his pack and used it to get a look around the tree without exposing himself. *Where the hell is Griff?* He thought to himself, wishing his backup would arrive.

Not seeing anything in the mirror, he took a peek around the tree. Afraid the man had changed positions during the exchange of gunfire between him and the second assailant, Daryl began to scan the area adjacent to the downed tree, looking for any signs of movement. Feeling as if his situation had been compromised by possibly losing track of the first assailant, Daryl fell back, one tree at a time, getting some distance between himself and his adversary.

Once in a safe position, Daryl topped off the tube magazine of his rifle, replacing the two cartridges that he had fired, giving him a total of eight rounds in the tube and one in the chamber. He might not have the magazine capacity of a modern tactical rifle, but Daryl appreciated the knock-down power that the heavy projectile the old .45-70 Government cartridge provided. One hit was all he needed to knock someone down, body armor or not.

After a few more moments of silence, Daryl decided to circle around to the left to try to either flank or get a better view of his adversary. He knew that he just could not break off the pursuit, as the other homesteads in the area would be in danger as long as this murderer was on the loose. Daryl crept through the woods, as he had done countless times, ground-stalking deer the old-fashioned way, and got to a position where he could see behind the man's cover; he was indeed gone.

Daryl crouched down behind some vegetation surrounding a mature walnut tree, visually scanning all around, trying to figure out where the man might have gone. As he peered through the weeds with his rifle clutched tightly and pointed out in front of him, he heard a twig snap behind him and immediately rolled to the ground, releasing his rifle, and drew his model 1875 Remington revolver, aiming it underneath his arm as he turned to see the man creeping up behind him.

He fired an unaimed shot, striking the man in the shoulder, causing him to drop his rifle. Daryl then continued turning toward the man, who was now unarmed except for the knife in his belt, which he clutched with his left hand. Daryl slowly cocked the hammer of his revolver and said, "I told you that you were gonna die today."

Just as the man began to pull the knife, Daryl fired a shot directly into the man's abdomen, dropping him to the ground. He then walked over and looked into the eyes of the dying man, who had dropped the knife as he fell in order to grasp his devastating stomach wound. Without breaking his stare, Daryl walked over, picked up the knife, put it to the dying man's throat, and said, "You have ten seconds to make your peace with God." After counting to ten, Daryl slit the man's throat, ending his suffering without wasting another bullet.

He then stood up, scanned the area, and listened, hoping that there were no other intruders in the area. He walked over to the other dying man and ended his life in the same manner. He took the two rifles from the attackers and leaned them up against a tree so that they could return for them later when they came back to dispose of the bodies. Daryl then hiked back through the woods toward the Lewis home, finding his horse near the body of poor Beth Lewis.

"Where the hell are you, Griff?" he said, mumbling to himself while looking around.

Chapter 14: Pressing On

As Evan drove the tractor and trailer up Route 107 toward U.S. Highway 70, their first obstacle was the bridge that crossed the French Broad River. As they approached the bend in the road just before the bridge, Evan brought the tractor to a stop and shut off the engine to contemplate the situation.

"Chokepoint," said Jason as he picked up his binoculars to look from a distance. He then continued and said, "There is an old, burned up car on the bridge. It could be a trap, or it could have been a trap. Either way, we need to check it out before we get any closer."

"Yep, I agree completely," replied Evan. Jason climbed down from the tractor and walked back to the trailer to talk to the men in the back. He wanted to avoid using their handheld radios, just in case someone was listening to learn their intentions with the bridge. He walked up to one of the open windows and said, "Two of you guys come with me to check out the bridge up ahead; the other two cover us from here and guard our ride."

"I'll come," replied Ed enthusiastically.

"Me, too," Nate also replied.

As Ed and Nate joined Jason and began to walk toward the bridge, staying along the edge of the road for cover, Charlie took up a position at the rear of the trailer, while Jimmy joined Evan on the tractor. Once they reached the bridge, Jason dropped down over the side of the hill for a moment to clear the area and the underside of the bridge for any potential hostiles. After just a few moments, he climbed back up to the road and said, "No trolls that I can see."

"How do you want to approach the car?" asked Ed.

Jason replied, "I'm the only one with a scope, which means I can provide the best long-range cover, but I don't want to volunteer you guys to get out on the bridge to check the car out up close."

"That's no problem," Nate answered. "I'll take point. You got my back, Ed?" he asked.

"Sure thing," Ed replied.

The two men then approached the bridge, hugging the left side's concrete railing while Jason covered them from the right in order to get a clear firing line onto the bridge without them being directly in front of his muzzle. Nate and Ed worked their way across the bridge to the center where the disabled car was located, occasionally looking back to Jason for hand signals in the event he had spotted something through his scope.

When they reached the car, Nate remained low to the ground and left the cover of the railing to get a look inside. To his horror, he found the partially burned remains of what appeared to be three adults. He also noticed four bullet holes in the driver's side door and one in the rear passenger's door just behind it. He could only assume the unlucky travelers were ambushed while crossing the bridge. He scurried back to the railing where Ed was covering him and informed him of what he had seen. Ed then relayed to Jason that there were no visible threats, via hand signals.

Once they rejoined Jason at the beginning of the bridge, Nate explained the scene in detail. After a moment of deliberation, Jason said, "I'll cover the crossing from here. Ed, you've got the next level of reach with that M1A. You drop down the hill and cover the riverbanks, and Nate, you head back and update the others. Tell Evan to go ahead and proceed toward the bridge. Once he gets here, take up a point position, walking along with the tractor at least until he gets to the car. Tell him to use the loader bucket on the tractor to push the car out of the way. Have Jimmy and Charlie each take a side during the crossing. Once you're all across, Ed and I will form up and meet you on the other side when you're clear."

With a nod to the affirmative, everyone took up their positions in accordance with the plan. As the tractor neared the bridge, Jason gave Evan the thumbs up and the tractor proceeded across. When Evan reached the car, he lowered the loader to just about a foot off the ground and easily pushed the car off to the side as they passed. From his vantage point on the tractor, he could see down to the grizzly scene inside the car and shook his head in disgust that the world had come to this.

As Ed watched Evan cross the bridge from underneath, he noticed an abundance of spent shell casings. They were mostly 7.62x39 Russian and 5.56mm NATO and appeared to have been from various different occasions, as they had different levels of weathering and contamination. *This must be a popular hunting stand,* he thought to himself in a morbid sort of way.

As the tractor reached the other side of the bridge, Ed rallied on Jason, and the two joined up with the group on the north side of the river as planned.

Once they all met back up and took their respective positions on the tractor and trailer, Jason looked at Evan and said, "Getting around sure is a lot of work these days."

Evan replied, "It is if you want to stay alive." He eased out the clutch and they got underway.

Looking at their map, Jason said, "Looks like we just go straight for a bit and then hang a right on U.S. Highway 70."

"What are you thinking for the night?" Evan asked. "We've not got a lot of daylight left before we need to consider hunkering down somewhere."

As Jason looked at the map and pondered Evan's question, he ran his finger over their proposed route and said, "Once on U.S. 70, after the fourth road that shoots off to the left, there is a stretch of the road that may have a few agricultural fields, with mountains to the left and the river to the right. I would sure rather be backed up to the mountains with lots of escape routes, than the river. Once we get to that point, let's start looking hard for a place to shut down for the night."

"That sounds good," Evan replied. "What about watches?"

"On it," Jason replied as he picked up the handheld and said, "Nate, you up?"

"Yep," replied Nate over the radio from inside the trailer.

Jason said, "You guys work out who's gonna stand the first watch tonight and take naps accordingly. One of you up and about should be good, for now.

"Roger Roger," replied Nate.

Evan just chuckled at the reply. Jason gave him a dirty look and then asked Nate, "Are you making fun of me?"

Nate simply responded, "Yep."

Evan busted out laughing and said, "You just make it too easy sometimes, Jason."

Jason just shrugged it off and they continued pressing forward. Just as Jason had said from his reading of the map, they soon passed by several roads on the left of Highway 70 where a few homes remained. Some looked like they may possibly still be occupied, but others were clearly abandoned.

Jason sighed and said with dismay, "I just don't get why so many homes around here are vacant. It's not like this is the kind of place you would need to migrate from in these times. Where did they all go?"

Evan answered, "I'm sure some left to link up with family that may have been in a better position somewhere. Others probably fell victim to the crimes of humanity that we see all too often, like the family on the bridge. Others probably were just not in a position to make it. If you were being kept alive by prescription drugs, for example, unless you were well connected like the ruling class, you probably simply didn't last that long. Throw in other formerly treatable illnesses and injuries, with suicides and crime, and the mortality rate is surely catching up with the local population."

"Yeah... I guess," replied Jason.

In just a few more miles, the stretch of Highway 70 they were on began to become more remote, as Jason had thought. Jason scanned the terrain up ahead and to the left, looking for a place to get off the main road for the night. He noticed a dirt road that ran between two overgrown fields and led off into the woods and the hills. "Stop here," he directed Evan. "Let's check this out."

As Evan pulled to a stop, Jason climbed down and walked back to the trailer where he saw Jimmy awake, with Charlie and Nate trying to catch a nap on the floor. "What's up?" asked Jimmy, enquiring as to why they had stopped.

"We're looking for a place to bed down for the night," replied Jason. "Can you guys hop on your ATVs and scout a dirt road out for us? It would be best if we cleared the way before putting the tractor and trailer at risk," he explained.

"Sure thing," Jimmy replied smartly as he kicked Charlie's boot to wake him. "Rise and shine, Old Man," he said.

Once Charlie cleared his head from his nap, Jimmy explained what they were being asked to do. The two men fired up their ATVs and rode them out of the back of the trailer, headed off on their scouting run. They rode down the road and turned left onto the dirt road that Jason had pointed out to them. Soon they were just sounds off in the distance, and then nothing.

After about five minutes, Charlie's ATV came back down the dirt road, but Jimmy's was nowhere to be seen. The men just looked at each other with the same look of concern, but waited for Charlie to get to them and give them a debrief before jumping to any conclusions. They were relieved to see that Charlie did not look at all distressed as he shut his engine off and said, "Looks good. If you go about a half mile up the road, you come to a clearing with a little stream that runs through. It looks like people have stopped to camp there more than once, but not too recently. I imagine we aren't the only people that have been looking for a place to bed down while traveling this highway."

"Where's Jimmy?" asked Nate.

"Oh, he's fixin' dinner," Charlie replied with a smile.

"Fixing dinner?" Ed queried.

As Charlie climbed off the ATV, he said, "Yep, good thing that boy had his crossbow mounted on his ATV rack as usual. He's always killing something for dinner back home with that thing. He nailed a good-sized rabbit from about twenty yards away. He's skinning it now and washing it in the stream. He said he will be looking for some wood to build a fire with and to make a skewer while we're setting everything else up."

"Outstanding!" replied Jason.

Evan just smiled and said, "Tell me about it. I thought we were gonna be eating jerky and beans for dinner. Now it will be hasenpfeffer."

As the men climbed back onto the tractor and trailer, Ed said, "Yep, or rabbit on a stick, rabbit and beans, rabbit stew, grilled rabbit, oh... or fried rabbit; we did bring a skillet, right?"

Chapter 15: Daryl's Dilemma

Daryl shouted for Griff a few times, but never heard a reply. He mounted his horse, went back, made a quick, cursory look around the property, and then headed back into the woods to search for Griff. A frontiersman at heart, it was easy for Daryl to put his skills, which were once merely an obscure hobby, into practice to track Griff and his horse. As he picked his way through the woods, slowly looking for signs of Griff's trail, he came upon Griff lying face down in a very awkward position.

"Griff!" he yelled as he leapt from the saddle to get to him as fast as he could. At first, he thought Griff might be dead, as his skin had lost a lot of its color. Upon checking his pulse, he immediately noticed that Griff was alive but badly injured and unconscious. His right arm was either broken or dislocated, as it was in a very unnatural position. He also appeared to have had some sort of impact to his face. Daryl turned and looked up to see a tree branch with scuffed up bark, and realized that he must have not only suffered injuries from hitting his head, but more than likely had multiple injuries from the unprotected fall as well, landing on several jagged rocks. Griff's breathing was laborious and shallow, and his lips were beginning to turn purple.

"Damn it!" Daryl yelled aloud. Afraid to move Griff by himself in this condition, he climbed aboard his horse and rode like a madman back to Linda Cox's home, as she was the closest neighbor. Daryl pushed his horse as hard as he could, thinking to himself, *just hold on, Griff, hold on. I've already lost one neighbor today, and I'll be damned if I'll lose another.*

Linda was outside working when she saw Daryl riding like a madman up her driveway. In his traditional frontiersman attire, it looked like a scene straight out of an old western movie. She dropped what she was doing and ran out to meet him, fearing the worst.

Daryl pulled back on the reins and brought his horse to a stop; he was out of breath and could barely get the words out. "C'mon... get your horse... Beth's dead and Griff's hurt... bad," he said, ashamed that he had let down his neighbors whom he had vowed to protect.

Linda's eyes immediately welled up with tears at the news of the death of Jimmy's wife, Beth. Then she quickly wiped the tears away and realized Daryl clearly needed her to help with Griff. "I'll be right back!" she shouted as she ran for her house.

In what almost seemed like an instant to Daryl, Linda was running back out of her front door, not even closing it behind her, with a bag over her shoulder, and running for her barn. She came racing out of the barn on her horse and said, "Let's go!"

Daryl spurred his tired horse back into action and rode hard alongside Linda as they raced back to the Lewis home. Arriving at the Lewis home, Linda came to a stop alongside Beth's body, looking down at her in horror. Daryl rode alongside her and gently said, "Come on, Griff needs us. There is nothing we can do for her. We'll tend to her later."

Linda snapped out of it and said, "Of course," and rode off with Daryl into the woods toward Griff.

When they arrived, his skin was pale and his lips were blue. His breathing was now rapid and shallow and he was still unconscious. After giving him a good look-over, Linda said, "We need Rachel. You stay with Griff; I'm gonna ride back to the Lewis home and try to find their CB radio and start relaying a call for help. Rachel is going to have to come our way. We can't risk injuring him further by moving him by ourselves right now, without medical oversight."

Daryl nodded as Linda raced back toward the Lewis house. "Hang in there, buddy," Daryl said. "Hang in there. We're gonna need you around this place a lot in the future, so you can't leave us now."

When Linda reached the Lewis home, she quickly dismounted and hurried inside. She ran through the hallway, from room to room, opening doors, searching for their radio. She finally found Jimmy's workshop, where he had his CB radio hooked to an old car battery. It was kept charged with a simple solar panel that was designed to trickle charge an unused battery and keep it topped off while in storage. She picked up the mic and said, "Mayday, Mayday, Mayday—who's on here? Mayday, Mayday, Mayday! This is Linda; we need help at the Lewis home!"

She heard Robert Brooks answer over the radio, "Linda? What's wrong? This is Robert."

"We have a medical emergency at the Lewis home. Can you make sure Dr. Stewart gets out here as fast as she can? I've got to get back to helping Daryl."

"Who's hurt?" he asked.

"Please, just send for the Doc," Linda replied, not wanting to give out too much information over the radio. She didn't know how to deal with such a situation, and taking things one step at a time just seemed like the right way to handle it.

"Of course," Robert replied.

Linda ran back outside, mounted her horse, and raced off to help Daryl with Griff. When she arrived, she found Daryl kneeling over Griff with a tear in his eye. She was taken aback, seeing Daryl so full of emotion. His big, rough exterior had disguised his warm and loving heart. Prior to the collapse, no one in the area had gotten personally close to Daryl. Except for his outings to various Frontier Days activities, which were similar to renaissance fairs, but with a focus on frontier living and bushcraft, he pretty much kept to himself.

Daryl wiped the tears from his eyes and said, "Oh, God, I hope he makes it."

"How's he doing?" she asked.

"He's got something going on internally; I don't know what, but it's just not right. There's no telling how bad he got banged up inside, taking a hit and a fall like that onto these rocks and roots. I was gonna roll him over, but was afraid he might have blood in his lungs or something, so I just left him be."

"That's probably the right thing to do," she said. "Except maybe we should reposition his arm. We don't want him to have nerve damage or something from a prolonged loss of circulation from it being in this position."

Daryl agreed and helped Linda by holding Griff's body in place while she manipulated his arm into a more natural position. "Oh, that would have hurt so bad if he was awake," she said, commenting on the unnatural sounds his bones and ligaments made during the repositioning of his arm.

After a few moments of silence waiting for help to arrive, Daryl said, "We can't just leave Beth out there like that. If you'll stay here with Griff, I'll go and get her moved inside of the house or something."

"Yes, of course," she replied.

He then noticed that in her haste to leave her house, she had come unarmed. He removed his 1875 Remington from its holster, topped off the cylinder, replaced the spent cartridges with new ones, and handed it to her, along with his holster belt. Without saying a word, she just looked up at him and smiled, taking his gun to keep with her. He picked up his rifle, climbed up onto his horse, and rode back to the Lewis home to deal with Beth's remains.

When he arrived at the house, he saw several birds gathering around her body as if they were inspecting a potential meal. In disgust of what he saw, Daryl leapt off his horse, pulling his rifle from its scabbard as he went. He gripped the barrel with both hands and began swinging the rifle wildly at the birds, scaring them away while screaming, "Get the hell out of here!" repeatedly, in a fit of total rage.

After the last bird was gone, in a state of total mental and physical exhaustion, Daryl dropped to his knees and began to cry aloud. He, like everyone else who grew up in the peace and stability of pre-collapse, modern America, was getting fatigued by the constant suffering and misery that seemingly lurked around every corner. It was all beginning to take its toll, even on strong men such as himself.

After a few moments, he regained his composure and walked back over to Beth, knelt down to her, and whispered aloud, "I'm so sorry." He picked her up and walked into the house, where he went into her and Jimmy's bedroom and laid her on the bed. He retrieved some water and a washcloth from the bathroom and cleaned her up the best he could. He knew the wound was a horrible sight, but he did not want the horror magnified for Jimmy by having her covered in blood as well if he should return before they had to bury her. He then pulled the covers over her head and left her in the room, closing the door behind him on the way out.

Chapter 16: Rabbit Stew

As Evan, Jason, and Ed arranged the trailer and the tractor into a proper defensive position for the night, as well as surveying the surrounding area for potential threats, Charlie got a fire going while Jimmy built a homemade rotisserie to cook his catch. They had packed a few basic cooking utensils for the trip, as well as salt and pepper, green beans, potatoes, carrots, and venison jerky. The beans were canned in jars and the carrots and potatoes were stored in buckets of sand to keep the air and the pests away.

Jimmy pulled out the campfire kettle that Evan's wife, Molly, had packed for them, and while the rabbit cooked over the fire, he prepared a stew base with water, beans, sliced potatoes, and sliced carrots. Once the rabbit was mostly cooked, he removed it from the fire, cut it up into stew pieces, and added it to the kettle, which he had cooking over the fire.

"Dang, that smells good, Jimmy," Jason said as he came over to the fire to check out Charlie and Jimmy's handiwork.

Jimmy smiled and said, "Just because you're roughing it, doesn't mean you can't be civilized. It'll be ready in a few more minutes if you guys want to be getting yourselves one of those stainless mugs to eat out of," he said, pointing at a box of supplies in the back of the trailer.

Ed grabbed each of them a mug and they all gathered around the fire. They simply enjoyed each other's company for a few moments and chatted about the day's events before Evan said, "Well, gentlemen, like Jimmy said, there is no reason not to be civilized. If none of you mind, I would like to say grace."

Everyone unanimously agreed, and they all bowed their heads as Evan said, "Lord, thank you for giving us the abilities to take care of ourselves in this dangerous world we now live in. Thank you for these friends, who we each trust with our lives, and please help us to look after one another during our journey away from home. Also, Lord, thank you for our friends back home who are watching out for our families and please keep them safe in doing so. We also thank you for this rabbit that has been provided for us; please use the nourishment that it provides to help carry us through our journey to be able to better provide for our friends and family back home. In your name we pray, Amen."

"Amen," the others said in unison.

"Okay, guys, dig in," Evan said as he raised his mug.

Jimmy dished out a mug full of rabbit stew for each of the men. They enjoyed their hot meal and their jovial conversation for the next half hour. They shared with each other thoughts of home and their hopes and dreams for their families in this new world. The fathers expressed their concern for the world their children would inherit, while the potential future fathers, such as Nate and Jimmy, just soaked it all in.

As the men continued to talk about their families back home, Jimmy said, "Beth and I have been keeping a little secret for a while now. Maybe when we get back home, we'll announce it to the community."

"What's the secret?" Jason asked.

"We're having a baby," he said with an uncontrollable smile.

"Well, why the heck would you be keeping that from us?" asked Charlie, pleasantly surprised by Jimmy's news.

"Beth has miscarried before," he explained. "She said she would rather keep it to ourselves until things looked a little more certain. She doesn't want to face the pity of the other women if it doesn't work out. She's just funny that way. She keeps her feelings wrapped up pretty tight. I think her rough childhood instilled her with that as a defensive mechanism. I think we are far enough along now, though, that it seems like a sure thing. She's even starting to show a little baby bump."

"Outstanding, Jimmy," replied Evan. "With all of the darkness in this world, here is to you and Beth bringing in a little light." He raised his mug of rabbit stew to give a campfire toast, followed by everyone joining in.

"Heck, if we keep this up, and if Nate ever gets off his butt and proposes to Peggy, and they get started, we may end up with enough kids to have our own school," Jason said in a half-serious and half-joking manner.

In agreement, Charlie added, "Yeah, and a school that doesn't ban the Bible and the Constitution. It's no damn wonder how easy this country was to knock down, the way our foundations were being eroded away."

Everyone agreed, and after a little more banter, Charlie said, "Well, I'm first watch, so I guess I had better get my butt up and get with it before I get lazy with this belly full of hot food."

Jason replied, "So we've got six of us; let's do three three-hour watches of two guys. One can stay close to camp while the other roves the nearby area. The two watch-standers can take the two radios we have to communicate. Let's make it Charlie and Jimmy, Ed and Nate, and then Evan and me." He turned to Ed and Nate and asked, "Since Charlie and Jimmy are up first, do you want mid or morning shift?"

Ed looked at Nate, and Nate just shrugged in reply. Ed then answered, "Heck, we'll take the mid shift."

"Well, guys, hit the sack. Jimmy and I have it from here. It's gonna be a long day tomorrow and we'll need our rest," Charlie said as Jason handed him the radios.

Everyone agreed and found a place to bed down in the trailer, as it was their only form of shelter. After they all got situated, Jason sat up and said, "Ah, heck, I'm gonna drag my sleeping bag out in the bushes. There's no need to have us all here in one spot like a gift-wrapped present for hostiles.

"Oh, great, Jason, way to help a guy fall asleep, thinking about getting ambushed," joked Ed.

"Never drop your guard in this world, Ed," Jason replied sharply as he carried his sleeping bag out of the trailer.

"Well, hell, that's my watch partner, so I guess I should go too," replied Evan as he, too, rolled up his bag and went outside.

Jason found a good flat place to sleep, just barely out of their clearing, off into the woods while Evan took shelter underneath the tractor. "Good luck with the critters over there," Evan joked to Jason.

"Good luck with the oil drips from that leaky old tractor," Jason replied with a chuckle.

"Touché, brother. Touché."

As Evan lay under the tractor, he peeked out at the stars and wondered if Molly was looking out of a window back home at the same sky. He missed her dearly, as his love for her was as strong as ever, and had been truly strengthened by the struggles they had shared since it all began.

The next thing he knew, he felt someone shake his shoulder. He flinched out of reflex and reached for his 1911 pistol, which he had taken out of its holster and laid next to himself while he slept, when he heard Jason's voice say, "Relax, man; it's me. Time to get up and get ready for school, young man."

Coming to his senses, Evan replied, "Ah, Mom, I don't wanna go to school today."

Jason chuckled in reply and said, "Our watch is in ten."

Evan yawned. "Roger that," he said as he worked his way out of his sleeping bag and to his feet. The two had never lost their ability to joke with each other, even during trying times. They felt that keeping a sense of humor was one of their most important mental survival tools. If you stay too serious and stressed for too long, depression can set in and cloud your judgment.

Evan and Jason met with Ed and Nate on their way back to the trailer to sleep. Their debrief was short. It had been an uneventful night, with the exception of a few animal sightings and some coyote calls that seemed not too far away.

Jason handed Evan a radio and said, "Rover or base?"

"Let's split it," Evan said. "I'll take the first base watch, and then you can swap me halfway through."

"Roger Roger," Jason replied. "I'm gonna take a walk down the road a ways and then duck into the woods to make a sweep of the perimeter. This moonlight tonight should make it easy enough, without having to burn my light."

"Don't get lost," Evan said with a smirk.

~~~~

After about a half hour of nothing but the sounds of nature, Evan got a double click on his radio that caught his attention. He listened intently, holding the radio close to his ear to see if he could hear anything else without turning up the volume and waking others. He then heard Jason's voice in a whisper say, "Movement on the road."

Evan immediately stood up and grabbed his rifle. He heard Nate whisper from inside the trailer, "Ev, what's up?"

Evan walked over to the trailer and whispered back, "I just got a faint call from Jason about movement on the road. Can you cover things here while I go see what's up?"

"Sure thing," replied Nate. "I can't sleep anyway."

"Thanks," Evan said as he handed Nate the radio. "I just hope Jason doesn't shoot me for sneaking up on him in the dark," he said as he slipped off into the darkness.

As Evan made his way slowly up the road, using only the moonlight to guide him, Jason saw him approach and waved him forward. Once they were joined up, Jason said, "I was watching the main road for a while and then saw some people passing from left to right. I think they may have turned up our little hideaway here. I can't really make out where they are at the moment, but I know for a fact that they didn't continue down Highway 70. They either stopped or turned in here with us."

The two stared off into the darkness for a moment, listening intently, when they began to hear voices that seemed to be getting louder as if they were approaching. "This is gonna get awkward real soon. We can't let them just walk right into camp."

"Yep," replied Jason.

The two men sat there listening to the footsteps of the strangers as the talking had now subsided. Once Jason felt they had gotten close enough, he said aloud, "Good morning."

A young girl screamed and a man's voice yelled, "Leave us alone!"

Jason answered, "We aren't here for trouble as long as you aren't."

"We are just looking for a place to sleep. We've been walking all night," the man said.

"Who are 'we'?" asked Jason.

"This is my wife and daughter, and I'm Tyrone. Tyrone Gibbs. We'll just turn around and find somewhere else to sleep. We didn't mean to bother you."

Evan spoke up and said, "No need for that, sir. We're gonna be packin' up and hittin' the road soon. We've got a good, safe spot and you're more than welcome to it. There's no need to keep those ladies out on this cold night any longer. We'll even get our fire going for you to warm up if you want."

The man just stood there for a moment, and then said, "Why would you do that?"

"Do what?" Evan asked.

"Go out of your way to build us a fire and give us your camp. That seems a little iffy to me," the man replied.

"Thinking like that is probably what's kept you all safe," answered Evan. He went on to say, "Look, if we wanted to hurt you, we could have done that already. We don't need to fool you with our intentions to do that. There are more of us than there are of you, and we are all armed. The fact is, Jason and I, as well as the others in our group, have wives and children back home, and we would want them to be able to find a warm place to rest if they were out here. We would want the same for yours, as well."

The man looked at his exhausted young daughter, who was maybe thirteen years old and said, "Okay, lead the way."

Evan and Jason led them back to camp, giving Nate the heads-up over the radio. It was nearing sunrise anyway, so he woke the others before their guests arrived to avoid any awkwardness. When they arrived, Evan introduced the guys, who were now all up and about, to the family and then said, "Oh, I'm sorry, I didn't catch the ladies' names."

"Oh, yes," Tyrone said. "This is my wife, Michelle, and my daughter, Rhonda."

They all exchanged pleasantries and then Charlie rolled a log near the fire that Jimmy was starting, and said, "Here, have a seat and warm up for a few."

The exhausted family was more than thankful for the hospitality and all took a seat on the log. Evan asked, "So what brings you out here in the middle of the night?"

Tyrone answered, "Traveling with women and girls isn't exactly safe right now. Some friends of ours, a married couple who also had a teenage daughter, were attacked in broad daylight." He paused, cleared his throat, and continued. "A group of men took his wife and daughter; he tried to fight them off, but they killed him right in front of everyone. I should have helped." Tears welled up in his eyes and his wife squeezed his hand. "I should have helped, but I was scared for my wife and daughter, so I just took them by the hand and we ran with every ounce of energy we had, for as long as we could. We only travel at night now. We've been basically hiding from the world ever since. I just can't let anything like that happen to them," the man said with strength and resolve.

In a concerned voice, Evan then asked, "Where and when did that happen?"

"Last week," Tyrone responded. "I forget what day, exactly. We've sort of lost track of time, just focusing on life from moment to moment, just worrying about what's around the next corner, and not tomorrow."

Everyone could see the pain and fatigue in the man's eyes. Jason looked at Evan; they shared a nod, and then Jason said, "We'll heat you up some food so that you can go to sleep on a full stomach for once. Then, you all three get some sleep. Even you, sir. We'll keep watch while you're catching up on some much-needed rest. You're no good to your family if you're not healthy. When you all wake up, we will pack up and be on our way."

Tyrone looked at his wife and daughter with relief. Evan asked, "By the way, where are you headed?"

Tyrone replied, "West is all we know for now. Our troubles were east, so we are going west."

"There is a Baptist church in the little town called Del Rio that's just up ahead," replied Evan. "The pastor there is a good man, and he's got other men helping him keep the place safe. He's providing shelter for women and children, and I'm sure he could help you out. If you want, we can give you directions and some more info on it when you wake up and are ready to go."

Tyrone just looked at his wife, smiled, and said, "Absolutely, sir, absolutely."

With that, Jimmy cooked up a delicious, warm dinner for the hungry family. There wasn't any rabbit left, but he made do with what they had. Any warm meal for people on the run like the Gibbs family was a true blessing during these difficult times. After they had eaten, the men set the trailer up as a shelter for the family and let them get their much-needed rest.

As the Gibbs family snuggled together, wrapped in the sleeping bags that Evan and the men provided them, Tyrone kissed his wife and daughter on the cheek and said, "See, there are some good people left in the world."

Chapter 17: Helping Hands

As Daryl walked out of the Lewis home, he heard the sound of a diesel engine roaring up to the house on the gravel road. He quickly realized it was Molly, driving Evan's Dodge pickup with several other people in the cab. As the truck came to a stop, the doors flew open and in addition to Molly, out came Luke, armed with an AR15, followed by Rachel, and Griff's wife, Judy.

Luke and Rachel ran up to Daryl as Luke shouted, "Who and where?"

Daryl replied, "It's Griff. Linda's with him in the woods now. He seems hurt pretty bad. I'll take you."

Judy frantically asked, "Who? Who is hurt?"

"It's Griff, ma'am," Daryl responded with a somber tone. "He had an accident with his horse while pursuing the thieves that attacked Beth."

"Where's Beth?" Molly asked. "Is she all right?"

He just shook his head *no* in response and said, "C'mon; Griff is this way."

Everyone knew by Daryl's behavior that something tragic must have happened to Beth, but Griff was the priority at the moment. Daryl led them on foot, through the woods in the direction of where he had left Linda with Griff. When they reached them, Linda looked up and said with relief, "Oh, thank God."

Judy ran to Griff's side and began crying as Molly tried to pull her to the side to allow Rachel and Luke to assess the situation. Rachel and Luke quickly got to work as a team, like they had countless times before when working with the Texas State Guard, as wounded soldiers and civilians were brought into their makeshift hospital.

Noticing his skin color and lips, Rachel quickly said, "Get a rate and BP." She then listened to his chest with her stethoscope and began to look him over for obvious signs of trauma.

"BP is seventy-six over thirty and his heart rate is ninety-eight," replied Luke after taking Griff's vitals.

Rachel looked up at him and said, "I think he's got a pneumothorax on his left side, possibly some broken ribs."

"A what?" shouted Judy through the tears.

"A collapsed lung," Luke replied, while Rachel was digging around in her bag. She quickly pulled out an IV needle and began running her fingers down the left side of his chest from his clavicle, counting his ribs. She inserted the needle and listened to his chest with her stethoscope.

Luke turned to Molly and Judy and said, "She's trying to allow the air trapped around his lung to escape so that it will re-inflate. It's okay. It's not hurting him."

"It's working," Rachel said to Luke as she continued to listen.

They could almost immediately see the difference in the rise of his chest. Luke looked at her and said, "Should I tape up the needle for transport?"

"Yes, we'll put a chest tube in back at the farm, where we can get him stabilized while we analyze the extent of the rest of his injuries. For now, though, let's get him out of here." She looked at Daryl and said, "Is there anything around here we can use for a stretcher, to get him out of the woods and into the back of the truck? We don't know the extent of his other possible injuries just yet, so we need to stabilize him before we move him."

Daryl quickly replied, "I'll find something," and ran back toward the house.

While Rachel and Luke continued to assess Griff's situation, Molly comforted Judy and did her best to assure her that Rachel and Luke were very experienced with trauma patients and would be able to get him back on his feet in no time. She hoped that was the case, but with the unknown extent of his head injury that still remained to be seen, she couldn't help but fear the worst.

After about ten minutes, Daryl came running through the woods, dragging along two long wooden poles and a scrap piece of plywood. As he dragged the items up to where Griff was lying, in an out-of-breath voice he gasped, "I found these poles in Jimmy's garden shed; I think they were supports for his beanpole strings. This scrap of plywood was leaning next to his garage."

He then pulled out of his pocket a screwdriver and some long wood screws, which he had also retrieved from the garage, and began to screw the poles along the long sides of the plywood. The screws went about halfway in; the resistance from the depth they were going into the wood began to cause the Phillips screw heads to strip. "Damn it!" he shouted in despair. "I really needed to drill a pilot hole. These screws are crap."

"It's okay, Daryl," replied Luke. "With the plywood on top of the poles, his weight will do a pretty good job of holding it all together. The screws are in far enough to keep the plywood from sliding off. That's all that really matters."

Daryl just looked at him with a defeated nod and put the screwdriver back into his pocket. They then placed the homemade backboard next to Griff and in unison, they all moved him as carefully as possible onto it and began to carry him out of the woods. Upon reaching the truck, they loaded him into the back, which was covered with a fiberglass truck canopy. Rachel climbed inside and said, "Judy, you ride with me and your husband. Luke, you ride shotgun with Molly upfront. Daryl, do you and Linda want to ride with us or are you going to ride your horse?"

"I'll lock up Jimmy's home and check to see if there is anything else I can do to secure Beth, and then I'll be on over," he said in a very somber voice. "Oh, and I need to go back out into the woods and deal with the bodies of Beth's murderers. That's not something Jimmy should have to come back home and deal with on top of everything else."

Rachel put her hand on his and said, "Thank you. You did a great job taking care of him, getting Linda to help, and getting us here. You made all the difference for him."

Daryl just nodded as a tear rolled down his face.

Linda said, "I need to head back to my place. I didn't come prepared for a trip. Please radio me if you need anything at all, and let me know how Griff is doing once you get it all figured out."

"We will," replied Rachel as she shut the back window. She gave Molly the thumbs up, and they began to drive away.

Linda turned to Daryl and didn't say a word. She just gave him a hug and patted him on the back. He hugged her back and began to cry. She didn't know what to think, seeing a big, burly man like Daryl, who had fought fiercely for them, today and in the past, break down like this.

"I'm sorry," he said as he pulled away and wiped the tears from his face with a sniffle. He cleared his throat and said, "Let me take care of things here and I'll escort you home."

"Okay, thanks," she said with a smile.

~~~~

After what was, thankfully, an uneventful drive back to the Thomas farm, they moved Griff into the house and stabilized him in Rachel's makeshift clinic in the basement. After as thorough of an examination as she could do without any real medical equipment, Rachel determined that the likelihood of any other serious internal injuries was low. His lungs had returned to a more normal level of function, and his blood-oxygen-content had returned to healthy levels. She removed the IV needle and replaced it with a chest tube to keep his chest cavity clear, preventing his lung from re-collapsing. At this point, she felt they just needed to keep him stable and hope that his head injury wasn't too severe to recover from on his own. She started him on an IV, gave him an anti-inflammatory, and started him on antibiotics to prevent infection from the wound around the chest tube. Having very limited medical supplies, it was all she felt she could do for him, other than just keep him stable and comfortable, and continue to monitor him. She was worried, however, that he had shown no signs of consciousness, and was fearful of the extent of his head injuries.

As Judy remained by his side, Rachel said, "I'll leave you alone with him for now. If you need anything at all, just yell, and Luke or I will come running. Can I get you anything?"

"No, I'm fine," Judy replied, wiping a tear from her eye. "Thank you so much for helping him. I can't imagine living without him, especially in this crazy world. He's my rock."

"We will make sure we take great care of him and get him through this."

Judy just nodded as she held back the tears. Rachel excused herself and joined the others upstairs in the living room.

"How is he doing?" Mildred asked.

"Stable for now, but still no signs of consciousness," she replied. "We've done all that we have the ability to do. At this point, we just keep him stable and wait."

Chapter 18: Return of the Guardians

Around noon the next day, as Evan and the men stood watch over the Gibbs family while they caught up on their much-needed sleep, Evan looked at Jason and said, "What are the odds they are still alive?"

"Who?" asked Jason.

"The woman and the girl Tyrone mentioned. Do you think they are still out there going through some kind of unspeakable hell in the hands of their captors?"

"If history has taught us anything... yes," replied Jason with a look of disgust on his face. "To scumbags like that, a female is a prized possession in a world where they don't have to worry about the threat of the authorities catching them. My guess is they will hang on to them until they are no longer useful. Look at how long the guys at the Muncie place kept poor Haley."

Evan kicked a rock and said, "Very true. Let's get some information from Tyrone before they leave, about the woman and the girl, as well as the men who took them. We are heading that way. There is no need not to keep an eye out for them. What kind of man, who has the means to do something about it, lets that stand?"

Jason just nodded, knowing exactly what Evan had in mind. "What if we find them? Do we take them with us?"

"We can cross that bridge when we get to it, but first we have to find the bridge."

Evan and Jason heard Charlie say, "Good morning."

They turned around to see Tyrone coming out of the trailer, looking much better than the night before. "That's the first sleep I've gotten in as long as I can remember," Tyrone said appreciatively. "Thank you, gentlemen, so much, for taking us in last night."

"No problem, sir," replied Jason.

Evan said, "If people didn't still strive to do what's right, this world would already be gone. Speaking of which, Jimmy is cooking up some lunch now. After you eat, if you could give us some information about the woman and the girl that were taken, we would greatly appreciate it."

"I can tell you now," he said. "But what do you plan on doing?"

"We'll keep an eye out for them," replied Evan. "If we see signs of them somewhere, we'll take it from there."

Tyrone just looked at them with bewilderment. *Why would these total strangers want to risk going up against some thugs to help people they'd never even met?* "The mother's name is Roxanne and the daughter is Sabrina. Roxanne is in her mid-thirties, and Sabrina is sixteen. They're both black, like us, and have slender builds and are average height."

"Where exactly were they taken?" Evan asked.

"We were heading west from Hot Springs, North Carolina. It was getting late in the evening and we were starting to look for a place to bed down for the night. That, of course, is when we still traveled during the day. Anyway, a little ways back, before you get to the point where seventy cuts across a peninsula made by the river, there was a bunch of old, abandoned eighteen-wheeler trailers and large shipping containers on the south side of the highway. It looked as if people had camped there before, those trailers and containers making the perfect temporary shelter. Anyway, we were checking out the containers when a truck pulled in. The Jacksons, that was the family name of our friends, had already climbed into a small shipping container while we were looking through what was still available to find one for ourselves."

"There were several men in the back with guns, and two up front, in the cab. They must have seen us looking around the containers. That or they simply use that place as a regular trap.

They seemed to operate pretty calm and calculated, like it was a routine."

Jason interrupted to ask, "Were you or the Jacksons armed?"

"No," he replied. "When it all started, I had a pistol and Ted had a shotgun. The kind you pump. He had gotten it for home defense when we all started to see the writing on the wall. Then during the initial stages of everything, the local city police went door-to-door, confiscating all of the legally owned weapons. Not wanting to become criminals ourselves by hanging on to them illegally, we complied. That was the biggest mistake we ever made."

"That's such bullcrap," Jason said in disgust.

Ed added, "They were doing the same thing in Ohio when I left."

The men all shared an equally disgusted look, and Tyrone continued. "Anyway, when we saw them drive up, we slipped off into the weeds to hide. The moon was really bright that night, so the darkness itself was no place to hide. We could have run then, but we didn't want to abandon our friends. The group of men moved from container to container, clearing each one with what seemed like military or swat team precision. When they reached the Jackson's container and opened the door, we could hear Sabrina's cries as the men dragged her and her mother, kicking and screaming, from the trailer. Ted, the father, tried fighting them off with everything he had. Two of the men pulled him out of the trailer and beat him mercilessly right in front of his wife and daughter."

Looking haunted by his memories, Tyrone cleared his throat and continued. "Sorry," he apologized for his pause. "So then, while he was down on his back, beaten nearly to death, he reached up with his bloody arm toward his wife and daughter, who were being restrained by the men. He told them he loved them as one of the men dropped a concrete block on his head, killing him."

Tyrone broke down into tears, weeping for his lost friend. Ed brought him a cup of water. He graciously accepted it and regained his composure. "His wife and daughter lost their minds. I've never heard such screams filled with pain and agony. I wanted to run out there and kill every single one of those men with my bare hands, but I knew if I did so unarmed, my wife and daughter would suffer the same fate. My wife and I held our daughter's mouth as she tried to scream out in agony from the horror of what she had witnessed. Luckily, the cries of the Jackson women drowned out her whimpers... huh... 'luckily.' I can't believe I just said that," Tyrone said as he hung his head down with shame.

Evan put his hand on the man's shoulder and said, "There was nothing you could have done for them, on your own and unarmed. You kept your wife and daughter safe from those horrors. Don't you ever regret that. Your family will always be your number one mission in life."

"Where did they take them?" Evan asked. "Could you see what direction they took when they left?"

"They loaded them up and headed back toward the east and then up a hill," Tyrone answered. "We waited several hours after it all went down before we started moving again. Since then, we've only traveled at night, staying hunkered down all day. Until we stumbled across your camp, that is."

"When we pack up and head out, we are heading east," Evan said as he stood up and took a sip of water. "We'll keep an eye out for the Jackson women. If there is anything in our power we can do to help, we will."

"Thank you guys so much," Tyrone said with tears in his eyes.

Evan then walked over to the trailer and dug around in his pack. He walked back over to Tyrone and handed him a .38

special revolver and a box of ammunition. "Do you know how to use a revolver?" he asked.

"Yes. Yes, I do. That's what I had before it was confiscated."

"Good," Evan replied. "Do as we said and head for Del Rio. When you get to the outskirts of town, you may encounter a roadblock guarded by some of the townspeople. If they are the same ones we encountered, they are good people, but have a right to be mistrustful. Tell them you are looking for Pastor Wallace... and tell him The Guardians sent you."

Chapter 19: Moving On

As Evan, Jason, Charlie, Jimmy, Nate, and Ed loaded up and headed out for the east, Tyrone's wife looked at him and said, "For the first time in a long time, I feel like God is looking out for us. It couldn't have been mere chance that we stumbled across those men. Their kindness to total strangers was like nothing I've seen since we started traveling."

He just squeezed her hand and smiled. She then noticed a concerned look on his face as he watched them drive away. "What is it?" she asked.

"Oh, nothing. It was just something he said," he replied.

"What?" she insisted.

"He said to tell the Pastor in Del Rio that The Guardians had sent us. I could see what that meant in his eyes."

"What did it mean?" she asked insistently.

"I'm probably just reading too much into little things these days. We had better get a move on. I'm anxious to get to this Del Rio place," he said as he pulled her by the hand, and the three of them started walking west.

~~~~

As the tractor rolled along with the trailer in tow, Evan and Jason were mostly quiet, both knowing what might await them ahead, and what that meant. The violence of the previous year had strengthened them, but had also left deep scars in their own hearts. They had not only lost good friends and neighbors, but they each carried a heavy heart for committing the deeds that had to be done. Even if the nation somehow returned to normal in the near future, they, along with most people who had survived the turmoil thus far, would remain forever changed.

In the back of the trailer, Jimmy and Charlie caught Ed up on the events of the previous year. Ed had heard the stories, of course, but not with the level of detail they were sharing with him.

The tractor eventually came to a point where U.S. Highway 70 took a turn to the left through a cut in the hills and no longer paralleled the French Broad River. Jason reviewed the map and said, "This must be the peninsula Tyrone mentioned. It looks like we are gonna be down between high terrain on both sides for a while. We had better keep our eyes peeled."

"Yep," replied Evan. "Especially knowing there are scumbags out there like the ones the Gibbs and Jackson families ran into."

"Stop the tractor for a minute," Jason said.

"What's up?"

"Oh, I just don't want to key up the radios and give anything away. That and I have to piss," Jason replied.

"Me, too, now that you mention it," Evan replied with a grin.

They pulled the tractor to a stop. Both Evan and Jason climbed down and joined the men in the back. They used the opportunity to take a quick break, as well as to discuss as a group how to mitigate the potential threats that might lie ahead. Charlie spoke up and said, "Maybe we should pull the ATVs out of the trailer and have one take point and one rear. There's no need to have them inside where, if we were ambushed, we would be sitting ducks trying to unload them. Spreading out would give our would-be attackers pause; if they fired on the ATV up front, they would know they could have fire returned from the other positions."

Jason replied, "That sounds good. I was thinking the same thing. I just didn't want to volunteer you guys to be out in the open like that."

"Hell, if they want to stop the convoy, they'll take Evan out first, since he's driving the tractor, not the ATVs," added Jimmy with a devilish grin while looking at Evan.

"You're right, Jimmy. Maybe you should drive the tractor," Evan said in reply.

They all shared a chuckle and then Charlie said, "Hell, I'll take point. You get it next time, though, Jimmy."

"Deal," Jimmy replied.

They unloaded their ATVs, checked their weapons, formed up in an appropriate tactical bound, and proceeded into the cut in the hills. As they continued up the road, Charlie would stop on occasion to glass the area up ahead before proceeding. Evan's pace was a bit slower, matching Charlie's stop-and-go cadence nicely, without having to do the same with the tractor. Jason scanned the hills to the left, Evan the right, and Jimmy kept an eye on things from behind. About halfway through the cut, Charlie came to a stop and gave Evan the signal to halt. Evan brought the tractor to a stop as they readied their weapons, unsure of what Charlie had seen up ahead. Jimmy saw that Jason was giving him the rally-on-me signal, so he joined up with the tractor and trailer accordingly.

"What's up?" Jimmy asked.

"Not sure," replied Jason. "Charlie stopped suddenly, gave us the halt command, and then dismounted. He's checking something out now."

Charlie then gave the signal for Jimmy to join him. Jimmy said, "Well, I guess I'm about to find out," as he started his ATV and rode ahead to meet up with Charlie.

Evan and Jason could see Jimmy dismount up ahead while Charlie seemed to be explaining something to him, pointing at various places on the ground. Jimmy then got back on his ATV and rode back to the tractor, leaving Charlie standing guard up ahead.

"What's up?" Jason asked.

"There are signs of a scuffle up ahead," he replied. "There are skid marks on the road where someone seems to have slammed on their brakes and swerved. There are also a lot of shell casings on the ground. Mostly 7.62x39 Russian and a few .223 Remington. There is something that may be a spot of dried blood, but it's kind of weathered and hard to tell for sure. Either way, something went down up ahead."

"That's the perfect choke point," Jason said, pointing at the map. "Well, no one is shooting at us yet. Let's keep moving, but keep your game face on."

"Roger that," Jimmy replied as he rode his ATV back behind them, re-establishing his position in the rear.

Jason gave Charlie the thumbs up and the convoy resumed its forward progress. Before long, the group was almost out of the cut in the hills and could see the terrain open back up ahead with the French Broad River once again visible on the right side of Highway 70. They all felt relieved to be out of what they considered a dangerous area, an assumption backed up by the evidence Charlie had found on the road.

Once they were in the clear, Evan stopped the tractor to allow the group to form back up. Jason gave the signal to Jimmy and Charlie to return. Once they were back to the trailer, they loaded their ATVs back inside to save fuel, and continued their journey east.

As they continued along the highway, they saw several homes on the right side of the road. The homes sat in the thin strip of ground between the river and Highway 70, and looked abandoned and in disarray. They could also see a home on the left side of the road just up ahead, tucked into the hillside with a tree line just behind it. There were signs that it was occupied. They did not want to linger too long to find out, just in case there was a trigger-happy resident who didn't like the sort of things that had been taking place on their once tranquil country highway.

After traveling a few more uneventful miles, they came upon a fork in the road where Tennessee 107 split from U.S. Highway 70 to the left. As they slowly approached the fork in the road, Evan brought the tractor to a stop while leaving the engine running. He looked at Jason and said, "Well, the original intent of this outing was for trade and barter. Do you think those houses up there are worth checking out?"

"Let's give it a shot," Jason replied. "If nothing else, maybe they can give us some good intel on where to look, or on the scumbags that might be preying on unsuspecting travelers up ahead."

"Let's send an ATV up ahead before taking the tractor and trailer there where we'd have a hard time turning around if things went to hell in a hurry," Evan added.

"Roger that," said Jason as he climbed down from the tractor and went back to talk to the guys in the trailer. "Charlie," he said through one of the windows, "would you mind running up ahead and checking out some homes that we may be able to do some trading with? We can get both ATVs out and have Jimmy on standby to assist if you get into a bind. I'll cover you from the top of the trailer with my .300 Win Mag. I can definitely reach you from here if need be. I'd just prefer to have Jimmy stay back a bit at first; a lone ATV rider won't appear to be much of a threat to any of the occupants of the houses."

"Sure thing," replied Charlie as he and Jimmy opened the trailer doors and once again unloaded their ATVs.

"Take the other handheld radio so we can communicate. You can call us on up if things look and feel right, and if anyone wants to barter or trade."

"Thanks," said Charlie as he reached out and took the radio from Nate, who had been holding onto the one they had been using from inside the trailer.

Charlie fired up his ATV and headed up the road. He had a pistol on his side, but chose not take a long gun; he did not want to appear to be a threat to the residents that might still live in the homes. Jason watched anxiously from a distance through his Nightforce scope as Charlie approached the cluster of houses.

Charlie stopped on the road in front of one of the houses that appeared occupied. He could see smoke coming out of the makeshift pipe chimney that looked as if it had been added to the house in a very crude manner. He climbed off his ATV and walked up to the driveway. He paused at the entrance to the driveway, allowing himself to be seen, assuming the occupants were watching him from within. After a few moments, he saw the front door open slightly as a voice yelled down to him, "Can I help you?"

"Yes, sir," he replied. "My friends and I are looking to do some trading if that is something that you may be interested in. We are from a community in the hills near Del Rio. We're practically neighbors."

"What do ya got?" the man yelled from inside the house, remaining out of view.

"We've got some canned goods and some alcohol," shouted Charlie in reply.

After a brief pause, the man inside the house opened the door and said, "Come on up, this yellin' is gettin' to my throat."

Charlie did as the man asked and walked toward the house while Jason watched from below. The man inside the house was a weathered-looking fellow in his mid-to-late sixties, with a thin build and of average height. As he reached the front of the house, the man said, "So you're from Del Rio, you say?"

"Not exactly Del Rio, although I used to run the little hardware store there," Charlie replied as he reached out to shake the man's hand. "Charlie Blanchard; nice to meet you."

"Fred Simpson," the man said, returning Charlie's handshake.

"My friends you see down by the road, with the tractor and trailer, and I live in a little homesteading community in the hills outside of Del Rio. We've been doing pretty well by ourselves up there and have a few things we can spare. We thought we might be able to form some relationships and trade with folks who are still around these parts."

"You say you've got alcohol?" the man asked.

Charlie smiled and said, "Yes, sir. We have a few bottles of whiskey and a stash of shine distilled right there in our own neck of the woods. Our master distiller is the man on the other four-wheeler down by the tractor."

Mr. Simpson squinted to try to see Jimmy at a distance, but it was clear to Charlie that his eyes were beginning to fail him in his old age. "Come on in and let's talk business," he said, ushering Charlie into the house and closing the door behind him. This made Jason nervous, as he was not able to see what was going on.

As Charlie entered the house, he noticed that the living conditions were an unsanitary mess, to say the least. A house cat clearly had free rein of the furniture, and it appeared as if its waste had not been cleaned up in quite some time. An elderly woman sat in a rocking chair in the corner and rocked back and forth without saying a word. "That's Ruth," Fred said as he pointed toward the woman. "She used to live a few houses up the street before this crap all started. She's been staying with me ever since. We brought her food and supplies down to my house and we've been keeping each other going. My son used to visit every couple of weeks, but he stopped coming about six months ago. I don't know why," he said as he looked down to the floor, clearly distracted by his own thoughts. "But anyway," he said, regaining his composure, "my son used to work at one of those big club stores where you buy everything in bulk. He always watched that show about those crazy people that stocked up for the end of the world. He started bringing home lots of stuff in bulk—to prepare, I guess. Anyway, he didn't want to keep it all at his apartment in Asheville. He knew if it all fell apart, he would, more than likely, come running this way; he started bringing it out here and took up all the space in my shed. If there is anything out there you want, we could work out a deal for some of that booze you've got. I've been out the stuff for a while, and cranky ol' Ruth over there could sure use a good, stiff drink every now and then, too."

"Well, sir, let's take a look," Charlie replied.

Watching intently from the fork in the road, Jason observed the front door of the house open. Charlie and a man from the home exited and walked around back to a storage shed. "Something is going on," Jason said to the others on the ground below.

"What's up?" Evan asked anxiously.

"Charlie came outside with the man from the house and they went around back. They are in a large shed now. I would guess they are looking for barter items—at least that's what I hope is going on." Just as Jason finished his sentence, he saw them come back out of the shed, carrying a cardboard box. "Charlie's got something."

"What is it?" asked Evan.

"All I can see from here is a box... okay; they set it down on the front porch. Charlie is walking back out to his ATV now. It looks like he's coming back."

"Without the box?" asked Evan.

"Yep, but the box is on the porch still, so we may have a trade to work out."

Charlie rode back down the hill toward the fork in the road, where the others waited. He pulled up alongside the trailer, shut off his engine, dismounted, and said, "Well, guys, you're gonna be quite pleased with our first little negotiations session."

"How so?" replied Evan.

"Coffee," Charlie said with a smile.

"Coffee? Great. How much?"

"Forty pounds of whole bean coffee. It turns out the man's son was sort of an amateur prepper and just happened to work at a club wholesale store. He's willing to trade ten pounds of coffee per jar of Jimmy's moonshine. He wants at least four jars, so that's a hell of a lot of coffee. He's got more than he can ever drink, which means we may be able to come back through some other time for more."

Ed smiled and said, "His son was smart—stocking up on things like coffee, that is. Coffee will always be useful as a form of currency."

The men shared a laugh and then looked at Jimmy to get his approval. Jimmy smiled and said, "Well, hell, yeah! Get that man his shine."

They put the four jars of moonshine into a box on Charlie's ATV rack to take back up the hill. Charlie made the trade and then came back down the hill to join the others. After loading the coffee into the trailer, Charlie said, "I asked if anyone else up there may be interested in working out any deals. Unfortunately, he told me it would be best if I didn't let the other folks know we had barter items unless we were willing to give it away for free. He said no one else had anything to give and that they were a bit trigger happy with strangers after a few less-than-desirables have been through as of late."

Jason interrupted to ask, "Did you ask him about what's on down the road this way?"

"Yes, he said after a few more miles we're gonna find a stretch of road that most of the locals won't go down. It's uninhabited, with no outs if you run into a problem. He said most of the locals here continue up Route 107 to get anywhere, but steer clear of 70 from here to the bridge that takes you back across to the other side of the river."

"Why is that?" asked Evan.

"Probably the same reason the Gibbs and Jackson families didn't fare so well down that way. He said there are some low-life folks that stay up in the hills and come down to prey on passersby."

"Did he know exactly where they stay?" asked Jason.

"No, unfortunately, the locals just know somewhere up on the hillside, overlooking the road. All they have to do to pin someone in is block the bridge and the other end of the road. Whoever is on the road in between, gets trapped with no way out without going through them. He said he thinks they are from Richmond or Asheville. Acting like that, they are definitely not local folks, according to him."

"Yep, probably out-of-towners looking for a small pond to be a big fish in," Nate replied.

"Well, guys, I say we press on into the spider's web and smash it. We need to get to Hot Springs. Along the way, we'll keep any eye out for the Jackson women. Are you guys still up for that?"

"Hell, yeah!" they all replied.

"Well, let's load up and get rolling, then. Daylight is burning," Evan said as he climbed back onto the tractor.

Chapter 20: Living in Hell

She could hear her mother's screams from the other room. She curled up on the floor behind the bed, bound to it by handcuffs and chains, trying to pretend the horrible events weren't happening. She knew all too well the hell her mother was enduring, as she herself had gone through it repeatedly since they were taken from their father. She was a virgin before this all started, but she knew she would never be able to wear that moniker again.

She had been brutally beaten and repeatedly gang raped by the band of thugs who had taken them. Their rhythm seemed to be to take one at a time into the other room while the other recovered for a few hours. They would then trade them off and do it all over again. She was bleeding from inside and was in terrible pain. She hadn't eaten in days and had barely been given anything to drink—just enough to keep her alive. She had been stripped of her clothes and was forced to shiver in nothing but the cold of her own blood and tears. They had done terrible things to her—twisted things that she never imagined would please a man—things she would never be able to get out of her mind. She prayed for God to take her, to let the next time a man hit her be the final blow that sent her off to Heaven to join him.

The door swung open as one of the men carried her naked mother into the room, throwing her on the bed. She was unconscious from the vicious beating she had received while trying to fend off her attackers, and smelled of their alcohol, cigarettes, and sweat. The man looked at the young girl and said, "Don't worry, darlin', you're not gonna miss out on all of the fun. It'll be your turn again next." He then leaned down and handcuffed her mother's limp wrist to the metal bedpost. He stood up, spat on her, and turned to walk out of the room.

Before he left, he turned and said, "We're gonna have to hose you beasts down. You're starting to stink."

As soon as he was gone, the young girl climbed up from the floor, where she was attempting to stay out of the man's way, and checked on her mother. "Mom... Mom," she said as she shook her.

She heard her mother whisper, "Is he gone?"

"Yes, he's gone. Please wake up, Mom."

Her mother opened her swollen eyes slowly, her eyelids flickering from her disoriented state. "Oh, baby, I'm so sorry this is happening. I've failed you. I'm supposed to protect you, and here you are in this living hell."

"Shhhh, don't say that, Mom. It's not your fault. Daddy tried to save us. Daddy tried. We all tried," she said as she broke down crying.

Her mother reached up with what little strength she had left and held her by the hand. The young girl noticed that her mother had burns all over her body. They looked like cigarette burns. They had even burned her genitals with whatever it was they used. The young girl shook in agony for the pain her mother must be enduring, and for the horror that she might face the same abuse the next time they come for her.

As her mother drifted back out of consciousness, the young girl laid her head on her mother's shoulder and closed her eyes, once again praying to God for help. "Please God, if you're there, please help my mother. Take my life if you must, but please don't let them continue to hurt her like this. And if you aren't able to send us help, then please just let us die. Please take us to Heaven with you and get us out of this hell on Earth."

Suffering from severe fatigue, she slipped off to sleep with her head on her mother's arm. She dreamed about her father, and about the happy times they once had as a family. She loved her parents dearly and could not imagine making it in this cruel and ugly world without them.

She awakened at the sound of two men arguing in the hall. *How long was I asleep?* she thought to herself as she looked around the room in her disoriented state. She listened closely in an attempt to hear what the men were saying.

"It's my turn, damn it!" one of them yelled. "I was on watch when you had your last go. It's my turn, and I'm taking the young one," he again yelled.

"Mom... Mom, they're coming," she whispered as she shook her mother's arm, trying to wake her. She noticed that her mother felt colder than before. A sudden panic went through her body as she realized her mother was no longer breathing. "Mom! Mom! Wake Up!" she screamed aloud as tears ran down her face. "Mom, please don't leave me here all alone! Please don't leave me!" she continued to yell as she shook her mother by the shoulders.

Hearing the commotion from within the room, the door swung open and two of the men entered. "What the hell?" one of them shouted as they walked over to see her pale, lifeless mother and the panic in the young girl's face. "Damn it! Dog told you not to be so damn rough with them. We've got to make them last for everybody to get least a few goes at them. You're missing your next turn for that, asshole!" he shouted. "I'm taking the young one again while we've still got her." He unchained and dragged the screaming girl out of the room while she desperately reached for her dead mother. "And do something with that damn body before it stinks any worse than it already does!" he added as he took the young girl down the hall.

Chapter 21: The Spider's Web

As Evan and the men proceeded into what Evan jokingly referred to as "The Spider's Web," they could sense the danger in the air. There were just too many warnings about the type of individuals that might lie in wait, for them not to heed. After they passed the last road prior to the bridge that they could see on their map, they knew they were coming up on the area where the Jackson women were more than likely taken. Evan pulled the tractor to a stop, shut off the engine, looked at Jason, and said, "Okay. . . game plan?"

Jason thought for a minute, and then replied, "Unless we run across them prior to reaching it, I think we need to focus on the area where the containers and trailers are that Tyrone mentioned. If those guys come down and check on them at night on a routine basis—hoping to find travelers seeking refuge—we could use that to our advantage. We know some of the things they've done and what kind of people they are. They, however, have no idea we are coming, what we know, and what actions we are willing to take. It may be their home court, but we are the only ones who know there's about to be a game."

"I like where you're going with this," Evan said. "Go on."

"Looking at the map, we know the containers are just before the bridge that crosses back over the French Broad to the south. After we round this last bend, we'll be in the kill zone all the way there. They will have the position of elevation with woods for cover, and we will be in the open on the road below. There *is* an option we can take to catch the spider in its own web."

Evan said, "Let's get the other guys in on this."

"Right on," Jason replied.

Evan and Jason climbed down from the tractor and joined the other men at the back of the trailer. Jason caught them up on what he and Evan had discussed so far and then said, "Here's what I think we should do. What we've seen, so far, is uphill terrain to the left and the river to the right. Up ahead, there is wooded uphill terrain to the left and wooded downhill terrain to the right before you get to the riverbank. If they are watching the road, and not the river itself, we can ditch the tractor in a secluded area on the last road we just passed. Then we quietly hike down the riverbank with the lower stand of trees as cover. Once we find the containers, we can figure out what we want to do from there based on what we see. From what Tyrone described, they very deliberately and methodically drove down to the containers and cleared them one-by-one, looking for people. We can use that pattern if they repeat it."

"I like it," said Evan, in complete agreement with Jason's plan.

"Me, too," said Nate. "Let's do it."

"Hell, yeah," said the others as everyone got on board with Jason's plan.

With their new plan in mind, they unloaded the ATVs and hid them in the brush alongside the road the best they could. They then began backtracking with the tractor and trailer to leave them hidden on the side road they had just passed. They did not want to lose their entire cache of supplies in one fell swoop if someone found the tractor while they were away. Having the ATVs stashed in a different location would at least give them some form of transportation in the event that happened.

Once everything was in place, they all suited up with their tactical gear they had brought along. Each man's loadout was different, based on his weapon and ammunition of choice, but they were all ready for anything that might come their way: from first aid, to ammunition, to emergency food in the event things took longer than expected. The events of the recent past had forced people such as them to think about all possible eventualities every time they undertook such a challenge, and these men were ready for anything.

Jason rallied the men together and said, "Okay, guys, let's travel down the riverbank via a bounding overwatch. Let's split up into two groups. Evan, Ed, and myself in one; Charlie, Nate, and Jimmy in the other. One group will move down toward the objective while the other lies low in the tree line, providing cover. When the first group on the move hunkers down in the trees, the second group will move forward while being provided with cover. It will slow us down a bit, but we won't be caught off guard that way. As long as we get there before dark to get the lay of the land and set up accordingly, we should be fine."

With that said, Jason led the first group while Nate led the second. They entered the lower tree line, worked their way toward the riverbank, turned east, and hand-railed Highway 70 from the river, continuing toward their objective. Along the way, they would occasionally stop as a scout would climb back up through the lower woods and to the road to scan the area for threats and to look for their objective. The scout would then rejoin their group and both groups would proceed.

Just as the sun was going down, the groups were getting close to the bridge. They couldn't see any movement on the bridge and decided to move through the lower woods and back up to the road while maintaining their bounding overwatch. Once they reached the road, they could see the scene that Tyrone had described. "This must have been some small time trucking company's base before things went to hell," said Jason as he checked the area out with his binoculars, lying low in the trees with the others.

"So what do you think?" asked Evan. "Should we put a moth in the web and wait for the spider?"

"But who gets to be the moth?" asked Jason with a crooked grin.

"Why, us, of course," Evan replied. "We are dragging these guys into this mess; we can't volunteer them to be the bait."

"My thoughts exactly," replied Jason.

Evan and Jason then shared their plan with the others. Upon reaching a consensus, Evan and Jason stripped their tactical gear off to try and look like two ordinary travelers. They put their pistols inside their waistbands to hide them from plain view, and then pulled their jackets over top of them. They quickly doubled back down the riverbank, confident, now, that it was clear of threats. They rejoined the road above as if they were merely two travelers heading east toward the bridge.

As they walked down the street in plain view, Evan said, "I feel naked without my VZ."

"Ditto, brother," replied Jason. "Imagine how I feel; you only had half a rifle to start with."

"Ha," Evan said sarcastically.

"Besides," Jason said, "only a fool takes a pistol to a gunfight."

"Well, nobody ever accused us of being smart," Evan chuckled in reply.

As they approached the containers and semi-trailers, Evan said, "Well, which of these luxury accommodations do you want to spend the night in?"

"Let's go for a trailer instead of a container. The height of the door will give us an advantage if emergency egress is necessary," he replied.

"Roger Roger," said Evan with a chuckle, poking fun at Jason's signature phrase.

"Keep it up and I might just let one of those scumbags have you," Jason replied in jest.

The two selected a trailer, opened the door, and climbed up inside. They closed the door loudly to make sure they sent a message to the spider that it had indeed caught a moth.

After about an hour, as the two men sat in the pitch-black darkness of the trailer, out of the silence, Jason said, "Are we there yet?"

"Don't make me pull this car over," Evan replied.

"I wonder how long it will take those scumbags to come check on their prey."

"Dunno," answered Evan. "Heck, they may not even come, for all we know. We're making assumptions based on limited information. You've got to do more legwork than this to pattern a deer, much less a gang of thugs."

"Hell, don't give them so much credit. The deer are probably way smarter," replied Jason with a chuckle.

Just then, over their own laughter, they heard a truck coming down the road. The truck came to a stop right in front of the trailers and containers just like Tyrone had described.

"Game on," whispered Jason.

"It's about damn time," whispered Evan in reply. "I'd go nuts if I had to be cooped up in this thing with you any longer."

As they heard footsteps headed in their general direction, they double-checked that their pistols were concealed, but ready. The sound of a metal door swinging open was followed immediately by it slamming shut. Then more footsteps and the sound of another metal door on rusty hinges being opened and closed. The footsteps then grew louder and closer as their door swung open abruptly, followed by a strong spotlight shining in their faces, temporarily blinding and disorienting them. They put their hands in front of their faces, out of reflex, to block the light, struggling to see.

"Jackpot!" a crude voice yelled out to the others. Evan and Jason squinted in the blinding light as another voice said, "Walk slowly toward us, and maybe we won't hurt you."

Evan and Jason began to comply when the voice ordered, "Empty your pockets. What do you have on you? Are you armed?"

In an attempt to stall the men, Jason answered the men in a fake foreign language. "Kaba dosta teno dringas monghumar! Monghumar! Monghumar!"

"What the hell did you say? Speak English, asshole!" the man demanded.

Jason again answered, "Monghumar! Monghumar!"

The man then said to one of the others, "Get up in there and check them out."

Before the other man could react to the demand, Ed's voice rang out from the darkness, yelling, "Drop your weapons or die where you stand!"

As the assailants turned around in surprise to engage Ed, Evan and Jason both drew their handguns as Jason yelled, "Monghumar means 'wrong trailer, scumbag'! Now drop your weapons or die, like he said."

The men then heard the sounds of Charlie's, Nate's, and Jimmy's actions all cycle a round into the chamber, verifying that they were surrounded and in the line of fire.

Jason and Evan took the spotlights from the men and illuminated the assailants, while they each stayed in the darkness, intensified by the blinding light for cover. Evan walked up to the one who seemed to be in charge and pistol-whipped him on the back of the head, knocking him to the ground. He then looked at the others and said, "One wrong move and you're wasted. Now drop to your knees."

Each of the men reluctantly complied while Jimmy and Charlie came along behind, tying their hands to a metal bar, keeping all of the men secured together.

Once they were all secure, Evan went to the first man and said, "Where are the women?"

"What women?" the man answered. "We don't know what you're talking about. We don't have any women."

"I don't think you realize who you're messing with. Two of my whores got away. Some man who claimed they were his family came and took them in the middle of the night. Those women were worth a lot of money to me—especially the young one. I have reason to believe you took them from him. If you have them, let's work a deal for me to get them back and I'll let you live. Hell, maybe I can even give you a job and cut you in."

"Were they black? An older one and a younger one in her teens?" one of the men asked.

"Yeah, that's them; so do you have them?" Evan replied.

"Ah, yeah, man. We've got'em. Them some good lookin' ones. That young one, she's got it goin' on. We popped that guy that took 'em from ya, too. They may not be as fresh as when you had them, though. We've damn near used them up," the man said with a laugh. "But hey, we can get them back to you and maybe even help you get some more. Just cut us in."

"Where the hell are they?" Evan demanded, trying to hide his growing rage.

"Up on the hill behind us. At our place. Let us go and we'll take you," the man replied.

"Shut the hell up, T," the man whom Evan had pistol-whipped said to his cohort.

"Is he your boss?" Evan asked.

"Yeah, man, he's in charge," the man replied.

Evan went over to the leader of the group, pulled his knife from its sheath, and slit the man's throat, spilling his blood to pool at the feet of the other men.

"I'm your boss now," Evan said as he pointed the bloody knife at them. "Anybody got a problem with that?"

"Na, man. You're the boss. You're the boss," the men replied.

"Now, how many more are on the hill that I might have to cut in on this?"

"There's three more. They're all cool, though. They'll be in. They'll be in," the talkative one said.

"What are they doing up there right now?" Evan asked.

"They're supposed to be keeping watch over the place and the women, but knowing those bastards, they're probably riding your whores right now," the man said with a laugh.

"Three, huh? Well, hell, that's too many. I can't cut so many of you in; I guess I'm gonna have to cut some of you out," he said as he slashed the throat of the first man, with Jason killing the other in the same fashion.

"What the hell, man? What the hell was that?" yelled Ed, aghast at what he had just witnessed.

"Ed, relax," said Nate. "These scumbags just admitted to murdering the father and kidnapping the mother and daughter to use as their sex slaves. What else were we supposed to do? Let them go? I can tell you that's just not gonna happen."

"Yeah, we've seen this before," Charlie added. "And we're not gonna let it happen again. That's how we got young Haley back at Mildred's place. That poor girl went through hell. I had a hard time coming to terms with this sort of thing at first, too, but trust me, these guys only do what's necessary for the good to survive. The bad simply reap what they sow, the way I see it."

Ed adjusted his hat on his head and said, "No, you're right. I'm sorry, guys. That was just a lot to take in visually. I mean, I've shot people. I've had to, but this was up close and personal on a level I just hadn't been to yet."

As Evan wiped the blood from his hands with a cloth, he looked at Ed and said, "It doesn't get any easier to deal with on the inside. We just get better at getting through it on the outside. If we act screwed up at times, it's because we are screwed up on the inside and just need a way to get it out."

Jason changed the subject by saying, "Well, guys, the scum up on the hill are gonna be expecting their cohorts here to return soon. We've got to regroup and get something going quick."

"What do you propose?" asked Evan.

"Well, there were three of them in the truck," Jason started to reply. "Were they all in the cab when they pulled up? We obviously couldn't see from our position."

"There were two up front and one in the bed," replied Charlie.

"Well, then, I think we should split back up into our two groups. My group will hump our way up to the house to do a little recon. Give us about an hour to get into position, and then drive right up to the place in their own truck. It's dark, so they won't notice it's not their guys until you're on them. Each group take a radio so we can adjust on the fly, but I anticipate you drawing them out front while we flank them or take them out from the inside. But, then again, you all know how plans go when it all hits the fan."

Everyone agreed to the plan as Jason recommended. Ed handed Jason and Evan the tactical vests and gear they had removed before the ruse. They quickly donned their gear and grabbed their rifles as Jason said, "Let's hit it."

Chapter 22: Killing the Spider

Jason, Evan, and Ed quickly began their ascent of the hill. They knew it would take some time to reach the house quietly on foot, and wanted to be in position with a plan long before the truck was expected back. They had to jog just shy of a half mile down the road toward the bridge and then take a gravel road that led off to the left and up the side of the hill. The road was steep, with many switchbacks as it wound its way up the side of the mountain. The moonlight that illuminated their way was quickly being replaced by darkness as a thin layer of clouds moved in, blocking out the night's sky.

As their useful ambient light faded, Jason quietly said, "C'mon moon! Get back out here."

"Tell me about it," whispered Evan. "I really don't want to have to flick on a flashlight at any point."

They could see the house off in the distance as they rounded the next switchback. The house had a generator running somewhere in the background, keeping the lights on both inside and on the front porch.

"These guys must be cocky," Jason remarked. "I'd have this place dark and quiet at night. If you light up your interior perimeter, your enemy can easily see you, but you can't see them hiding off in the darkness."

"Well, let's be thankful that's the case and use it to our advantage. Speaking of which, that noisy, old gas generator is providing good cover, as well."

"Let's not get too cocky like them, though, and assume it's gonna be easy," added Evan.

Once they got close, they ducked into the tree line to establish a plan. Jason said, "Okay, we need to try and get a look inside. We don't want to be shooting directly into a part of the house where the women are being held, and risk injuring them. Evan, you go around to the right. Ed, you go around through the woods to the left. I'll cover you from here and keep an ear on the radio for the guys down below. Don't shoot unless you have to. We don't want to give up the initiative too soon. In about fifteen minutes, work your way back to me so we can nail this down."

Evan and Ed both nodded in the affirmative and began to creep around the darkness of the wooded perimeter in their assigned directions. Evan, being on the downhill side of the house, had the clearest path, but also had the disadvantage of having to get elevation to see inside the first floor windows. Without leaving the security of the woods, he threw his VZ58 across his back and climbed a tree to try to get a better vantage point. He hoped to be able to see into what he assumed was a bedroom window on the side of the house.

Meanwhile, Ed crept around the uphill side of the house, being careful not to make a sound. An awning over the house's back deck blocked his view inside from his elevated position. He decided he needed to get lower and closer to get any real intel on the situation. With that in mind, he carefully crept down the hill, using caution to avoid making too much noise in the dead leaves that still covered the ground from the previous fall and winter. As he crept slowly toward the unlit rear deck, he stumbled on something in the darkness along the edge of the tree line. Nearly tripping and falling onto the ground, he caught himself and knelt down on all fours, being still, making sure he didn't inadvertently make a sound to give his position away.

What the hell is this? he thought as he pulled back a plastic tarp covering the object. It was too dark to see, so he tried to feel inside with his bare hand. As he felt the cold, soft object, the smell from within the wrapped bundle hit him. He flinched and jumped back, falling to the ground as he realized, with horror, what he had just touched; it was a woman's body, cast outside like the trash. The smell and the feel of the corpse sent chills up his spine, causing him to vomit as he instantly felt nauseated. His stomach was already twisted into knots from the stress of the situation, and his morbid discovery sent him over the edge.

After he regained his composure and wiped the vomit from his mouth, spitting on the ground, Ed crept closer to the house, inching up to a window next to the deck. The light from inside the house illuminated his immediate area so he could get a good look around. He did not want to step onto the deck itself, as he was afraid a creaky or loose board would give him away. The deck looked a few years beyond some needed TLC, and he didn't want to chance it.

As he peeked in the window, he saw that it looked into the laundry room, adjacent to a bathroom. Just then, the generator sputtered to a stop, followed immediately by the lights in the house going dark.

He heard a man yell inside the house, "Damn it! Did you forget to top off the gas in the generator?" followed by a muffled reply coming from further inside the house. He heard the first voice yell, "Then get your ass out there and get it going! And hurry the hell up before Dog gets back up here. He'll ride you like one of them whores if you don't!"

The door leading off the deck, just a few feet away from Ed, swung open violently, causing him to flinch and raise his rifle. Out burst a scuzzy-looking man, cursing under his breath while stomping his way over to the generator. "I'm getting so sick of this crap!" the man said aloud as he poured gasoline into the generator from a jug that was sitting on the ground. "I'm gonna pop somebody if they don't chill the hell out and get off my back," he said with rage and disgust.

Ed did his best to duck into the shadows below the window as the generator started back up and the lights came on. He knew he could engage and take the unsuspecting man out with little trouble, but didn't want to blow their cover and risk their chances of recovering the Jackson women.

~~~~

Evan saw the lights go off, followed by the man out back getting the generator going again. He wondered how far around Ed had made it. He then turned his attentions back to the interior of the house, as he could now see through the window on the side. He saw a door open inside the room; a man entered and then walked out of view. After a brief moment, the man passed back in front of the window and appeared to be yelling at someone in the corner, against the exterior wall. He then left the room, slamming the door behind him. *I wonder if that's where the women are,* he thought to himself. He wanted to get a better look, but it was time to join back up with Jason and Ed. He slipped out of the tree and quietly backtracked to Jason's position.

Once the three had regrouped, Ed and Evan both reported what they had seen and heard. Ed explained, "The rear of the house has little to no security. When the generator shut down, I was within mere feet of the man who got it going again. He could have easily spotted me, but had his head so far up his own ass with his disdain for his fellow scumbags that he didn't have the presence of mind to even look around."

"That's something that we can use to our advantage," Jason said, taking it all in.

Ed continued, saying, "Now to the bad news."

"Bad news?" queried Jason.

"Well, I stumbled across something in the dark, out back in the tree line. I stopped to check it out and it was a dead female body, wrapped up like trash and just thrown outside."

"Damn... Was it one of the Jacksons?" Evan asked.

"I dunno. I was kind of freaked out when I realized what it was. I didn't use a light or look very close. In hindsight, I know I should have, but..."

"Don't sweat it," Jason interrupted, getting them back on track. "We'll figure it out soon enough. Here's the plan: Ed, you stay on the high side in the woods with your M1A, to be able to lay down a harassing fire at their flank wherever necessary to keep them from being able to focus on either of the advances. We'll call in the truck from below, and when they arrive, the enemy's attention will be focused on what they think are their returning comrades. Evan and I will make entry from the rear of the house and rush them from behind. We've operated in close quarters together quite a bit, so we should be up for the close and personal stuff. We'll have Nate, Charlie, and Jimmy hold them down from the front. As loosely as they are organized and hitting them from three points, we should be able to roll them pretty easy. Just don't assume that, though, and we'll be fine."

"Sounds good to me," affirmed Evan.

"Me, too," seconded Ed.

"Alrighty, then. Ed, be making your way to your spot on the hill. I'll call in the truck, and then Evan and I will get into position."

Ed complied and began to move into position as Jason relayed the plan to the team waiting with the truck down on Highway 70. Once the plan was thoroughly briefed, he and Evan made their way to the back of the house.

Still in the tree line, but in the backyard, Evan said, "Let's hold here until we see the truck getting close. Then once their attention is on the truck, we can make a move across the yard and position by the door for our entry."

"Roger Roger," Jason sharply replied in his typical fashion.

It wasn't long before they heard the old pickup truck lumbering its way up the hill, slowing for the sharp switchback turns along the way. As the truck rounded the last corner and its lights shined on the front of the house, Evan made his move for the back door, followed by Jason, once Evan was in position and providing cover.

As the truck pulled to a stop out front and shut off the engine, there was a moment of uneasy silence for Evan and Jason, not being able to see what was taking place from their position. Then all of a sudden, gunfire erupted at the front of the house, giving Evan and Jason their cue. Jason patted Evan on the shoulder and Evan pulled open the door and rushed inside, with Jason following along behind. Evan took a knee on the floor a few feet inside and covered the hallway leading toward the front of the house. Jason went right, to check the first room on that side. He kicked the door open, scanned the room, and yelled, "Laundry... Clear!" He then moved into position with Evan and patted him on the shoulder to initiate the leapfrog.

Jason now covered the hallway while Evan kicked in the door on the left and scanned the room. As he started to yell clear, he noticed a young girl's arm, cuffed to the metal bed frame, reaching up from behind. She appeared to be hiding behind the bed, but her restraints were keeping her partially in view. Just as Evan yelled, "Girl!" Jason began firing his Remington down the hallway, cycling the bolt and re-engaging as fast as he could. It was times like this when the long-range advantage of his large, bolt-action rifle was lost in the tight confines of close-quarters battle. Evan partially reentered the hallway and laid down a rapid cover fire with his VZ58 as Jason's next shot took down his assailant.

~~~~

At the front of the house, the man who appeared at the front door was quickly dispatched by Nate, before he could figure out it wasn't his friends returning, after all. Nate continued to fire from the bed of the truck while Charlie and Jimmy moved to positions of cover. Using the shots from Nate, Charlie, and Jimmy as his cue, Ed fired into the side of the house, near the windows, to confuse the occupants and force them to divide their attention.

A second man appeared at a window and opened fire on them with a fully automatic machine gun, ripping into the truck and sending debris flying in all directions. Nate had left the tailgate of the truck down for ease of egress; he dove out of the back of the truck, taking cover underneath to avoid the barrage of bullets tearing the truck to shreds.

"SAW! He's got a freaking SAW!" yelled Nate to Charlie and Jimmy as they took cover behind a group of oak trees.

Nate was pinned down by the machine gun fire and unable to move. Fearing for Nate's predicament, Jimmy exposed himself to lay down cover fire for him. Not long after, he was hit by the incoming fire and knocked to the ground. He felt a searing heat in his left shoulder and a dull pain in his chest. He could barely breathe and was nearly hyperventilating.

Nate had taken advantage of Jimmy's momentary suppressing fire and leapt from the truck. He nearly dislocated his prosthetic leg upon hitting the ground. After re-securing it, he crawled on the ground and took cover in the trees with the other two men. Realizing that Jimmy was down, he dove behind Jimmy's tree, pulling him out of the line of fire.

"Are you hit? Are you hit?" he asked.

Jimmy nodded yes, but didn't reply verbally. That was when Nate saw blood seeping through the jacket sleeve of Jimmy's left bicep. Knowing it wasn't life threatening, he quickly began looking Jimmy over for other wounds. The rapid fire of the fully automatic M249 Squad Automatic Weapon (SAW) would most likely have made multiple hits. Amidst the continuing barrage of machine gun fire that ripped bark and splinters of wood from the surrounding trees, Nate aggressively unbuckled Jimmy's load-bearing vest and opened his jacket, looking for other serious wounds while Charlie attempted to return fire at the house.

Jimmy began to catch his breath, and said faintly, "I'm okay. I'm okay."

It was then that Nate found a fully loaded magazine in Jimmy's vest that had been penetrated by the high velocity 5.56mm NATO round from the SAW. He followed the path of the projectile into his jacket and found it, mushroomed and distorted from the impact, in Jimmy's Bible that he carried in his left inside pocket. As Nate looked at the Bible in amazement, he noticed that the bullet had almost completely penetrated the pages before coming to rest at Psalms 82:4, which reads, *Rescue the weak and the needy; rescue them out of the hand of the wicked.*

As Nate flipped through the pages, at a loss for words, a photograph of Jimmy's young wife, Beth, fell to the ground. Jimmy quickly grabbed the picture, kissed it, and held it close to his heart, realizing that he had almost been taken from her in an instant.

Nate simply said, "She saved you, man," noticing that the picture had also been pierced by the bullet as it came to rest in the pages of the Bible.

~~~~

In the back of the house, after dispatching their immediate threat, Evan said to Jason, "Stay with the girl; I'll try to take out the machine gun."

Jason nodded and fell back to the bedroom where the girl was restrained to the bed. The young girl was terrified as Jason approached. He slung his rifle over his shoulder and held both hands in the air as he approached her, saying softly, "Shhhhh, it's okay. The Gibbs family sent us for you. Are you Sabrina?"

The young girl nodded yes and began to cry uncontrollably as she realized her ordeal might be coming to an end. The horrors she faced had caused her to hold back much of her emotion until this very minute. Jason looked around the room for something he could use to cover the girl. The sheets and blankets on the floor were all bloodstained and filthy, so he removed his gear and took off his own jacket, placing it over her. He then looked for something he could use to break the thin metal tubing of the headboard to free the girl. They could worry about getting the cuffs off later, but for now, he needed to get her mobile.

His search was to no avail. Her captors had already cleared the room of everything that was usable as a weapon. In his desperation to get the girl free, he remembered the small chain-type survival saw he kept in his pack. He removed his pack and quickly dug around until he found what he was looking for. He pulled out a chain-type saw with a nylon loop for a handle on each end. He wrapped the chain around the metal tubing of the headboard, which was there mostly for decorative reasons, and quickly sawed through it, freeing the girl from the bed. He pulled the bed away from the wall a few feet and said, "Get down here on the floor with me. We'll wait here until Evan gets back." Propping his rifle up on the bed and using it for cover, he kept his aim on the doorway in the event Evan did not achieve his objective.

As the man in the front of the house focused on Nate, Jimmy, and Charlie, Evan crept up the hallway leading toward the living room and kitchen area. Unsure if there were any other assailants in the house, he proceeded slowly toward the sounds of the gunfire, scanning for threats as he went.

Upon approaching the living room, he saw a large man firing an M249 SAW out of the front windows of the house.

With all of the glass blown from the windows, he had the SAW propped up on the back of a loveseat and was laying down a barrage of fire toward the pickup truck. Evan slipped into the kitchen, which was just to the right of the living room, popped up from behind the bar, and fired three rounds into the man's back, ending the fight.

Outside in the woods, as the barrage of bullets ceased, Charlie and Nate took advantage of the lull to refocus on the front of the house and assess the situation for continuing threats. "Is he out of ammo?" asked Charlie.

"That or the guys got him," replied Nate. "Let's lie low for now. He could be waiting to tear into us as soon as he sees movement."

As Jimmy regained his composure, he took up a defensive position to cover their rear in the event some of the other men from inside of the house were trying to maneuver against them. Nate then yelled to Ed's position, "Ed... report!"

"I've got nothin' from here!" he yelled in reply.

After a few minutes of silence, they heard a familiar voice over the handheld radio say, "Clear!"

Nate asked in response, "Evan?"

"Yes, clear in here! How about out front?"

"Two down that we can verify, including the machine gunner," said Nate.

"I think that's it then. We got the rest inside. I'll cover you from here while you make a move for the house, just in case," said Evan as they saw him move into position in the front window.

One at a time, the three men made a move for the house, covering each other as they went. First Charlie and Ed proceeded out of their hunkered-down positions to the house, followed by Nate, and then Jimmy. Once they were all inside the living room and Evan advised him that the house was secure, Jason brought the young girl out of the bedroom. His jacket, oversized for her, covered her torso, but left her bruised and battered legs exposed in the cold night air. "We've gotta find a way to get these cuffs off," said Jason, looking around the room for ideas.

Nate dug around in his pocket for a second and then pulled out a Tool Logic SLP4 multi-use knife. "How about a key?" Nate said with a grin. "I was military police in the Navy, remember? I've got cuff keys stashed all over me."

Jason, not believing something could actually work out so easily in their predicament, took the key from Nate with a look of relief, and freed the young girl's wrists from the pain of the handcuffs. Her wrists were raw and bruised from days of struggle while wearing them, and she was thankful to have them off.

"Thanks, man," he said, handing the key back to Nate. "Okay, guys, let's get ourselves together here. Is anyone hurt?"

Nate and Charlie looked at Jimmy as Jimmy said, "My arm, but we can worry about that later."

"Nonsense," Evan replied. "Let's get that wrapped up, at a minimum, for now. Nate, if you can help him with that."

Nate nodded in the affirmative, led Jimmy over to the sofa, and sat him down; he had him remove his load-bearing vest, jacket, and shirt so they could get a good look at the extent of his wound. While they were dealing with Jimmy's injuries, Charlie said, "Where's Roxanne?"

He immediately realized the full extent of the situation when the girl looked down and broke into tears once again. Ed then realized his fears were true, and knew exactly whom he had stumbled across in the woods earlier. Their moment of glee from having defeated the predators quickly turned dark once again as they let the full extent of the situation, as well as what the young girl and her mother had gone through, sink in.

"Let's get her out of here," Jason said, interrupting the somber mood.

"Jimmy's not in a position to hustle on foot at the moment. Ed, how about you and Charlie go get the ATVs," Evan said to get the ball rolling once again. "We'll get her back to the trailer on one of them and get her some clean clothes. They won't fit, but they'll be warm and clean. We can use the other ATV to transport her mother somewhere so we can give her the respect she deserves. We can't leave her here, not after what she went through in this place."

Everyone nodded in agreement as Charlie looked at Ed and said, "Let's get moving."

"Roger that!" he replied.

Jason sat Sabrina down on the sofa and offered her some venison jerky and a drink of water. She was desperately hungry and tried to eat, but was so distraught she got nauseated after only a few bites. She took a few drinks of water and with a mere whisper from her sore, dry throat said, "Thank you," as a tear rolled down her cheek.

Evan sat down next to her and said, "The Gibbs family is on their way to somewhere safe. A place where women and girls are sheltered and protected from atrocities such as this. We will get you there to them. I'm sure they would love to have you with them. They were very worried about you and were devastated about what happened to you."

"Did they pay you to come?" she asked.

"Pay us? What do you mean?" he asked in reply.

"Why did you come for me? Why did you risk your lives and get hurt to save me? You didn't even know me."

"Why wouldn't we?" he said softly. "I know you've seen and gone through a lot of horrible things since this all started happening, but I promise, there are still some good people in the world. The Gibbs family are good people, and we just want to get you back to them."

She tried to smile in appreciation for what he said, but simply harbored too much pain. She laid her head on the arm of the sofa and closed her eyes, falling asleep for the first time in days, knowing that she had her own guardian angels keeping her safe.

Chapter 23: Intensive Care

He could hear muffled voices, but the relentless pain made him unable to focus on the words being said. The light in his eyes blurred his vision; he squinted, trying to see. A blinding light in his right eye sent shooting pain through his already pounding head, and then it moved to the left. "Griff... Griff..." he heard from a voice behind the light.

He tried to speak, but merely moving the muscles in his face to make his jaw work caused blinding pain. Struggling to open his eyes, he saw a figure standing over him. "Honey, it's me. Are you in there?" said the voice of his wife, Judy, as he felt a woman's touch on his forehead, gently dabbing a cold, damp cloth to ease his pain. "I think he's awake," she said as others crowded around him.

"He's still in a lot of pain. I don't think he's ready," another voice said. He then felt a stinging in his arm followed by the voice saying, "This will help him sleep. He'll come out of it in time..." as he faded into darkness.

~~~~

Opening his eyes once again, he saw that the room was now dark, which was pleasing to his pounding head. He struggled to figure out where he was, but it hurt too much to move his head to look around. His neck was sore and stiff and his head throbbed with pain. "Griff?" he heard again as a female's soft touch caressed his arm.

"Baby," he quietly mumbled.

"Yes, yes, honey, it's me," sobbed Judy as she kissed him on the forehead. "Oh, thank the Lord you are awake. I've been so scared I was going to lose you."

"Where... Where is Daryl? Beth... Where is Beth?" he struggled to ask.

"Daryl is fine," she said as she stroked his hair and gazed at him with watery eyes. "He's out on patrol with some of the others, keeping us safe."

"Where's Beth?" he asked through the pain.

"She didn't make it. There was nothing you could do."

He just lay there, soaking in what she said as he realized it wasn't just a bad dream. It had all really happened, although he had no memory of how he had gotten where he was now or what had happened to him.

Just then, Rachel entered the room and said, "Oh, thank goodness he's awake." She checked his pulse, listened to his chest with a stethoscope, and said, "How are you doing, Griff? Are you feeling any pain?"

"Yes, all over, but especially my head, my chest, and my shoulder," he sluggishly answered.

"That's to be expected," she replied as she took his temperature. "You took a nasty fall off of your horse and got banged up pretty bad. We were worried about you for a while."

"I need to help Daryl. I need to get back out there and help Daryl," he said.

"Daryl and the others have everything under control. They'll be fine. You're in no condition to even get up, much less go running off again. You hit your head pretty hard. You also collapsed a lung and possibly broke a few ribs. How do your arms and legs feel? Do you have any pain anywhere else?"

"My neck and shoulders ache, but my right shoulder really hurts," he replied.

"You may have torn something in your shoulder. Without any real diagnostic equipment, it's hard for me to tell. We will work with you as you begin to get up and about, to see if we can tell the extent of the damage and try to figure out how we can best rehabilitate you, but for now, we have to focus on the more important stuff."

She then began to check his pupils and basic eye function to assess the extent of his head injuries. After completing her exam, she gave him an anti-inflammatory and said, "This should help a little. I'll leave you with your family now." Rachel turned to Judy and said, "Just give us a yell if you need anything. I'll bring you something to eat when Mildred serves dinner later, so you don't have to leave his side."

"Thank you so much, Rachel. You're a godsend," Judy replied.

As Rachel left her basement office and joined the others upstairs, she gave them the good news that Griff was awake and responsive, and updated them all on his continually improving condition. She turned to Luke and said, "If you hear anything from Daryl, please let him know Griff is doing much better and is on the road to recovery. I know he's been worried sick about him."

"Of course," Luke replied. "The last time he checked in with us, he said he was riding back out to Jimmy's place to see what he could do with Beth's remains. He wants to make sure she is well taken care of until Jimmy gets home. We really need to get her buried soon, but Daryl doesn't want to take the moment away from Jimmy. He doesn't just want him coming home to a gravestone."

"What did he have in mind?" she asked.

"He said something about wrapping her in some industrial-type shrink wrap. The stuff that comes in a large roll. I guess he wants to wrap her up nice and tight to keep the air and pests out. He wanted to start working on a grave for her, but he decided that Jimmy may want a say in where she's laid to rest."

"Thanks for that, Luke," Judith said as Mildred and Rachel nodded in agreement. "Daryl means well, but he's not thinking straight right now. He blames himself for letting this all happen, and is trying a little too hard to carry the entire burden."

"We are blessed to have a man like Daryl Moses as a part of our community," Mildred added, taking a break from cooking. "Ollie always thought highly of him, and every man didn't automatically get his respect; it had to be earned the old-fashioned way, but he sure loved Daryl."

Chapter 24: A Fork in the Road

As they waited for Ed and Charlie to return with the ATVs to transport Sabrina to the trailer, Jason took up an overlook position on the roof with his Remington 700 while Nate covered the rear of the home after he had done his best to treat Jimmy's wound for the time being. While Jimmy stayed with Sabrina, Evan searched the house to look for anything that could be useful to them. The first item of interest to him was the M249 SAW that was used by the assailants at the front of the house to keep Ed, Jimmy, and Nate pinned down outside. A SAW, or Squad Automatic Weapon, is a light machine gun that fires the same 5.56mm round as a military M16 and M4, as well as a civilian AR15. The M249 is used to enhance the firepower of smaller military units and has never been available to the public.

Evan walked over to the sofa where Jimmy was resting while keeping an eye on Sabrina, and said, "I wonder where these bastards got this thing?"

"That's the damn gun that shot me!" exclaimed Jimmy. "It was like a bee's nest of bullets being unleashed on us."

"There were two other ammo cans of 5.56 green tip over by the scumbag that used it on you. Looks GI to me. I wonder where these boys came across this stuff."

"Those bastards probably stole it or did some other dirty deal to get their hands on it," remarked Jimmy as he rubbed his bruised chest.

"Well, it will surely come in handy on our little journey, as well as to help fortify the homesteads when we get back. I'm gonna go through the house and look for other weapons and ammo. Keep an eye on her," Evan said, nodding toward Sabrina, who was still asleep.

"This poor girl could probably sleep for days and not catch up on what she's lost," said Jimmy softly, trying not to wake her.

Evan then went around the house, retrieved the weapons and ammunition from the dead kidnappers, and staged it all in the living room. In all, he found a cheaply made 12-gauge Chinese pump shotgun, two Beretta M9 9mm pistols, two government-issued select-fire M4 carbines, a Romanian semi-automatic WASR-10 AKM, a 9mm Glock 19, and a Turkish made Sig Sauer clone in .40 S&W. He also found two 840 round ammo cans of 5.56 NATO green tip, several boxes of various commercially available shotgun shells, several boxes of 9mm pistol cartridges, and twenty-three government-issued 5.56 NATO STANMAG magazines for use in AR pattern rifles as well as other NATO compliant 5.56mm weapons.

"That's quite the little weapons cache you've got there, Ev," Jimmy commented as Evan tossed the last box of ammo onto the pile.

"Tell me about it. If these guys weren't so undisciplined, we'd have never been able to take them. They had a serious firepower advantage," Evan said, looking at the pile of weapons. "The SAW, the two M4s, the 5.56 ammo, and magazines are all military issue. These guys either had a serious connection, or they stole it. Either way, these would be hot potatoes if a man were caught with them by the feds."

"I guess it's a good thing we're here in the sticks, where the feds don't tread," replied Jimmy with a grin.

"Yeah, for now. Anyway, there was some food and water in the kitchen. We'll take the food that's in sealed packages, but the rest of it doesn't look so good. The water doesn't look clean either. I don't trust these scumbags' hygiene enough to risk it. I'd rather filter river water, if it comes to it. When we roll back through here with the tractor and trailer, we'll stop by and load it all up. We'll hide the weapons, of course, just in case someone else comes along while we are on our way to get it. By the way, I've got an idea... and a favor to ask."

"What's that?" asked Jimmy.

"We've come to a fork in the road here," Evan explained. "You're injured..."

"I'm fine, I'm fine," interrupted Jimmy.

"Well, you may be fine, but you still need to get that cleaned out and closed up right—and maybe get some antibiotics. We don't want your arm turning green and falling off on us while we're out here. We also need to do something to get Sabrina to Del Rio with the Gibbs family. I would like to ask you and Charlie to get her there to safety on your ATVs, and then for Charlie to accompany you back home so Rachel can look at that wound and treat it properly. You've got a pregnant wife at home and don't need to be out here, dying on her from infection when she needs you the most."

"But what about you guys, though? You'll be down to four men and no four wheelers," Jimmy said in protest.

"Four guys and no ATVs are better off than six guys with a young girl to protect if it all hits the fan. We really need to get her to the Gibbs family," Evan said in a serious tone. "Do this for us, Jimmy, and then get home to Beth and get yourself taken care of."

Jimmy knew Evan was right, and from the look on his face, he would not be taking no for an answer. In a reluctant voice, Jimmy said, "Okay, Ev. You're right. We'll get her there safe and sound."

"Thanks, Jimmy," Evan said with a smile as he patted Jimmy on the shoulder.

"Crap!" exclaimed Jimmy, flinching with pain.

"Oh, sorry, man, wrong shoulder," Evan said with an embarrassed grin.

Up on the roof, Jason was glassing the area with his riflescope when he saw Charlie and Ed returning with the

ATVs. He covered them until they drew near and then climbed back down from the roof to join the others below. "How'd it go?" Jason asked as Charlie and Ed shut down their engines and began to dismount.

"Uneventful," replied Ed.

Evan then joined them out front, leaving Jimmy inside with Sabrina, to work out a plan. "I've got an idea that I've already got Jimmy on board with. I just need you guys to sign off on it."

"Shoot," Jason replied.

Evan explained what he had discussed with Jimmy about taking Sabrina to Del Rio to get her reunited with the Gibbs family, and then for Jimmy to seek medical care at home with Rachel. He assured Charlie that even though they would be returning home early, he and Jimmy would both share in the spoils of whatever supplies they acquired along the way, as they were part of the team through the end. He then explained, "By the way, guys, in addition to the SAW, I found two select-fire M4s, two M9s, a bunch of mags, and some ammo, all of which, of course, were probably stolen from a guard unit or a regular service component. There was also a crappy pump shotgun and some shells, but the mil-spec stuff has me concerned. We can definitely use it in the current state of things, but if the pieces start getting put back together, or if we encounter any federal forces, they would be a huge liability."

"The mil what?" asked Charlie.

"Oh, mil-spec means military specifications. In other words, the government-issued weapons we found, the long guns of which would be restricted class III weapons regardless of the state of affairs."

"That SAW sure would come in handy back at the homesteads if we encountered any more major trouble like last fall," said Jason. "But we would need to keep that stuff stashed for the reasons Evan stated, only to be pulled out in the event that it all hits the fan again."

"We won't have room on the four-wheelers for any of it, so you guys just hang on to it all for now and bring it when you come home. Besides, you might need to fight your way out of a mess down the road for all we know," Charlie added.

"Well, let's get the show on the road," Evan replied. "I don't want to keep that poor girl in this hellhole for one minute longer. This place has got to be a nightmare for her."

"What about the mother?" Jason asked.

"Oh, yeah. I figured we could put Sabrina on one ATV and her mother on the rack of the other, following behind, of course; Jimmy on one and Charlie on the other. Just run the quads slow, and the rest of us will hoof it and take up point, rear, and flanking positions to escort you to the trailer. Once we get there, we will make camp until the sun comes up. We can then give her mother the proper burial and respect before we go our separate ways."

"What about the guns?" asked Charlie.

"We'll be coming back this way to head east toward Hot Springs. We can duck back in and get them then. For now, we can hide what we want to take with us in the woods in case someone comes along behind us between now and tomorrow, after the burial."

Jason looked at Charlie and said, "Does all that sound good to you? You and Jimmy are the ones being put out the most."

"That sounds fine with me. We need to get that girl taken care of. If we keep dragging her along with us, there's no telling what will happen, so let's go with Evan's plan."

After a brief discussion of specifics, Evan, Jason, and Ed moved the weapons into the trees and covered them with brush the best they could, while Charlie stood watch out front. Once that was accomplished, they turned their attentions to the least desirable task at hand, which was dealing with Mrs.

Jackson's body. While Ed and Jason retrieved her body from the woods and brought her to the front porch, Evan began searching for something rigid to place on the rear cargo rack of the ATV to support her body, as they wanted to be able to transport her in a dignified manner. After a few moments of scavenging around the house, he realized he was forgetting the materials that were all around him. He went out to the tool shed by the carport and found an old, rusty axe. He pulled the axe out and said, "Hell, I think I'll take these tools with us, anyway." Swinging the axe at the hinges on the door, Evan quickly separated the door from the shed, creating the perfect backboard to transport her to the trailer. He then took a few extra swings to the side of the shed before throwing the axe to the ground, and thought, *I needed that.*

Chapter 25: Rendering Honors

Once Sabrina and her mother were aboard the ATVs, Jason took up the point position and took along one of the handheld radios; Evan took the rear position and carried the other, while Nate and Ed took the left and right flanks respectively. Sabrina rode on the back of Jimmy's ATV, bundled up in a few of the cleaner blankets they were able to find in the house, while her mother was loaded onto the wooden door, attached across the rear cargo rack of Charlie's ATV.

Jason led the way and began walking down the hill to get a comfortable distance in front of the lead ATV. He could communicate with the rear of the convoy via the radio to Evan while he could simply use hand signals with Jimmy up front. Once Jason got into position, he signaled Jimmy and off they went. Nate and Ed walked alongside, pacing with the idling ATVs while Evan waited until they were far enough ahead and started marching along behind.

Being ever on guard, the men led the slow convoy west on Highway 70, toward the location where they left their tractor and trailer, watching for threats along the way. As Jimmy watched Jason up ahead, barely visible in the darkness of the night and almost out of reach of the illumination of his ATV's headlights, he saw Jason stop abruptly and raise his rifle. Jimmy slammed on the brakes, bringing the convoy to a halt. Nate and Ed both took up defensive positions to cover the ATVs. Just as Evan started to key the mic to ask Jason what was going on up ahead, he heard the loud crack of his .300 Win Mag's muzzle report and saw the flash of light in the distance.

He immediately dropped to a knee and spun around to cover them from the rear when he heard Jason say over the radio, "Hot damn! Dinner is served, gentlemen."

"What? What the hell are you talking about?" Evan asked in an excited voice over the radio, in reply.

"A mature doe just walked right out in front of me. I guess it was the headlights from the four-wheelers. I popped her. I couldn't resist."

"You jerk; you scared me to death," replied Evan.

"Sorry, man, but if I had keyed up the mic to talk, she would have bolted. I had to take the shot."

"Okay, just toss her on Jimmy's front rack and we'll gut and dress her out at the trailer," Evan replied.

"Roger Roger!" Jason replied with a rejuvenated spring in his step.

Evan just chuckled to himself and thought, *It's the small things in this new world that keep people going.*

As they neared the small dirt side road, where they left the tractor and trailer, Jason signaled for the group to halt. He then motioned for Ed and Nate to rally on him out front while the ATVs and Evan remained in position. As Ed and Nate arrived at Jason's position, Jason said, "Ed, come with me to make sure everything is still secure before we get Sabrina in the area. Nate, go back and tell Evan and the others what we're doing. He's got the other radio. Tell him we'll call when we've secured the area."

"Roger that," Nate replied as he turned to join back up with the others.

Jason then looked at Ed and asked, "Point or rear?"

"I'll take point."

"Alright then, let's get on it," said Jason as he and Ed proceeded toward the dirt road.

As they crept up the road, Ed in the front and on the left shoulder, with Jason bringing up the rear and off to the right, they could see the sun about to come up over the eastern horizon. *Damn, it's morning already,* Jason thought to himself. After being hit with that realization, the fatigue began to set in and rear its ugly head. Jason forced himself to stay alert, however, as the last thing they needed was to be caught off guard and have their plans derailed.

As they arrived at the tractor, he and Ed both cleared the area and set up an overwatch before calling in the others. Once everyone had arrived, the first order of business was to get Sabrina taken care of and get her some rest. Evan dug around in the supplies they had brought along and gave her a fresh set of clean clothes, "They'll be a bit big, but you can roll up the sleeves and legs for now. Here are a couple pairs of socks as well. We don't have any extra shoes, but these will at least keep you warm. I'm sure the church can get you some shoes in Del Rio. Oh, and here are some alcohol wipes from our first aid kit. You can use them to clean up a little if you like."

"Thank you," she said with a quick smile as he led her into the trailer to change. Evan closed all of the windows on the trailer for her privacy. Just before he closed the door, he asked her, "Is there anything else we can get you for now?"

"No, sir. Thank you so much," she said quietly. Although she was happy and relieved to be free of her captors, she knew it would be a long time before she would feel normal again. She had a lot of suffering yet to do inside before she could begin the healing process.

~~~~

The birds were chirping and the beautiful sounds of nature were all around. The light of the day was shining brightly through the gaps around the windows of the trailer. She yawned and looked around, flinching at first from her unfamiliar surroundings, though she quickly remembered that she was in the safekeeping of her rescuers.

She could smell something delicious cooking. She hadn't had a true meal in at least a week, making the scents of freshly grilled meat overpowering. She gained her composure and went to the door of the trailer, cracking it slightly, and peeked outside. She could see Evan, Jason, Jimmy, and Nate sitting around a campfire, grilling some kind of meat directly over the fire on a skewer.

Jimmy looked over at the trailer, saw her peeking out, stood up, and waved her over with a smile. She slowly opened the door and nervously walked over to the men. She knew she could trust them, yet just couldn't shake the feeling that it was all too good to be true. She felt as if her newfound freedom was just a dream and she would awaken in her previous hell at any moment. As she approached the campfire, all of the men stood up and took their hats off as Evan said, "Good morning, ma'am; or rather good evening. You slept pretty well."

Charlie brought her a small folding camp chair and said, "Here you go, young lady. Have a seat and we'll get you a plate of food."

She complied with a nervous smile as Jason handed her a plate of freshly grilled venison, green beans, and some cornbread they had brought along from the homesteads. It was a feast for her, as her captors had barely even taken efforts to keep her alive, but even before that, she and her parents often had to scavenge for food.

"Are you doing okay today?" asked Evan. "If there is anything at all you need, or if you have any concerns, please just let us know. We can't even begin to imagine what you must have gone through and what you might need because of it..." Evan said, suddenly at a loss for words. He assumed she may have some health concerns or feminine needs, but didn't know how to approach the situation, after what she had been through.

Sabrina just nodded that she understood him, looked around, and then asked, "Where are the other two men... and my mother?"

"Ed and Charlie are standing watch right now. That's why we are able to sit here and cook and eat without the stress of looking over our shoulders. There is no better security than friends you trust," he said. "We've got a place prepared for your mother. We just wanted to let you get some sleep today, as well as a bite to eat so that you would feel up to seeing her off properly. We also wanted to get your blessing on the location we found for her resting place. She's your mother, so you have the final say."

Sabrina didn't know how to feel about what was going on around her. For as long as she could remember since the attacks triggered the collapse, she known the world to be an ugly and unforgiving place. With the exceptions of a few rare instances, people only seemed to be out to take from you, to hurt you, to use you, or simply disregard your needs. Yet, there she was with a group of men who risked their lives to save her from her unspeakable hell. They were feeding her, caring for her, helping her with her mother, and they promised to reunite her with the Gibbs family—the closest thing left on earth that she could consider family. They did all of this for what gain? She simply wanted to mourn her mother and lay her to rest so that she could move on, but she didn't know what to accept as real. The actions of these men, who were total strangers, just didn't make sense to her.

She finished her plate of food and in a quiet, sheepish voice said, "Thank you all so much." A tear rolled down her cheek. "I don't know what to say or what to believe anymore, but thank you for everything." She paused for a moment to regain her composure. "Thank you for not hurting me like the other men," she said as she broke down into an inconsolable cry.

Evan wanted to hold her and comfort her as if she was one of his own daughters, but after what she had gone through, he was afraid to make any physical contact with her. Trying to console the girl, he said in a gentle voice, "It's okay to cry.

You've got a lot of pain that you need to deal with. Everyone here knows that."

Then, unexpectedly, she got up out of her chair and ran straight into his arms, breaking down into a gut-wrenching cry. She was having a total release, finally giving in to all of the pent-up emotions from her terrible struggles and from the loss of both of her parents. Evan hugged her and began to cry with her. In that moment, he saw her as if she was his very own little girl, and would have done anything to be able to take the pain away.

Jason, Jimmy, and Nate quietly got up and walked away to give them some privacy in the moment. Jason whispered to Evan as they passed, "We will be at the site... for when you two are ready, of course," referring to the grave they had prepared for her mother while she slept.

Evan just nodded in reply and off they went. After about another ten minutes, Sabrina began to regain her composure. "I'm sorry," she said as she wiped her eyes in an attempt to dry them of her tears.

"Don't be. No one could have gone through what you did without feeling a mountain of pain."

"So what are you going to do with my mother?" she asked.

"With your blessing, we've prepared a grave for her with a beautiful view of the river. It's in a place that will be easy to find after the country gets itself sorted out if you want to come back and visit. It's on a hill facing west, with what should be a beautiful view of the sunset each day."

"Okay, I'm ready. I would like to see it," she said.

Evan led Sabrina to her mother's grave, where all of the men were gathered; even those currently on watch were there so that proper respects could be paid. Evan led them all in a prayer while Sabrina clung to his arm and cried. She then said goodbye to her mother, and they lowered her into the grave. Once the grave was covered, Sabrina laid a bouquet of wild spring flowers that she had gathered from the area and said her final goodbyes. In that moment, she knew deep down inside, her days as a young girl were officially over. She must find the resolve to carry on the family torch so that her mother and father's legacy did not die, but would live on forever, and their memory be passed on to their future generations.

Chapter 26: Keeping Watch

Back at the Thomas farm, Griff awoke to the smell of fresh, hot coffee. For a moment, he was lost in his memories of a wonderful spring morning, still in bed from a hard day's work the day before. His wife, Judy, would surely be making breakfast, he thought. He opened his eyes and found the harsh reality of his injuries and the memory of what happened to Beth Lewis. He looked over and saw Judy sitting in a recliner that they had moved down to the basement so she could stay with him in a little more comfort. Once she saw that he was awake, she quickly got up and came over to his bedside. "Good morning, handsome," she said as she pushed his hair back out of his face. She chuckled and smiled.

Griff looked at her with scrunched up eyebrows and said, "What's so funny?"

"Your hair," she replied with a giggle. "I thought I would be stuck with that Marine Corps 'high and tight' forever, but now you're all shaggy."

"Yeah, well... the barbershops are still all closed."

"We've got our own clippers, you know," she replied in jest.

"No need to start a generator and burn fuel just to power a set of hair clippers," he said defensively.

"You must be feeling better. You're getting your grumpy bulldog back."

"That's me, baby," he said with a proud smile. "So has anyone heard from Evan and the guys?"

"No. Nothing yet. Judith has been keeping her ears glued to the radio. She's been worried sick since her son, Nate, is out there with them. That, and I think Peggy is driving her nuts asking her for updates."

Griff just chuckled and then winced in pain. "Damn... laughing still hurts."

Rachel entered the room, smiled, and said, "Glad to see you're chatting away. You must be feeling better."

"I sure am, Doc," he replied smartly, never wanting to be seen as weak. "Where's Daryl?"

"Luke's leg is feeling better, so he is out doing a patrol on horseback today. Daryl didn't stop by and we couldn't reach him on the CB radio, so Luke went to check on the families at the Homefront, and then is going to head out Daryl's way to check on him."

"By himself?" Griff said in a concerned voice. "He really shouldn't have gone by himself."

"We're spread a little thin right now, with so many out on the run and you down-and-out. We've got a lot of ground to cover. It's come to that point, at least until the others get back."

"Damn it. How long till I can get back out there?"

"It takes at least six weeks for broken ribs to heal. The head injury should be behind you soon, but you're gonna have to take it easy physically for at least the next month. Your shoulder still remains to be seen, but it looks like the swelling has gone down, and you are able to put weight on it, so I think you'll be fine there."

"Can I at least get out of here so I can stand watch at the Homefront? There are no men over there without me," he said, trying to sit up.

"No men?" exclaimed Judy. "What about Greg and Jake? They've been holding down the fort just fine. Either one of those boys are more fit to defend the Homefront than you are right now, so put your pride away and just get better. We'll get you back over there in a few days. Besides, once we are in our new place, it will always just be you and Greg, so you had better get used to it now."

Griff just laid his head back on the pillow and huffed and puffed at Judy's statement, unable to disagree. "What's for lunch?" he asked, changing the subject.

"That's more like it," said Rachel with a smile. "I was looking for an appetite."

~~~~

Luke passed by the Homefront to check on Molly, Peggy, Sarah, and the kids, to find that all was well. Greg and Jake had both stepped up to the plate and were pulling alternating twelve-hour shifts in Griff's absence. He knew this news would be welcome to Griff, who was really taking being down and out to heart.

After leaving the Homefront, Luke rode on out to Daryl's place to find out why he hadn't stopped by, as was his routine of late. He proceeded with caution, not knowing exactly what might have held him up. As he arrived at Daryl's house, he rang the bell as Daryl's sign requested. He did not want to be accidentally shot as an intruder by the very man he had come to check on. After a few moments of silence, he rang the bell once again. *Damn it, Daryl. Where are you? Don't shoot my ass out here,* he thought to himself.

Ten more minutes passed and nothing, so he once again rang the bell. *If he doesn't come out this time, I'm gonna have to risk it and just walk up to the house.* He thought for a moment, trying to come up with what to do next. After adequate time had passed, he decided it was time to violate Daryl's own rule for visitors, and proceeded to the home to check on his dear friend.

He climbed back on his horse and slowly proceeded up the gravel and dirt driveway. Looking at the freshest horse tracks he could see on the ground, it appeared that Daryl might have ridden away from the house and had yet to return. This was just a guess, as Luke, admittedly, was no skilled tracker. As he approached the house, he shouted, "Daryl! It's Luke! Don't shoot!" He stopped his horse and waited for signs of noise or movement, but nothing. He shouted again and still received no reply. He dismounted his horse and slowly walked it by the lead up the drive to the house, where he noticed there was no smoke in the chimney and no sign of Daryl's horse anywhere.

He tied his horse up to the porch railing and walked up to the door, listening before knocking. After three consecutive knocks, he reached up and attempted to turn the knob and found it locked. *Where the hell are you, Daryl?* he thought as he stepped off the porch and began to look around the property. Walking out to Daryl's goat lot, he noticed the animals were nearly out of water. *That's not like Daryl to leave his animals inadequately cared for.* Assuming Daryl must be away, he filled all of the drinking troughs and gave the goats and chickens some grain to help tide them over until their owner returned.

Concerned about Daryl at this point, Luke decided to ride to the other homesteads in an attempt to find someone who might have seen or heard from him. Following a hunch, he rode to the Lewis home first.

Upon arrival, he found Daryl's horse tied to a shade tree in the front yard. Luke tied his horse up alongside Daryl's, looked around the property, and then limped to the front door of the home. His gunshot, although healing nicely, was beginning to cause him pain from overuse. As he reached up with his right hand to knock on the door, it pulled open, causing his heart to skip a beat. To his relief, he quickly found it was Daryl on the other side.

"Holy crap, man! You scared me half to death," joked Luke as he greeted Daryl with one hand on his chest as his heart pounded from the scare. "I stopped by your house and it looked like you hadn't been around in a while. Is everything okay?"

"I've been here," he said, looking exhausted.

"Doing what?"

"Keeping an eye on the place mostly. As well as tending to Jimmy's animals," Daryl replied as he stared off toward the woods.

"You don't have to do this all yourself. You've got animals and chores to tend to yourself. Speaking of which, I watered and fed your goats and pigs, so they should be good for today," Luke said as he tried to peek inside the house. He could see that Daryl had a bed made on the sofa, looking as if he had spent the night there.

In a somber, yet defiant voice, Daryl replied, "Jimmy has already lost enough. I'll be damned if he loses so much as one more animal or item from his home. This all happened on my watch and I'll not let it happen again."

"I understand how you feel, Daryl; just please, let us help. If you want to stay here and keep an eye on this place, fine, but let the rest of us chip in and help. If not here, then at your own home. The guys on the supply run are there for all of us, and those of us back here all have an obligation to each other in their absence. You're not in it alone."

Daryl looked at the ground for a moment and said, "Thanks, Luke. That means a lot." He then changed the subject by saying, "We need to bury Beth. At first, I thought it proper for her husband to be here to make the decisions, but this time of year, with it getting warmer and all... it just needs to be done. We can't let Jimmy's last memory of Beth be one of horror."

Luke nodded in agreement and said, "So what do you propose?"

"There is a beautiful spot on the hill just beyond his pond. It's close enough to visit, yet far enough away to not have it always in his face, reminding him every day of his loss. I think we should do it there. We can wait to have the ceremony, getting everyone together to pay our respects properly when he is home."

Luke put his hand on Daryl's shoulder, looked him in the eye, and said, "You're a damn fine man and a damn fine friend to everyone here. Don't you ever forget that."

Chapter 27: The Encounter

After the small ceremony for Sabrina's mother, Evan explained in detail their plan to have Charlie and Jimmy escort her to Del Rio to meet up with the Gibbs family at the church. She was relieved to be rejoining her family friends after all the suffering and loss she had gone through in recent days. They were, after all, the closest thing to a family she had left in this world.

Evan and Jason each wrote a letter to their wives back home, letting them know they were okay and they loved and missed them dearly. Nate wrote two letters, one for his love, Peggy, and one for his mother, Judith. They bundled the letters together and gave them to Charlie for delivery when he and Jimmy reached home. Taking the letters and putting them in his cargo vest, Charlie said, "We hate to leave you guys out here. If you need us, just send word and we'll come running like the cavalry."

Evan reached out and shook Charlie's hand, saying, "Thank you, sir, and please take good care of this young lady."

"Will do, Ev, will do," he replied.

"Are you up for the trip with that arm there?" Evan asked, pointing at Jimmy's wound.

"It's not gonna get better on its own. It's throbbing pretty good right now, but I can deal with it until I see Doc Rachel back home," he replied. "But at least it's not my shootin' arm," he replied jokingly to lighten the mood.

Jason yelled down from the top of the trailer, where he was using the vantage point to scan the area with his powerful riflescope, and said, "It looks clear as far as I can see from here. Do you want me to hike out ahead of you to clear the area before you leave?"

"No, that won't be necessary," Charlie replied. "Jimmy's gonna ride out in front of Sabrina and me to clear the way as we go. Besides, we'll make good time on the four-wheelers without you guys slowing us down with that slow old tractor."

"Did you top off your tanks?" Evan asked.

"Yep, and Jimmy is gonna haul one of the gas cans on his rear cargo rack, just in case."

Sabrina ran over to Evan, sensing the time for departure growing near, and gave him a hug and whispered, "Thank you. Thank you so much," as she began to cry. "Be careful out here; your families may need you like I did, some day."

Wiping the tears away, she turned and waved to Jason, as he was still on top of the livestock trailer, then turned to Nate and hugged him as well. Charlie took her by the hand and helped her mount the ATV. With a wave, they started their engines and rode away. Evan, Nate, Jason, and Ed all watched silently as they rode off out of sight.

"Okay, ladies," Jason said as he climbed down from the top of the trailer. "Let's get a move on. All this time on the road, and all we've got so far is coffee. It's gonna be dark soon and we need to get to our stash at the house on the hill and get back to making progress."

"Roger that!" replied Evan. "Okay, guys, you heard the man; let's break down camp and roll on."

Once everything was packed up and put away, the men checked the readiness of their weapons and got underway, driving the tractor out of the wooded dirt road back to Highway 70. Once on Highway 70, they made good time back to the stash of weapons they had taken from Sabrina's kidnappers and rummaged the house one last time, throwing anything of use into the trailer. With most of the items in the house considered tainted, they mostly looked outside for items to scavenge. Not finding much of value, other than a few tools and hardware items in the shed, Ed looked up at the top of the shed at the sheet metal roof and asked, "Don't we need roofing?"

"Sometimes you just can't see the forest for the trees," replied Jason. "Let's find a ladder and use the hammers we brought along to pop it loose."

"I've got your ladder and hammers right here," Evan replied with a sly grin as he climbed up on the tractor, fired it up, and switched on the lights, illuminating the shed brightly in the fading light of the day. He then yelled over the noise of the engine, "If we're not gonna use this thing, we might as well have brought a pickup truck." He then raised the loader bucket to the level of the roof and positioned the arms just shy of the building. With an upward flip of the bucket, he peeled the metal sheets from their rafters with ease. He repeated this around the shed until the roofing was completely loose. He then lowered the bucket and drove straight through the side of the shed, collapsing it to the ground like a house of cards. The men smiled, as they could now simply pick up the sheets of roofing from the ground with ease.

"Since it's in large sheets, let's strap it to the top of the trailer," Evan said as he shut the engine off and climbed down. "It won't take up any space inside the trailer at all that way."

"Roger Roger," replied Jason as he took out a roll of scavenged rope to secure it to the trailer. After they lifted all of the sheets to the top, Nate and Ed held them in place while Jason and Evan lashed them on securely with the rope.

Standing back, admiring their handiwork, and with the other items now loaded in the trailer, Evan said, "That'll do it. Let's roll," and with that, they were off.

Once back down on Highway 70, Jason said, "The next bridge crossing is just up ahead."

"What do you think?" Evan asked.

"I say Ed, Nate, and I quickly move on foot to secure it and then you just blast right across. The cover of darkness can be a blessing or a curse in a choke point like a bridge; we just need to hope it's a blessing tonight."

"Sounds good to me," Evan replied.

As they drove past the abandoned semi-trailers and shipping containers, Jason said, "I can't help but think about the horrors that began for young Sabrina and her family there, and how many others there may have been."

"Yeah, I know," Evan replied in a somber voice. "But at least those perpetrators are no longer in the picture. Think of how many won't have to go through that now." Jason nodded in agreement as he looked off into the distance, trying to forget about it and move on with the task at hand.

Upon reaching the bridge, Evan pulled the tractor to a stop, shut off the lights, and killed the engine. Jason climbed down from the trailer and briefed Ed and Nate on the task of clearing the bridge ahead. He said, "I'll take point and cross the bridge while you cover me, Ed. Nate, you ride shotgun with Evan as he drives across, then I'll cover Ed as he joins back up with us on the other side."

With no objections to the plan, Jason moved quietly across the bridge in what was now the complete darkness of the night. He stayed low, using the concrete and steel railing as cover, pausing on occasion to look and listen for potential threats. Once in position on the other side, Jason signaled with a double click of his handheld radio mic for Evan to cross.

Evan fired up the tractor, and while leaving the lights off for stealth, began a slow drive across the bridge. After about twenty yards, he thought, *Screw it. It's too damn dark to drive across this bridge with the lights off tonight. The last thing I need is to go over the side.* With that in mind, he flicked the lights back on and proceeded across.

Everything seemed to be going well until at about halfway across the bridge, when a helicopter came out of nowhere, shining a spotlight down on Evan and Nate on the tractor. Ed and Jason watched in horror, as they were still hidden in the darkness of the night. Both Jason and Ed held their aim on the helicopter, prepared to retaliate if any hostile actions were taken. After a few moments of hovering, the helicopter extinguished its lights and once again, slipped off into the darkness, flying over the ridge and out of sight.

With his heart pounding in his chest, Evan accelerated the tractor and raced across the bridge to the other side. Breaking from the plan of using Jason for cover, Ed ran across the bridge behind them, as all bets were now off. Once they met up on the south side of the river, Ed and Nate climbed back into the trailer without saying a word, and Jason rejoined Evan in the cab.

"What the heck was that about?" exclaimed Jason.

"Don't know, but I'd feel better if we got some distance between us and that bridge before we shut down again."

"I second that!" Jason replied.

"I couldn't make anything out. I was blinded by the spotlight. Who the hell was that? Feds? State? Civilian?"

"I couldn't make anything out. It was all blacked out. Nothing but the spotlight. Not even NAV lights," Jason said in a stressed voice.

For the next few miles, the men were silent as Evan drove the tractor while Jason scanned the skies for any further signs of the helicopter. The visibility, however, was rapidly deteriorating, as a rainstorm seemed to be building. The terrain on the south side of the bridge was getting very mountainous and the twists and turns of Highway 70 limited forward visibility. It soon began to rain and Jason broke the silence, saying, "On the bright side, with this weather and terrain, it's becoming a not-so-helicopter-friendly kind of night."

Evan just responded with a nod as they came around a blind corner at nearly the tractor's full speed. Catching a glimpse of something blocking the full width of the road just in front of them, he quickly slammed on the brakes, sending the tractor into a skid on the slick pavement, nearly jackknifing the trailer behind them as they slid to a stop.

"Ag tires suck on wet pavement!" he shouted.

"What the hell?" Jason responded.

Ed and Nate quickly egressed the trailer as Evan and Jason climbed down from the tractor. Both men had their rifles at the ready, not knowing what brought the tractor to such an abrupt and dramatic halt.

Evan pointed in front of the tractor into the darkness of the increasingly dreary night and said, "There's a damned tree in the road."

"Trap?" Nate queried.

"I don't think so," Evan replied as he walked closer to the tree to get a better look. "It hasn't been cut; it looks like it fell over from its roots. Probably during a storm, and there just isn't anyone to clear it out of the way anymore."

"I guess that's us," added Ed.

"Yep, I guess so," replied Evan as he walked back toward the trailer. "Jason, help me grab the saw and tow strap. Ed and Nate, if you two could cover us while we work, just in case, I would appreciate it."

"Roger that," replied Ed. "I'll take this side of the tree; Nate, you get the other side."

"Will do," Nate replied as he moved into position.

Using the headlights of the tractor, Evan illuminated the downed tree as the deteriorating weather conditions and the darkness made it increasingly difficult to work. As Jason started the chainsaw, Evan yelled over the noise of the rain and the saw's engine, "If you section it up, I'll use the loader and the strap to lift and drag the sections out of the way."

"Roger that!" replied Jason as he got to work on the large tree. He found it difficult to run the saw in the heavy rain. The water slinging from the chain, mixed with the wood particles, made it difficult to see with no safety goggles. He squinted his eyes, occasionally peeking to check his progress.

While he cut the tree into sections, Evan lifted them out of the road with the loader, placing them off to the side. As Jason made his final cut, Evan gestured for him to move out of the way. Once clear, Evan lowered the loader and drove straight through the remaining debris, pushing it out of the way. Jason then gave the signal for Ed and Nate to join back up with them, and they once again got underway.

"I can hardly see anything in this rain," Evan said as he struggled to see out of the cab of the tractor in the blinding rain. "We need to find a place to hunker down for the night."

"Looking at the map, we're approaching the North Carolina border," Jason said as he struggled to read with his penlight in the dark. "We're in the hilliest terrain we're gonna encounter tonight. Anyone would have a hard time landing or maneuvering a helicopter close to the ground in this area, especially in this weather. There are some small country roads off to the right up ahead. I suggest we pull into one and try to find a defendable position to hunker down until this blows over."

"I agree. Let's do it."

After another mile of navigating the dark and twisty mountain road, Evan said, "Looks like a road off to the right just up ahead."

"Yeah, I see that on here. Give it a look," Jason said, confirming their position on the map.

As they approached the road, Evan slowed the tractor to an idle and stopped just shy of entering. Just as he began to speak, lightening crashed nearby and the storm intensified. "I don't know how much scouting we could actually get done tonight. You can barely see a few feet ahead. I think we should just chance it and head up this road until we find a place to pull over and call it a night. I doubt many others would be out prowling around in this, either. We're probably safe riding the storm out in the trailer tonight."

"Agreed," Jason replied simply.

Evan turned up the small gravel road, which was bordered by thick woods and brush on both sides. After traveling a little more than half a mile, he found a pull-off where they could stop for the night. They felt the thick vegetation, trees, and mountainous terrain provided ample cover for the big green tractor and its trailer in the event of a random flyover by another helicopter.

As the men settled in for the night, Nate said aloud, "I wonder how Charlie and Jimmy are doing with Sabrina."

"I'm sure they're fine," Evan replied. "They should have made good time on those ATVs. If they pressed on, they should be nearing Del Rio by now. With luck, Sabrina will wake up warm and dry with the Gibbs family, where she can begin to put all of this behind her and begin her recovery."

"Speaking of putting things behind... let's hit the sack and put this day behind us," Jason said as he pulled his hat down over his eyes and lay back on his pack.

"Roger Roger," replied Evan with a chuckle from Nate and Ed.

Jason peeked from underneath his hat, tipping it up with one finger and said, "Keep it up, funny man, keep it up."

Chapter 28: Rude Awakenings

Evan lay awake, unable to sleep. He looked at his watch and saw that it was 4am. There were still several hours before the sun would be fully up. The rain had slowed to a trickle—just enough to provide a background noise as the raindrops impacted the sheet metal roofing strapped to the top of the trailer. The others seemed to be sound asleep as the snores and labored breathing told him all he needed to hear. At this point, Evan realized that for the first time he could remember, they had broken their cardinal rule about keeping a rotating watch while everyone else slept. *I guess it's good I can't sleep,* he thought.

Needing to relieve himself, Evan slipped quietly past the others, trying hard not to make any noises to wake them. *It's been a long day and these filthy bastards need some sleep,* he joked to himself.

As he opened the trailer door and stepped outside, he heard a gruff voice say in a slow, deliberate cadence, "Don't... move."

Although his Kimber 1911 was on his hip, he knew he didn't have a chance to deploy it before being cut to pieces by whoever had gotten the drop on him. He slowly raised his hands and said, "Good morning. What can I do for you?"

"You can start by explaining who you are and what you're doing here," the voice said calmly.

"I'm Evan Baird, and the other fellows in the trailer are my neighbors. We are on a supply run, hoping to do some scavenging and bartering. We're headed to Hot Springs, North Carolina. We've heard they have swap meets and barter markets there from time to time. Now, if you don't mind me asking, to whom do I have the honor of speaking?"

"We'll get to that. Where exactly do you live?"

"Within a day's walk of Del Rio," Evan replied vaguely.

"Exactly where?" the man asked.

"I can't get any more specific than that," Evan said bluntly.

"Give me a name from Del Rio."

"A name? Whose name?"

"Just give me a name so I know you're telling the truth," the man said with an insistent tone.

Not wanting to give away the position of anyone in particular, Evan responded, "Retired Gunnery Sergeant Wallace."

"Oh... Pastor Wallace. How do you know him?"

Evan was now curious as to how this person knew the Pastor was a retired Marine Corps gunny. "He's a friend," he replied.

The man in the darkness then asked, "Where is he currently located, and what supplies does he have?"

"He is where he is, and he's got what he's got," Evan replied in defiance of the question, not wanting to give anything away that might bring trouble to Del Rio.

The man then stepped from the darkness into view. He wore a plastic rain poncho over a multi-cam top, with old-style woodland camo BDU pants, and an olive green boonie hat. He carried a tricked out AR-15 with a well-worn finish and sported a chest rig with numerous AR-15 magazines. He also wore an old school M1911 .45 pistol in a drop-leg holster. "Ted Hawthorne's the name," he said, holding out his right hand.

"Nice to meet you," Evan replied with a firm handshake.

Evan then saw two other men, also well equipped, step out of the darkness behind him. "I'm a squad leader for the Blue Ridge Militia," Ted added. "We are out of a town to the east of here, to remain nameless at this point. We're scouting the area, as we've heard reports from travelers of foreign ground patrols and aircraft traffic operating under the flag of the United Nations in the region. Word has it the president has called them in to help—unlawfully, I might add—calling them peacekeepers."

"We've heard about that to a point. We heard they were staging in the cities, but this is the first time we've heard anyone say they were making their way out here to the sticks," replied Evan. "And why use U.N. soldiers? Wouldn't that just put the people off even more than if our own troops were patrolling the streets?"

"As far as the U.N. soldiers go, from what our sources tell us, the desertion rate has been so high in the federally controlled military, there are just barely enough domestic forces left to handle the security of key cities and government interests. Our own boys also might not be so keen on putting the smackdown on their fellow Americans who don't simply fall in line with the new order of things as they see it in Washington. The U.N. troops don't have a dog in the fight, so they are basically just acting as mercenaries. Being a U.N. soldier pays pretty well these days, considering the collapse of the world's economies. I'm sure they have no shortage of enlistees. As to the why here? We aren't exactly sure why," Ted explained, "but our theory is that they want to crush or prevent an insurgency before it happens."

"Before it happens?" Evan asked.

"Look at history," he explained. "Afghanistan, for example. If you rolled into a city and took over, the Taliban took to the hills. The same thing happened with the Mujahedeen during the Soviet occupation. They simply fled the cities and regrouped in the mountains where they could hide and prepare a resistance. Rural people also tend to be a little more loyal to their own, and are more apt to render aid to an insurgency than a downtown city dweller, since they are generally wary of outsiders. By showing force in the rural areas before they make a push to implement whatever it is they have up their sleeves, that natural fallback area will not be available. Applying pressure on the locals now may either deter them from joining a militia-type group or from providing support once they start to pop up or attempt to form."

"That makes sense," said Evan. "We had an encounter with a helicopter last night that you might be interested in, unless, of course, it was yours."

"We wish we were that well equipped, but no, that wasn't ours. We are in the process of negotiating an alliance with a few guard units that stayed loyal to their own states, but we aren't there yet. Where exactly did you see it?" Ted asked.

"When we were crossing the bridge on Highway 70, a few miles back. Once we got about halfway across, it appeared out of nowhere and hovered over us, spotlighting us for a few minutes, and then broke off and disappeared over a ridge."

"Did you get a type or see any markings?"

"No, it wasn't running any lights other than the spotlight it flashed on us. All we could tell was that it was substantial in size and turbine-powered. Aside from that, we were blinded by the spotlight and the sky was pretty dark, with the weather starting to turn."

As Ted began to reply, he heard the click of a safety selector from inside the trailer. He looked at Evan with a serious face as Evan quickly said, "No. No, guys, it's okay. Come on out."

The trailer door opened as Jason, Ed, and Nate exited the trailer with their rifles in hand. The militiamen tightened their grips on their guns due to the tension of the moment; both Evan and Ted diffused the situation. After everyone was at ease and introduced, they caught them all up on the discussion and Ted said, "Well, gentlemen, we will leave you be. I apologize for the intrusion. If you see anything, try to get as much intel on it as you can and pass it along to us as soon as you get a chance. We've got eyes everywhere to the east of here, so that shouldn't be hard to do."

Evan shook Ted's hand and said, "Will do, sir, and thanks for what you're doing."

With that, the militiamen disappeared into the woods as quickly as they arrived. They were clearly experienced operators from the way they moved and handled themselves. After standing there for a moment and processing everything they had just heard, Evan looked at the others and said, "Okay, I haven't slept all night. Who's got the next watch?"

"Next watch? Hell, we didn't set a watch last night," exclaimed Jason, realizing their lapse in procedure.

Ed shook his head and said, "We were all so exhausted and wet, I guess we subconsciously just wanted to get some rest and forget about it all."

"Maybe so," Jason added, "but if our early morning visitors weren't who they were, it could have quickly been game-over. We've got to get back on our game, especially after what they said."

"I've got watch then," volunteered Nate as he stepped forward. "I got plenty of sleep. Besides, I just sit on my butt in the trailer all day, anyway."

"Let's hope the day goes like that," Evan said as he walked over to the bushes to relieve himself. "And, Nate, thanks. I'll just take a power nap and then we'll get on the move again."

Jason looked around at the night's sky, which was beginning to clear and show the stars coming back into view, and said, "It sucks that we've gotta look up in the sky for threats now. That adds a whole new dimension to things."

They all just nodded in agreement as Evan walked over to the trailer and said, "Nite-nite, ladies."

As Evan slept and Nate stood watch, Jason and Ed decided to patrol the area properly since they had neglected that duty the previous night. They walked the length of the side road until reaching Highway 70 and then carefully scouted around the next few turns. Satisfied that they were not under any immediate threat, they returned to camp to prepare for the day.

Upon arrival at camp, Nate welcomed them back and said, "You know, I just realized something."

"What's that?" asked Jason.

"We sent our cook home."

Ed slapped his knee and said, "Damn. That's right. He was a damn fine camp cook, at that."

Jason and Nate looked at each other and simultaneously called, "Not it!" as if they were back in their elementary school days.

The three men busted out laughing as Ed said, "Okay, okay... I'll get to it. Just don't expect a gourmet meal."

"Luckily, I've got low standards. As long as it makes a turd, I'm happy," replied Jason as he leaned his rifle up against a tree. "Nate, I can take the watch from here," he added.

"Roger that," Nate replied as he began to help Ed gather some dry wood to start a fire.

Ed stopped what he was doing and said, "You know what, guys? Let's break out the multi-fuel camp stove. Starting a fire with damp wood will create a lot of smoke, as well as waste a lot of resources getting it going. Not to mention, now that there is the chance of being spotted from the air, maybe that wouldn't be the best idea."

Chapter 29: An Unbearable Loss

As Charlie and Jimmy waved goodbye to Sabrina and the Gibbs family, now safe and sound at the Del Rio Baptist Church, they anxiously began the last leg of their ride home. Charlie tried to convince Jimmy to stop and see Doc Stewart before heading home, with the Thomas farm being along the way, but Jimmy insisted on rushing home to his pregnant wife first. Not one to argue with a man over family matters, Charlie agreed to ride along with Jimmy until he made it home to his wife safely in his weakened condition. Charlie would then go his own separate way from there and would drop off each of the letters in his care once he was settled in.

The men rode as fast as Jimmy could comfortably go with only one good arm to steer. He still felt too much pain to put pressure on his left arm. Luckily, his ATV had an automatic clutch and linked brakes, making riding with one hand on the controls feasible. Charlie felt guilty for not stopping at the other homesteads as they passed them along the way, but Jimmy was a man on a mission.

As they approached the Lewis homestead, Jimmy's heart was nearly pounding out of his chest. His excitement to see his pregnant wife, Beth, could hardly be contained. He envisioned a young son or daughter running around outside, playing in the sun while he and Beth worked the land and tended to their animals. He finally had a glimmer of hope shining through the darkness of their harsh, new world.

As he and Charlie pulled up to Jimmy's home, they saw Daryl and Linda's horses tied up out front. *Oh, good,* he thought, *they have been stopping by to check up on her and to keep her company.* He pulled his ATV up to the house, shut it off, and dismounted. Charlie pulled up alongside and followed him to his house in order to give Daryl and Linda a debrief of their trip before proceeding to his own home.

As they stepped onto the front porch, the door opened, but instead of Beth running to his open arms, there stood Daryl and Linda with looks of great sadness on their faces. "Where's Beth?" he asked, trying to look around them both to see if she was inside the house.

"Now, Jimmy," Daryl said in a serious and solemn tone as he held up his hands to slow him down.

Jimmy stopped dead in his tracks and saw Linda's eyes welling up with tears. "What? Where is she?" he said, looking around. "Beth! Beth, where are you, baby?" he called out, hoping to hear her answer.

"Jimmy, something happened..." Daryl said, trying to break the news to his friend.

"Happened? What happened? Where is she? Beth, where are you?" he said in a panic, hoping that it was all just a bad dream and he would soon wake to a different homecoming. "Where are you, baby?" he yelled. He started pushing his way past Daryl as Linda stepped aside, covering the tears in her eyes with her hands.

Charlie watched it all happening as if in slow motion. He could see in Daryl's and Linda's eyes that something terrible had happened. This entire trip, his dear friend Jimmy only had thoughts of his lovely wife and the new baby they were bringing into this world, only to come home to some sort of tragedy. He reached out for Jimmy's shoulder as Jimmy pushed past Daryl and ran toward their bedroom, where Beth's body still remained, tightly wrapped to preserve her until she was buried.

Daryl desperately called out, "Jimmy! No! Wait!" trying to catch him before he saw the horror first-hand, but to no avail.

Jimmy shoved open their bedroom door to see his beautiful wife in her morbid state. Shockwaves of emotion rippled through his body. He screamed, "Noooo! Oh, God, please, no! She was pregnant, Oh, my God! She was pregnant! We were going to have a baby..." He dropped to his knees, taken over by a total emotional breakdown. He turned and looked at the others and mumbled through the tears, "We were having a baby... a baby."

Everyone in the room lost their composure. It was shocking news to Daryl and Linda that Beth was pregnant. Charlie broke down into tears for his dear friend as Daryl and Linda processed what Jimmy was saying.

"Oh, my God, Jimmy, we're so sorry," Linda said, struggling to speak through her own emotions.

Jimmy's emotional nightmare was now turning from sorrow to rage. He looked at Daryl and said, "What the hell happened? You were supposed to look after her! I trusted you!" He glared at Daryl with pure hatred.

Unable to speak for himself, Linda yelled, "It wasn't his fault. He tried to save her. He killed her attackers and Griff nearly died, too. He did everything he could!"

Jimmy just turned and looked at his beloved wife, rubbed his hand on her stomach one more time, and then looked back at Daryl with a cold-blooded stare and said, "May God damn your soul to hell." He drew his sidearm with the look of a madman.

Linda and Charlie both yelled, "Jimmy, no!" and reached out for his gun as he raised it to the side of his own head and pulled the trigger, sending blood and bits of brain matter and skull across the room. Droplets of blood splattered on Daryl's face and beard as if the whole thing happened in slow motion.

Daryl dropped to his knees, looked to the ceiling, and screamed out in agony at the horror of what had just transpired. Jimmy's body lay across that of his wife, blood soaking the once bright white bedding.

Linda ran to Daryl's side, afraid of what might happen next in his emotional state. Linda knew Daryl had not been well ever since Beth was killed. She knew he blamed himself for letting it happen and feared that the horror of the moment might send him over the edge.

Chapter 30: The New Reality

Evan awoke to the smell of hot coffee, fried venison, and potatoes. *Ahhhhh, that feels so much better,* he thought as he stretched and yawned. He wanted to lie there in the peace and quiet of the trailer for just a few more minutes, but his empty stomach demanded he investigate the delicious smells coming from outside. As he poked his head out of the trailer, the first thing he heard was Jason's voice saying, "Good morning, sunshine."

"Good morning," he replied, with another stretch and yawn as he stepped out of the trailer. "Did I miss anything exciting?"

"We solved world hunger, but other than that, nope."

Ed pointed at the stove and said, "Your food is getting cold."

"Ah, you broke out the Coleman. Good move," replied Evan as he walked over and took his plate and cup of coffee.

After he had eaten and the men shared some thoughts of home and the uncertain future, they loaded back up, fired up the tractor, and continued their journey toward Hot Springs. As they got rolling on Highway 70 once again, Jason said, "We should have brought some bikes to back up the ATVs. They would come in handy right now for scouting ahead. It would take way too long trying to scout everything out on foot first. We would never get anywhere like that."

"Yes, 'hindsight is 20/20,' as they say," Evan replied. "I think for now, the most important thing is to press on to Hot Springs and try not to get wrapped up in any more drama between here and there. We are the living definition of mission creep. We set out to do one thing, and then get involved in three others along the way. There have been a couple times I've forgotten this was supposed to even be a supply run."

"Yeah, well, getting involved is who we are. I would rather be us than the kind of people that would drive right on by that house on the hill, knowing Sabrina was being raped and tortured there."

"Me, too, brother. Me, too," Evan replied.

The stormy weather of the previous day had completely given way to a beautiful East Tennessee day and provided them a gorgeous view of the Blue Ridge Mountains. For the next few miles, things were relatively quiet. They stayed on their guard, but enjoyed the scenery of the new life the spring season always brings. Their only distractions were the occasional abandoned car on the side of the road. As they approached, they would slow down to take a cursory look, but from what they saw, most simply seemed to have been abandoned there, as if they ran out of fuel trying to cross the mountains.

Coming across a sign that read, *Welcome to North Carolina,* Jason said, "Well, this is the first time we've left the state of Tennessee since our escape from New York."

"Hopefully we won't be gone long. It feels weird already," Evan said as he drove past the sign and noticed it was riddled with bullet holes; once again, he began to feel uneasy about their journey.

Studying the map, Jason said, "Around the next bend to the right, we will be more out in the open, out of the densely wooded mountains, and in an area that might contain some farms. We could possibly find some barter stops along the way to Hot Springs. If there are working farms along the way, they may be sources of trade into the future as well," he added.

"Heck, if we find everything we need doing that, maybe we won't even have to go all the way there," Evan said as he looked up and saw a helicopter fly overhead from left to right. "Crap!" he said, startled by its low altitude.

As Evan drove the tractor, Jason tracked the helicopter visually as it seemed to arc back around toward them as if to get a better look. "What is it? Who is it?" asked Evan.

"Looks like an Mi-24. It's got grayish-white paint. Looks like... Yep, UN markings. It's coming back."

"Crap. Wait... did you say an Mi-24... as in a Russian Hind?"

Jason lowered his binoculars and said, "Yep, a Hind, and it's coming."

Evan looked in front of the tractor and saw a Humvee, also with UN markings, pull into the road in front of them, blocking their path. "Hang on!" he exclaimed, slamming on the brakes and bringing the tractor to a halt. Ed and Nate had been looking out of the trailer at the helicopter and were thrown forward with the sudden stop.

Several soldiers got out of the Humvee, armed with AK-74M Russian service rifles. The AK-74M is the modern Russian service rifle for its ground forces. It is an updated version of the famous AK-47/AKM platform, but chambered in the 5.45x39 Russian cartridge and has a synthetic stock and handguards, instead of the traditional wood of the previous models.

The helicopter landed in the clearing off to the right of the tractor and another Humvee pulled up behind the trailer, blocking them from backing away.

"If it wasn't for that damn helicopter, I'd drive right through this damn Humvee. We can't get away from or fight a Hind with a John Deere, though," Evan said in a defeated tone.

Jason looked around and said, "We don't have any options. We're gonna have to ride this out." He then clicked the mic on his handheld radio and said to Ed and Nate. "Just comply. Only fight if you must."

Evan begrudgingly shut the tractor off and placed both hands on the steering wheel in plain view as the soldiers approached. As they came up alongside the tractor, he noticed one of them carried an M4 carbine instead of an AK-74.

The soldier with the M4, who had no name tape or rank insignia on his uniform, gave the order, "Place your hands on your heads and climb down."

Evan replied, "But I can't climb down with my hands on my head; I need them."

"Would you rather stumble and fall with your hands on your head, or be shot for non-compliance?" asked the soldier in perfect English with an American accent.

"Damn it," Evan mumbled as he started down with his hands on his head.

"What was that?" the soldier demanded.

"I said 'damn it,' damn it!" Evan said in an angry tone. "Who the hell are you, anyway, and why the hell are you pointing guns at us? This is a public road. We have every right to use it as U.S. citizens."

"I'll determine what your rights are," the soldier replied. "Right now you are suspected domestic terrorists and insurgents. You will be treated as such, in accordance with the Insurrection Act, until cleared. Is that understood?"

Biting his tongue, Evan reluctantly muttered, "Yes."

Soldiers from the rear Humvee cleared the trailer and removed Ed and Nate at gunpoint, bringing them up alongside Evan and Jason after patting them down and disarming them. The soldiers then searched Evan and Jason, removing their knives and handguns as well.

Hearing several of the other soldiers talk with a heavy accent amongst themselves in the background, Evan asked, "You sound American, but who the hell are those guys, and why are you working together doing this?"

"We are here under the direction of the President of the United States, in accordance with his orders and at the direction of the United Nations, operating as peacekeepers to quell the violence and instability caused by right-wing extremist insurgents," he answered. "That's all you need to know for now. Your compliance is mandatory. Resistance will be treated as hostile intent. Do you understand?"

"Very much so... traitor," answered Evan with contempt.

The soldier then nodded, and out of the right side of Evan's view, came the butt of an AK-74—and then total darkness.

Chapter 31: Insurgents

Evan awoke to a pounding headache, a swollen lip, and pain around his eyes. He tried to move but found himself bound to a chair by both his hands and his feet. A bright light shined in his eyes as a voice with a heavy eastern European accent chuckled and said, "Good of you to join us, kind sir. We thought maybe we had been much too hard on you, but here you are. Now, I'm going to ask you again, where are you from?"

"I'm from Kentucky... Harlan County, Kentucky," Evan reluctantly answered as he spit blood onto the floor.

"So you are with an insurgent militia from Kentucky?" the voice inquired.

"No, that's where I'm originally from. I don't live there now."

"Stop playing games with me or you may not wake up next time. Where do you currently live? Who lives with you? How many of you are there? Who is your leader? What is the name of your organization?"

"You are seriously overestimating us," Evan replied. "It's just me and the other guys. We don't really have a home. We live in the back of that trailer and are on the move all the time."

"Where was your destination when apprehended?"

"Hot Springs, North Carolina," Evan replied, again spitting blood on the floor. The more he moved his mouth to speak, the more the bleeding seemed to intensify.

"What was your business there? What militia unit were you going to meet with there?"

"I told you. We aren't associated with a militia. We were on our way to Hot Springs for the swap meets. That's our deal. We scavenge and trade," Evan insisted, hoping if the others suffered the same interrogation that they, too, did not give away any information about their loved ones back home.

"If you are not associated with an insurgent militia, then where did you get the weapons?"

"What weapons?" Evan asked, confused and still uncertain of his surroundings.

The voice demanded, "I'm only going to say this one more time. Where did you get the weapons you were smuggling in the trailer that you were pulling?"

It was then that Evan remembered the guns recovered from Sabrina's captors. "Oh... those weapons. We got them from a gang of thugs that were kidnapping people and doing horrible things to them. We were gonna turn them back in as soon as we found a proper authority, and here you are. So I guess we can turn them back over to you now."

"Those weapons were stolen from a peacekeeping unit during a raid on a convoy. Peacekeepers were killed by the insurgents during the raid."

Evan shook his head and said, "The scumbags we took them from were nothing more than common criminals. They were not part of any insurgency or militia. They're dead now, anyway, so justice for your men has been served."

The lights in the room came on and Evan got his first look at his surroundings. He was in a damp room with brick walls. He assumed he was in a basement somewhere, but could not be sure. His interrogator spoke with another soldier quietly off to the side. They appeared to be speaking a language similar to Russian, but he could not be sure. Once the interrogator was finished talking, the other soldier nodded and left the room. He returned after a few moments with two other soldiers both armed with AK-74s.

The two armed soldiers stood in front of Evan while the third untied him from the chair. The interrogator looked at Evan and said, "We require your cooperation. This level of indignant behavior simply will not do."

The unarmed soldier took him by the arm and pulled him to his feet. Still shaky from his period of unconsciousness, Evan struggled to walk. One of the armed soldiers shoved the barrel of his gun into Evan's back, coaxing him to walk faster. As they left the room, Evan was led up a flight of stairs where he entered what appeared to be an old farmhouse. He was then led outside, where the sunlight caused his throbbing headache to intensify.

"Is the firing squad this way?" Evan said to the soldiers with a sarcastic tone.

The soldiers both laughed and one of them replied in a choppy accent, "That will come with time. Not now."

They led Evan out to a barn with a guard posted on all four corners. As they led him toward the barn, he noticed the ground all around was covered with broken glass and shards of sharp metal. It crunched underneath his feet as they escorted him to the door. Upon reaching the door, they ordered him to remove and surrender his boots. He handed them his boots as ordered, then they shoved him inside, causing him to fall to the dirt floor. He raised his head to see several other people being held captive in the barn. They looked as if they had been there for at least several days. Flies swarmed around piles of human waste on the ground, giving him an idea as to what kind of stay he could expect.

"It's about damn time you got here," said a familiar voice from a dark unlit corner of the barn.

"Jason... thank God. Where are Ed and Nate?"

"We were split up when they took us at the tractor. You and I were put in the front Humvee, and Ed and Nate in the one that pulled up behind us. I never saw where they went."

Evan leaned on the wall, rubbed his eye, and said, "Damn. The room just started spinning on me."

Jason chuckled and said, "Just be glad you're not in a coma after that hit you took. Looks like they weren't very kind to you after that, either," he said as he got a closer look at Evan's face. "Damn, man, what did they do to you?"

"Let's just say they don't have a sense of humor," Evan said as he sat on the dirt floor and leaned back against the old plank wall.

"What they lack in technology, they make up for with creativity, don't they?" Evan said, referring to the debris on the ground and their bare feet.

"Yeah, I guess you could say that," Jason replied. "So what happened?"

"I think I blacked out during the first round of fun. When I woke up, they were demanding to know what militia we were with," Evan explained quietly as Jason sat down next to him.

"Militia?"

"The guns we took from Sabrina's captors—they were stolen from a hijacked peacekeeper convoy. They assumed we had some sort of connection with that." Being unsure who could hear the conversation, or if any of their fellow captives were moles, he said, "I told them the truth. That we were just simple scavengers that ran across some scumbags that needed to be dealt with, and they had the guns, so we took them. I mean, hell, who wouldn't take a SAW and select-fire M4s, given the chance these days?"

Jason looked around the room to see if any of the other captives seemed overly interested in their conversation, and said, "I just hope Ed and Nate are okay."

"Nate's one tough SOB. He went through hell just to get to us. He can take anything they can dish out. Ed is a hell of a guy, too. Let's just pray for both of them. I wonder why you haven't gotten the special treatment."

Jason just chuckled and said, "You mean *yet*. When they do, I think I'll just tell them you're a top militia leader and you kidnaped me because I was too loyal to the president."

"You go right ahead and do that, brother. I'll haunt you after I'm dead," replied Evan with a crooked smile.

The men's joking subsided as the harsh reality of what was happening sank in. They knew the odds of making it out of this predicament and getting home to their families were not looking good. Even if they were released, they had been stripped of everything they had. No shoes. No weapons. No food. Nothing.

The sun was now setting and the last of the day's rays of light that shined through the gaps in the old barn's planks were beginning to fade. Evan and Jason found the least filthy part of the barn's dirt floor they could, and tried to get in position for as good of a night's sleep as possible. The ever-present stench of human waste and the crying from some of the other prisoners made the chance of sleep seem like a fleeting fantasy.

"I hope everything is okay back home," Jason said, breaking his and Evan's silence.

"I'm sure they're all fine. Charlie and Jimmy should both be there by now to help keep an eye on things," replied Evan as he tried to convince, not only Jason, but also himself, that everything was all right.

"How quickly things can change," added Jason.

"How so?"

"Back on the homesteads, we are the kings of our world," explained Jason. "We settle injustices, protect the weak, and support the strong. We raise our own meat and grow our own crops. We are as free as they come. With the exception of being vigilant for threats, of course. That's the one thing we don't have a say about. Now here we are, lying on a dirty barn floor, swatting flies—barefoot, no less."

"Thanks for cheering me up, brother," Evan said sarcastically.

"That's what I'm here for," Jason replied.

~~~~

Sounds of spine-chilling screams echoed from across the farm, waking him in the middle of the night. Reaching for his watch to see what time it was, Evan realized they must had taken it while he was unconscious. "Bastards!" he mumbled aloud. His head still throbbed with pain from the beating he took; still, he tried to listen as best he could to the sounds of agony crying out in the darkness. *Is that Ed? Is it Nate? Dear God, please don't let it be.* He felt guilty for wishing it were someone other than his friends receiving what he assumed must be torture, as no man should have to face that hell.

"What the hell, man?" Jason whispered in the darkness.

"I know," Evan replied.

From across the room, one of the other men being held in confinement with them said, "I think he's one of ours."

"One of whose?" asked Evan, surprised by the statement from a man who had been silent until now.

"A man from our unit," he said as he crawled closer to them.

"Unit?" queried Jason.

"Yep, our militia unit," the man said, reaching Evan and Jason's side of the room. "I didn't want to say anything earlier because I didn't know who you were. You could have been moles or something for all I knew. I've been listening to you guys all day to try and figure you out. I don't know who you are, but I know you're not with them and that's all that matters to me at this point." The man then reached his hand out and said, "Quentin Elliot; nice to meet you."

Returning his handshake, Jason said, "Jason Jones."

Evan also returned the handshake, saying, "Evan Baird. Nice to meet you, too."

"So when is the cavalry coming?" asked Jason.

"I wish I could say they were, but I doubt they would have a clue where we are," Quentin said. "We've got to start thinking about our own way out of this mess. I'd rather be shot in the back trying to save my own ass than to die slowly rotting away in here, or be executed once they think they no longer need us."

"So who were you with again?" asked Evan.

"The Blue Ridge Militia. We were lying low as observers collecting data on their movements and tactics. Someone must have tipped them off to us."

"Damn, that sucks. Talk about a betrayal," Jason said in disgust.

"Yeah, probably someone who thought they could win their favor and be left alone, I guess. There were three of us. One of my men was killed when they ambushed us. The other... well, I'm afraid that may be who you're hearing right now," Quentin said in a somber voice. "They'll come for me next. Maybe I'll be tomorrow night. Who knows? Either way, I plan on getting the ball rolling before they get a chance. If you guys are in, we can work as a team and have a much better chance."

"So what do you know about this place? Where are the other captives? Why are they holding us here? If they are truly UN peacekeepers, what is the point of the harsh treatment?" Evan asked.

"Let's start with their motives for doing this," Quentin explained. "They aren't here to keep the peace. That's nothing but a ruse. They are here either to stake their claim or to ensure their influence during the reconstruction. These guys, in particular, are Russian, but there are a lot of countries that have not been all that fond of us in the past who are on our soil now as so-called peacekeepers. The UN always was a dirty organization hell-bent on equalizing the world. Well, they've got the ball rolling in their direction now. As to the *why*, if they squash any motivation or willingness for an insurgency now, they'll have a much easier go of it in the long run. They know we're a heavily armed population capable of putting up one hell of a fight, so they want to squash the fight before it starts by rounding up the possible instigators. As to why we are here, it seems to be for intel gathering purposes. Maybe they are hoping someone will crack and give up the location of militia units. From the pattern I've seen, they rough up one or two of a group, leaving the other alone. Then the interrogations get rougher and rougher, putting pressure not only on the one being questioned, but their counterpart who starts to realize he is next. The one being roughed up eventually cracks or is killed, then the one that has been witnessing the whole thing is brought into the picture, knowing he is about to suffer the same fate."

"Well, that explains why they haven't touched you, Jason," Evan interrupted.

"Yes, it would," Quentin continued. "There is another holding point somewhere on the other side of the farm, but I'm not sure where. By splitting groups up, they can work the same angle simultaneously, putting the same psychological pressure on more than one person at a time. It also makes us, or our friends on the other side, assume the worst, which also steps up the stress level."

"So, what's your plan?" asked Evan.

"Our immediate barriers are the four guards they keep posted on the barn twenty-four seven, and the glass shards they have all round this place. With our bare feet, even if we struggled through the pain of just running straight through it, we wouldn't make it far on mangled feet, and if we did, we would be leaving a blood trail." He paused before continuing. "This barn is made of some pretty long wood planks."

"Yeah, this thing is from back in the day when farmers ripped their own boards from the trees they cleared to make the pasture," added Evan.

"So if we can work one of these things loose ahead of time, we can lay it out on the glass and run on the plank to the clear," Quentin said.

Jason spoke up and said, "So when do you picture this happening? When could we get past the guards?"

"Our only opportunity to get our hands on one of the guards is when they pick up or drop off a prisoner. They slide that rancid food they bring us once a day under the door, so that doesn't provide much of an opportunity."

Evan said, "But when they bring someone in and out, their attention is focused at that moment. Short of fighting them all off, barefoot and unarmed, how do you propose that would work?"

"Oh, that's not what I propose; I just said that's the only time we could get our hands on one of them, which means it probably wouldn't work. This farm hasn't been put back on the grid, just like most rural areas, so the only electricity they have is from a generator somewhere near the house. They don't have searchlights or anything of that nature, so it gets pretty dark out here by the barn at night. If we could get some sort of diversion, and already had a plank worked loose that we could use as an egress point and a walkway to get over the glass and metal shards, we could slip out and make for the tree line."

"Diversion? What sort of diversion, and how do we do that from here, without drawing attention to the barn?"

"That's the part I haven't worked out yet. For now, let's get to work on our egress point, and when the answer presents itself, we'll be ready."

Chapter 32: A Tragedy Fulfilled

Charlie stood there in shock as the tragedy unfolded before him. His good friend, Jimmy Lewis, with whom he had been through so much, and whose bonds of friendship were strengthened by the journey from which they had just returned, now lay dead by his own hand. He watched as Daryl dropped to his knees, screaming and crying, and Linda just stood beside him, as if frozen in time. Unable to control his own emotions, Charlie ran out of the house and stepped off the front porch, where he vomited and dropped to his knees. *What about my family?* he thought. *Are they okay? Did my wife face such a fate while I was away?*

Unable to control his fears as they raced wildly around in his mind, he ran to his ATV, fired it up, and sped away toward his own home. Nearly running off the road several times, he rode like a madman. Hitting a large pothole in the now unmaintained road, he nearly lost control, having the handlebars almost yanked from his hands. Regaining his focus, he stowed his emotions and continued racing toward his home.

As he approached his homestead, he saw Luke untying his horse from the front porch railing. Fearing Luke might be at his home for the same reason Daryl and Linda were at Jimmy's, he slid the ATV to a stop, not even shutting off the engine, and yelled frantically, "Where is she? Where is Rebecca? Is she okay?"

Luke, realizing that Charlie must have been to the Lewis home, said in a calming voice, "She's fine, Charlie. She's just fine."

Rebecca ran out of the house to Charlie, who dropped to his knees in relief and began to sob. "Oh, thank you, Lord. Thank you," he said as he stood up to greet her, picking her up off the ground and joining her in an emotional embrace. "I thought I might have lost you. I couldn't go on without you. Please, don't ever leave me," he said, still in tears.

"Oh, my dear," Rebecca said softly. "You must have heard about poor Beth. I'm okay. Everyone else is okay."

"No. No, everyone else is not okay," he struggled to say through the tears.

This got Luke's attention, as he still hadn't been able to get an update about his brother, Nate, who had been on the run with Charlie.

"Is my brother okay? Are Nate, Jimmy, Evan, and Jason okay? Where are they?" Luke asked.

"They are all fine. Well, everyone except Jimmy was fine the last I saw them," said Charlie as he began to gather himself. "Jimmy was hurt, so I accompanied him to his house where we found Daryl and Linda looking after Beth's remains."

"I know, dear; it's horrible what happened to her. Daryl caught and killed them all, but he's been a mess ever since."

"That's not all," he said. "Beth was pregnant."

"Oh, my God," Rebecca said, putting her hands over her mouth in shock.

"It's all Jimmy could talk about while we were gone. He wanted to get back to her so badly, only to find her and their baby dead on his bed. He lost it. He completely lost his mind. He pulled out his pistol and took his own life. He's dead. The three of them are dead now, Beth, Jimmy, and their baby."

He then looked at Luke and said, "Luke, please go check on Daryl and Linda and give them a hand. It all just happened. They were falling apart when I left. Daryl especially didn't look so good."

"Yes, sir," Luke said, untying his horse, mounting it, and riding away without hesitation.

Charlie looked Rebecca in the eyes as he held her cheeks in his hands and said, "I will never leave your side again."

Chapter 33: Reprisals

The new day's sun shone through the gaps in the old barn once again, illuminating the horrid conditions in which the prisoners existed. "How you feeling today, old man?" Jason asked Evan, who continued to recover from his beating.

"A little better," he said. "My headache is finally gone. My entire face and my ribs still hurt, though."

Jason turned to Quentin and said, "Get much done in the dark?"

"A little," he answered quietly. "It's the plank with the mud smeared on the bottom. It's getting loose. It was hard trying not to make a sound, though."

Peeking through a gap in the wood, Evan said to the others, "Check this out."

"What's up?" asked Jason.

"Looks like our welcoming committee is bringing in a newbie. He looks pretty roughed up, too."

"Lemme see," said Quentin, pushing his way to the gap. "Holy crap! That's Wilkins," he said as he saw his fellow militiaman escorted across the field by two of the soldiers with the muzzle of a rifle in his back, prodding him along. He looked as if he had been worked over pretty thoroughly. Even from a distance, one could see the blood, bruises, torn clothing, and the pronounced limp in his step. He seemed to struggle just to stay on his feet as they moved him toward the barn. "Those filthy UN thugs beat him up pretty bad. Well, at least he's still alive."

Just then, a muffled thump, followed by an explosion, rocked the barn. "What the hell?" said Evan.

"Mortar," replied Quentin. "One of ours, no doubt."

The soldiers escorting Wilkins across the field to the barn dove for cover, assuming they were under attack. Wilkins took advantage of the confusion and tried to make a break for the tree line, struggling through the pain of his injuries, running as fast as he could. One of the soldiers shouldered his rifle in the prone position and fired three shots, dropping Wilkins to the ground.

"Those damn commies shot him in the back! Damn it to hell!" Quentin yelled as he punched the side of the barn.

"What's going on?" one of the other captives across the room asked.

"Not sure yet," Jason responded.

Several well-placed shots rang out from the tree line, killing the soldier who had shot Wilkins. The other escort then made a break for the farmhouse, making it merely a few steps before dropping to the ground, dead from another long-range shot. Machine-gun fire erupted from the farmhouse, aimed at suppressing fire on the tree line.

During the chaos, Evan, Jason, and Quentin observed the reactions of the guards around the barn and at the main house. Two of the guards took up prone firing positions in front of the barn, facing the tree line. They were unable to take cover up close, as the glass and metal shards placed as a deterrent for escape were now a hazard to them in any position except standing. The other two guards took up positions on the rear two corners of the barn, covering the area opposite the direction of gunfire.

After a few moments of suppressing fire, the machine guns went silent as they watched and observed. "That was a probe," Quentin said. "They wanted to poke the snake to see how it would strike. They plan to make a move. I'm sure of it. They are probably even more motivated now after what happened to Wilkins right in front of them. Look, when it all starts to hit the fan around here, and it will, we've gotta make our move. They have made it clear to the rest of us that they are coming, and they will expect us to be ready when the time comes."

Just then, a UN-marked helicopter flew overhead toward the tree line. After making a few wide orbits over the trees, it began firing its four-barreled 12.7mm machine gun into the woods. "Damn, I hope they are just using the spray-and-pray method. If our guys are under that gun, they are as good as dead," Quentin said.

After ceasing fire, the helicopter circled overhead for a few more moments before disappearing over the tree line to the south from where it came. "We won't make it far barefoot with that damn thing on our heels. When your boys come, I sure hope they can deal with that thing," Evan said in an uneasy tone

"Yeah, well... now they know. As for us, though, we just need to be ready to get the hell out of here when the time comes," Quentin replied.

"Agreed, but what about how the guards stayed put at the barn? There wasn't an unguarded side for us to make a break for it. They held pretty firm," explained Evan as he posed the question to Quentin.

"If they were able to get out of here to get the info back to the others, they would have noticed that the soldiers on the barn didn't break rank. That would tell them something of interest is in here. Hopefully, they will assume it's us and use caution not to level this thing. I think, at a minimum, though, it will make them focus on our guards. Our basic rescue strategy with our resources is just that. Hit the enemy and hold them under fire to allow our folks to escape. If an extraction team is required, they'll try, but with our limited manpower, equipment, and level of intelligence, in most cases we would be limited on what we could do."

Evan and Jason just nodded as they observed what was going on outside the barn. After what seemed like a quiet period of observation, a team of four was sent from the main farmhouse to recover the two dead soldiers. The team immediately took the bodies back inside. Another team was dispatched to the barn with an American-led patrol of four Russians guards. The team burst into the barn with the American leading the way, screaming, "What do you not understand? Do you think this is a game? Do you think taking a few shots at us and trying to run away will have any effect on us and make us turn away? You have a global power against your pissy, little right-wing militia movement. Take that one and that one," he said, pointing to two men cowering in the corner. Let this be a warning to your friends; if this happens again, we will kill you all and eliminate our liabilities completely."

The four Russian soldiers forced the two men out of the barn at gunpoint, marched them outside, and directed them toward a large mature chestnut tree. They then stood at a distance of about twenty yards and opened fire, riddling the bodies with bullets, continuing to shoot until their magazines were empty, even though their victims were dead and lying on the ground.

"God damn it!" Quentin yelled. "Those two were just random civilians. They had no ties at all to anything."

"Hey, keep it quiet," Jason said. "That's just the sort of thing one of the guards would hear you say, an admission of your own involvement. It sucks, yeah, but for now, you just need to eat those emotions and let the rage build inside until you can do what you need to do. For now, though, survival is your mission, and keeping your mouth shut is the only weapon you have."

"Yeah, I know," Quentin said as he stomped the floor in anger.

"You're militia?" one of the two other remaining captives said aloud. "Oh, my God, it's you they want; not me."

Quentin ran across the room, grabbing the man by the throat, squeezing on his windpipe, and said, "You shut your mouth. You say another damn word and I'll kill you with my bare hands. Without militia groups and autonomous guard units controlled by the states, free from federal control, there would be no America already. The rest of the damn world wants to carve us up and take their own piece of the American pie. Do you want your kids or grandkids growing up speaking Russian, Chinese, or some other language that the commie country that takes your piece of the pie dictates? Stand on your feet like a man and resist. Resist for the future. Resist for your children. These oppressive scumbags are not here for peacekeeping. You've seen that first-hand. They are here for control. If you are gonna go down the path of siding with them, I'll kill you myself for treason."

He then relaxed his grip on the man's neck and slowly let him go, staring him in the eye, making it clear the choice he had to make. The man just nodded and sat down in the corner. Turning to Evan and Jason, Quentin asked, "What's going on out there now?"

"They brought a tractor out from behind the house, looks like... Yep, they're throwing a rope over a tree branch and tying it to the bodies. Those sons of..."

"What?"

"They pulled the tractor forward and lifted them up into the tree, hanging upside down by their feet."

Quentin looked back at the man in the corner and said, "That could have been you. For no damn reason other than to control the rest of us, that could have been you. You think about that the next time you consider, even for a second, helping those scumbags."

The American who led the group that killed the men looked back at the barn for a moment, knowing his fellow Americans were watching him... knowing they considered him a traitor of the highest level. He then turned and walked back to the farmhouse with the murderers, pausing to take one more glance over his shoulder, riddled with guilt.

"That bastard is going down if it's the death of me," Quentin mumbled aloud.

Chapter 34: A Helping Heart

As Luke arrived at the Lewis home, he saw Linda sitting out front on the porch with her elbows on her knees and her face in her hands. She looked up as he drew close, exposing her distraught face. Luke dismounted, tied his horse to the porch railing, and asked, "How is Daryl?"

"He's just sitting in the bedroom like a zombie. I can't get him to leave and can't get him to talk. I'm afraid to leave him here. I don't know what he would do. I took his pistol. It's lying right over there," she said as she pointed to his model 1875 Remington that had become a part of Daryl's persona. "I unloaded it. I have his bullets in my pocket. After what Jimmy did... I'm just afraid."

Luke sat down next to her and put his arm around her. "How are you doing? Charlie told me everything that happened. That had to be hard to witness."

"I'll survive," she said. "I'll go to my grave with the image of what Jimmy did in my head, but I'll survive. It's Daryl I'm worried about. He used to be this large, burly man with a bulletproof outlook, but now—it's like he snapped. He's just a shell of who he used to be. He seems empty inside."

"I'll go and check on him," Luke said as he stood up and limped to the door.

"Thanks," she replied softly, putting her face back into her hands as she began to cry.

Luke walked into the room slowly, making sure Daryl recognized him. He glanced at the macabre scene on the bed and looked away quickly. "How are you doing, Daryl?" he asked. Daryl just sat there silently staring at the bed. "I wish I could say everything will be all right, but nothing is all right anymore. We have our ups and our downs, and our downs are pretty damn low. But the one thing that has kept all of us going and alive is that we don't ever intentionally let each other down. This community's strength lies solely in that. We will never be able to stop bad things from happening, but when they happen, we all need to continue to band together all the more tightly to pull everyone through it. This community not only needs you, it loves you. Everyone here looks up to you, and no one thinks any of this was your fault. You're the glue that binds us together. We just want you to know that."

"Thank you," Daryl said, breaking his silence.

"Why don't you come back to Mildred's farm with me," Luke said as he walked over to Daryl. "We can trade places for a few days. I'll deal with this and make the rounds. You can help out on the farm. Mildred really needs a strong man around there this time of year, and with the others gone, you'd be a big help. I'll make rounds through your place every day to care for your animals, too."

"I need that. Thanks," replied Daryl. "How are the others? Did Charlie say anything about Ed, Jason, and Nate?"

"He said they are fine. He's got more stuff to tell us later, but nothing that needs our attention right now, with this going on. You'll be able to get a radio update from him at the Thomas farm."

"Where's Linda?"

"She's out front. She's really worried about you. After seeing what happened with Jimmy, she is afraid of what might happen next," Luke explained.

Daryl stood up and closed his eyes for a moment as if he was saying a silent prayer, and then said, "I had better go talk to her."

"She really does need that," Luke replied.

Daryl walked out of the house, stepped onto the porch, and sat down next to Linda. She turned to look, thinking it was Luke. Realizing it was Daryl, she gave him a big hug, and the two just held each other for a while. "I'm sorry," Daryl said.

"For what?"

"For how I've been acting," he said. "I think I had done a pretty good job of not letting anything in this jacked-up world get to me all of this time. I put things away, and played it like it was a big game. When that happened to Beth, the reality and the suppressed feelings hit me like a ton of bricks." He kept his arm around Linda while she gathered her composure and said, "Thank you for taking my gun. I honestly don't know what I would have done in the moment, given any easy options. The horror and heartbreak of it all..."

"I know," she said. "I know. Jimmy had his reasons; only God knows the hell that was going through his mind in that moment, but those of us that are still here need to stick it out for each other. Maybe someday this screwed up world will straighten itself out. I mean, I'm sure it will. If you look at history, upheaval and strife are the norms. Peace and stability are the exceptions. We're just in one of those times—but to us and everyone in recent history, it seems apocalyptic. We'll get through it, though, if we stick together."

She patted him on the leg and said, "Can you escort me home? I need to get away for a bit. I don't want to walk back into this house right now."

"Yes, ma'am, absolutely," he said, standing and helping her to her feet.

Luke joined them on the porch and said, "I'm gonna try and get in touch with a few of the others. Robert Brooks, Lloyd Smith, to name a few. We will get this taken care of. You two have seen and done enough. So, Daryl, do you want to come stay at the farm for a while?" he asked.

Daryl looked at Linda, then turned and said, "You know, I think I'll be just fine. I've gotta catch up on a few things around my place anyway, and I would prefer to be able to check in on Linda from time to time. I'll be okay."

Chapter 35: Farmageddon

As the day drew on, it was quiet in the barn. They watched through the gaps in the wood as the occupying soldiers searched the surrounding woods for signs of the attacking militiamen, to no avail. There were no more interactions between the prisoners and the soldiers, either, which was a welcomed silence. As the evening approached, the sun began slipping off behind the trees, yet again. "Damn, I'm hungry," Jason said as his stomach pains began to grow increasingly noticeable, and he began feeling shaky.

"I wouldn't eat their food right now, anyway," Quentin replied. "They'd have probably pissed in it after today."

"Let's just hope we won't need to worry about them being the hand that feeds us for much longer," replied Evan.

Quentin walked over to the other two men on the far side of the barn, reached out his hand, and said, "Let's start over. If we stand a chance of dying alongside one another, I think it's only appropriate that we know each other's names. I'm Quentin."

The man Quentin had the altercation with earlier reluctantly reached out his hand, and said, "My name is Dustin, and I'm sorry about before."

"Don't sweat it. This isn't a place where every man is at his best. Just do what's right from this point forward, no matter what the circumstances, and you'll never have to apologize again. I'm glad to meet you and I'm sorry about before, too."

The other man then shook Quentin's hand, as well, and said, "My name is Kyle, sir."

"Nice to meet you, Kyle," Quentin said, returning the handshake.

Before Evan and Jason got a chance to make their introductions to the men, Jason looked around the room and said, "Guys, I hate to say this, but I think I'm gonna have to do the deed."

"You've gotta crap?" Evan asked.

"Yep, I've been hoping to avoid this, but... that only works for so long. I'm up against a wall here."

"Speaking of up against a wall, go find a spot on the far wall... way over there," Evan replied with a familiar sarcastic attitude, while pointing to the far side of the barn.

"At least they didn't beat your so-called sense of humor out of you," Jason said in rebuttal. "At least it's getting dark. It won't be as easy for you guys to stare that way."

As Jason began doing the walk of shame to the other side of the barn, the crack of a distant gunshot carried through the air, followed by another about ten seconds later. The soldiers all took positions of cover as best they could while trying to ascertain the origin of the shots. A third shot then rang out, cutting the rope being used to suspend the bodies of the two murdered civilians, dropping them to the ground. A few seconds later, an RPG round came streaking out of the woods directly at the farmhouse. The RPG entered a downstairs window and exploded inside.

Using the RPG's flight path as a tracer, the remaining machine guns inside the house opened fire on the woods, firing blindly in an attempt to hit or suppress their attackers.

Incoming small arms fire then began to focus on the barn from the right flank. "Hit the ground!" yelled Quentin as he and the others tried to avoid the friendly fire. They kept their heads down with their faces in the dirt as wood debris filled the air around them. Militiamen in the woods at the right flank of the barn were assaulting the soldiers guarding the barn in order to clear a path for the captives to escape.

Once the barrage of bullets hitting the barn subsided, Quentin crawled over to the front wall, peeking outside, and said, "Two down on this side."

Jason then crawled to the back wall of the barn, getting a look at that side, and said, "One barely moving, but hit pretty bad. The other is down hard."

"Let's make our move!" shouted Quentin over the intense sounds of gunfire all around them. "We can't go out the front. Let's go through the back wall," he said as he ran across the barn to the plank he had been loosening. He easily yanked on the board, freeing the few remaining nails holding it in place. They then used the opening to get a better hold on several of the surrounding planks and began ripping them loose, breaking them in half to increase the size of the hole.

Once there was a large enough opening, Quentin pulled the plank into the barn, laid it down flat, and fed it out onto the ground, over the glass, and toward the body of the nearest guard. He then scurried quickly out onto the plank, using it as a walkway to avoid the glass and metal shards with his bare feet, grabbed the guard by his load-bearing vest, and dragged him back into the barn.

Quentin removed the AK-74 that the man wore slung around his neck, while Evan stripped him of his load-bearing vest, containing his spare ammunition.

"Who wears a size nine?" Jason called out while removing the man's boots. "Too small for me."

"Nope," said Evan.

"Negative," replied Quentin.

Dustin, who was cowering in the far corner, said, "I can wear a nine."

Jason tossed the boots to Dustin and said, "Put these on; I've got a job for you."

As the man frantically donned the boots, Jason said, "Now, Quentin there is gonna cover you with the AK. You slip out the hole and drag the other body in here so we can strip him, too, before we make a run for the trees. You got it?"

"Yeah, yeah," Dustin replied nervously.

As Quentin got into position to cover Dustin through a gap in the wood, Jason said, "Okay, go!"

Dustin slipped through the hole in the barn, started to go in the direction of the body, then turned and ran straight for the tree line.

"Damn that coward!" screamed Jason as Dustin abandoned them, wearing the only pair of boots.

"If he was a soldier, I would shoot his pansy ass in the back," grunted Quentin.

Jason and Evan then quickly pulled the plank back inside and repositioned it to try and get close to the other soldier, but could not get to the steep angle needed from the opening to create a clear path all the way to him. Evan pulled the plank back inside, stood in the middle, and said, "Pick that end up to snap it in half."

Kyle and Jason both pried up on the board, using Evan to hold down the center until it snapped in two. Evan took both pieces of wood to the hole in the wall and said, "Cover me!" to Quentin, who kept watch out the front of the barn. Evan hurried out onto the plank, getting as close as he could to the soldier, carrying the second piece with him. He then tossed the second piece on the ground about two feet away, making the pathway long enough to reach the downed soldier.

Leaning as far as he could to reach the downed soldier's belt, he lost his balance and stumbled, falling off the board, stepping onto the broken shards of glass and metal, cutting his feet in multiple places. "Damn it to hell!" he yelled, grabbing the man and dragging him back toward the barn, leaving a bloody trail of footprints on the plank behind him.

Before he could reach the safety of the barn, a barrage of small arms fire focused on him from one of the side windows in the farmhouse. Evan dove to the ground, landing mostly on the plank, and pulled the corpse of the dead soldier up to himself just as he felt the sickening *thump, thump, thump* sound, as bullets impacted the dead man's chest.

Another RPG round streaked from the trees from behind Evan and smashed into the side of the house from where the gunfire came, ending the assault on Evan's position. Jason and Kyle took advantage of the lull in the fire from the RPG hit to reach out onto the plank and drag Evan back inside, still hanging on to the dead soldier's body.

Once inside, Jason screamed, "Evan, are you hit? Are you okay?"

"I'm fine. I'm fine," he insisted. "I got cut up a little bit, but I'll live."

"Damn, man, your feet are cut up pretty bad," Jason added, looking at Evan's wounds.

Quentin joined up with Jason, Kyle, and Evan in the rear corner of the barn to strip the soldier of his weapon, vest, and boots. "Boots are eleven," Quentin said. "Evan, what size do you wear?"

"Ten and a half to eleven, but you take them. Those are your boys out there saving our asses."

"No way, man; your feet are sliced up. We can't carry you out of here so put the damn things on!" Quentin insisted. He then turned to the others and said, "Okay, we've got two rifles and ammo for each. It's too dangerous to try and get outside in front of the barn in clear view of a majority of the enemies' positions, so we are just gonna have to make do with what we've got and leave the other two rifles behind. As Evan stood up, Quentin said, "Are your feet good to go with the boots on?"

"Oh, yeah, marathon ready," Evan replied.

"Good. Jason and I will cover you while you piggyback Kyle to the edge of the glass. He can sprint for the woods from there."

"Roger that," Evan said as Kyle jumped up on his back. Evan squeezed out of the now enlarged hole in the side of the barn, carried Kyle past the debris, and said, "Run, man, run!"

Kyle took off running for the tree line and never looked back.

Quentin and Jason provided cover with the rifles while Evan made his way back into the barn. "Who's next?" he asked. "Go, Jason, and give Evan the rifle when he puts you down."

Evan and Jason made it to the edge of the clear grass, handed off the weapon, and Evan returned to the barn, covering Jason's escape as he went. Once back at the barn, Evan joined up with Quentin and said, "How's it looking?" as he looked through a gap in the planks toward the front of the house.

"It looks like a majority of the gunfire is still between the front of the house and the front tree line off in the distance. Those bastards better start bailing out of that house soon though. That thing is on fire and that old wood is torching up fast. As much as I want to watch them burn or be gunned down while trying to escape, we need to get the hell out of here."

Evan and Quentin ran back over to the rear corner of the barn where their escape hole was located. Quentin jumped on Evan's back, and Evan ran like hell for the edge of the debris field. Once in the clear grass, Quentin jumped off and the two started a run for the trees, each taking turns pausing to return fire to cover the other man.

Upon reaching the trees, several militiamen waved them in their direction. Evan and Quentin joined up with them to find Jason and Kyle already hunkered down with them, when one of the men said, "Q, thank God, man! We know about Wilkins, but where are Thomas and Scott?"

"Dead," Quentin replied.

"Damn it," the militiaman said in disgust. "Well, let's get the hell out of here. Blue Team has the Hind tied up with a diversion, but I'm sure it's figuring out the ruse by now."

"I was wondering what was taking that bastard so long to get here to wipe us out."

Chapter 36: The Pursuit

As they turned to fall back into the woods following their rescue, Quentin yelled, "The Commie Cavalry is here! Move! Move! Move!"

The others turned to see three UN-marked MRAPs barreling across the field toward their position. The CROWS (Common Remotely Operated Weapons System), an M240 machine gun operated from the safety of the interior of the MRAP's armored hull, was blasting away at their position from all three vehicles. Two of the militiamen instantly went down while trying to return fire.

"Scatter!" one of the others yelled as every man ran for his life in a different direction. The small arms carried by the militiamen, Evan, and Quentin were no match for the armor of the MRAPs. Before turning to run, Jason picked up one of the downed militiamen's M4 carbines and ran off into the woods with the others.

Unable to pursue them into the densely spaced trees with their large vehicles, the soldiers continued the pursuit on foot, following closely behind. Running barefoot through the woods, Jason tried to avoid rocky and jagged surfaces, as a foot injury could be devastating given the situation, yet he could only be so careful while running at full speed.

Running through the pain of the lacerations on his feet, thanks to the protection of the boots, Evan looked back to see Jason lagging behind. He stopped and turned around, yelling out to Jason, "Go, I'll hold them off for a sec while you make some ground." He then took up a position behind a downed tree and began to fire on the pursuers, killing one and slowing the others as they changed course to take cover. Slowing their momentum, he turned and started running as the bark from a tree only inches from his head exploded from the impact of the high-speed 5.45x39 rounds, causing him to alter his course through the woods.

As he ran at a full sprint, he could feel blood pooling in the bottom of his boots as the lacerations continued to be pounded by each impact, worsening the injuries. *No time for pain, Evan. No time for pain,* he thought to himself as he ran, sloshing the blood in his boots.

Up ahead, Quentin saw Evan and fell back saying, "My turn! Go!"

Evan just nodded and continued the chase of those up ahead. He heard Quentin firing on their pursuers and immediately stopped, and turned around, popping off a few shots as well, giving Quentin a chance to break off and move ahead. As Quentin reached Evan's position, he said, nearly out of breath, "Too many. Just run. Can't keep stopping to engage."

Evan popped off a few more shots, nodded in agreement, and then joined him, running off into the trees, no longer having Jason in sight.

~~~~

Out of breath and not knowing were to run, Kyle slid underneath a downed tree that lay in a thick patch of heavy brush. He was nearly hyperventilating, trying to calm himself so that he could lie low while his pursuers hopefully passed him by. He heard rustling through the woods coming his way, and tried to silence his heavy breathing. He could feel an itch in his throat, urging him to cough as they approached.

Oh, God, no. Please, not now, trying his best to hold it in until they were out of earshot. He could see the legs of two of the soldiers approaching him. They came to a stop about ten yards away, realizing they had lost his trail. As they scanned the area, his struggle to contain his cough was futile. As the sound of his muffled cough gave away his position, the soldiers quickly turned toward him, aiming their rifles in his general direction. Afraid they were about to shoot, he cried aloud, "Don't shoot! Don't shoot! I give up."

One of the soldiers commanded, "Show yourself."

As Kyle began to climb from underneath the tree, he heard several rapid-fire shots, followed by the soldiers dropping to the ground, dead. He then heard Jason whisper, "Come on. Come on out. Let's get the hell out of here."

"Where did they all go?" asked Kyle, sheepishly.

"I don't know, just get your ass out here before they come," Jason said as he laid down the M4 and traded it for one of the soldier's AK-74s. Having not been able to take the time to pick up extra magazines in his hasty departure earlier, only three rounds remained in his only magazine. He was able to scavenge five magazines of 5.45x39 from the downed pursuers, as well as two rifles. Tossing one to Kyle as he emerged from his hiding place, Jason asked, "Are you familiar with an AK?"

"Yes," responded Kyle, "my cousin had a Romanian WASR. I've shot it a few times."

"Great—same thing, just a smaller bullet," Jason said, tossing him an extra magazine. "Now let's get moving."

As Jason and Kyle moved slowly through the woods, the first thing they noticed was the silence. There was no more gunfire anywhere, not even back at the farmhouse. "Either someone has been defeated or the Blue Ridge Militia has pulled back after achieving their objectives. They may still be on us, though, so we need to find the others and regroup."

"Let's just get the hell out of here," said Kyle. "This is our chance."

"Our chance to what?" Jason replied. "Abandon the people who just rescued us? Not a chance; we are making sure everyone that can make it out of here does make it out of here. Got it?"

"Yeah, sorry. I'm just not used to this sort of thing," Kyle replied.

"How the hell did you survive this long?" asked Jason, frustrated by Kyle's lack of fortitude.

"With a lot of help from my brothers," he said.

"And where are they?"

"Dead. They killed them. They tried to resist, but I didn't."

"Sorry," Jason said. "Now let's get going."

As the two men silently crept through the woods, pausing every few steps to listen and observe, Jason heard a turkey up ahead. He gave Kyle the halt signal and just listened. "You hear that?" Jason whispered.

Kyle nodded yes in reply.

"That's a turkey. A six-foot tall turkey, to be exact."

Kyle gave Jason a confused look and shrugged his shoulders to show that he didn't understand.

"Evan and I hunt together. I would recognize his jacked-up turkey call anywhere. He never does it right," Jason said with a sarcastic grin. He then motioned for Kyle to follow along quietly. They crept along in the direction of the call. Once they got close, Jason heard a turkey gobble. He said aloud, but quietly, "You can't be a hen and a tom... pick one and stick with it."

"Just get your ass over here," Evan said softly, from a washed-out ravine.

Jason and Kyle crept over to Evan's voice, and to their surprise, found Evan, Quentin, and four other Blue Ridge Militia members hiding in the ravine. "It's about time you got here," Evan said, thankful his friend had made it. "You guys are armed now, great," he said, noticing their rifles.

"Yeah, the guys that had these didn't need 'em anymore," answered Jason. "So what's the plan?"

Quentin spoke up and said, "We've got to hike a few miles north until we cross a road. Then straight over the next hill from the road is where our ride should be waiting. Are you all good to go for the hump with those bare feet?"

"Hell, yeah, let's get out of here," answered Jason.

Quentin then looked down at Evan's tan suede boots and said, "Damn, man, you've got blood soaking through your boots."

Evan replied with a grimace on his face, "Yeah, it's starting to really suck... beats being dead, though. Let's move. The longer I sit here, the more it hurts."

Quentin looked around, and once he was sure everyone was ready, he said, "Lead the way, Matt," to the senior militia member on the scene.

Matt gave the order, "Q, you and the civilians hang in the middle, and I'll take point with Spears. Jacob and Fletcher, you bring up the rear. Once we get moving, no stopping unless forced to. We're in the homestretch."

Everyone nodded in the affirmative, and off they went. The group kept a loose tactical bound as they worked their way through the woods. It was still very quiet—almost creepy quiet with all of the animals being hunkered down and silent after the hailstorm of bullets that had ripped through the forest. As they neared the road, Jason, Quentin, and Kyle were all feeling the effects of the day's events on their bare feet. Quentin said, "Thank God. There's the road. We're almost there."

As they approached the road, Matt surveyed the area and determined that the road seemed to be clear. Matt stepped up onto the road, looked both ways, and as he turned around to give the signal for the group to advance, a shot rang out from the woods behind them, and the top of Matt's skull shattered, sending blood and brain matter spraying onto the road. His body dropped like a rag doll as Quentin yelled, "Move! Move! Move! Across the road and into the ditch!"

Jacob and Fletcher spun around and laid down suppressing fire to their rear while the rest of the group hustled across the road and into the large drainage ditch on the far side. They had approximately one hundred yards of cleared pasture to cross to get into the woods leading up the hill toward their rally point. Knowing that would be a suicide run, Quentin decided the best thing to do was take cover and fight.

Evan, Jason, and Quentin began firing from across the road, creating an opportunity for Jacob and Fletcher to dash across and join them. "I was sick of running, anyway," said Quentin in a pissed off voice. "If I'm gonna die today, it's gonna be fighting, not by getting shot in the back while I run away like a coward."

Evan and Jason looked at each other and gave a mutually understood nod, and then refocused on the threat across the road.

Evan looked at the three surviving militiamen who were there to rescue Quentin and them and said, "Gentlemen, thank you for this. Thank you for coming. Thank you for everything you've done to resist this encroachment into our land and our freedoms."

They each just nodded and got their eyes back on target across the road. They could hear a man shouting out orders in plain English, followed by a translator reissuing them in Russian. Clinching the pistol grip of his rifle, Quentin said, "That damn traitor is here." His brow tightened from the rage he felt deep inside. "Bring it!" he yelled toward the trees, where the enemy took cover while they formed up for an offensive.

Kyle spun around and began to look into the sky frantically as he heard the horrific *SWOOP, SWOOP, SWOOP* of a helicopter's main rotor. In a panicked voice, he said, "It's back! Holy crap, it's back! That damned helicopter is back!"

From around the corner, following the road, a helicopter roared onto the scene, opening fire with its machine gun. Evan, Jason, and the others covered their heads in anticipation of a barrage of hot lead being rained down upon them, only to realize—it was an Apache. The AH-64 Apache attack helicopter emptied its 30mm M230 chain gun into the tree line, annihilating the enemy soldiers. Chunks of bark and wood debris filled the air as trees were shredded by the powerful high-speed gun. As an unsurvivable hell was unleashed on the invaders, Evan and the others could barely believe their eyes. What was certain defeat mere seconds before was now an overwhelming victory.

As the Apache ceased fire and circled the area overhead, a voice called out from the hill to which they were headed, "Hot damn! That was some good shootin'!"

The men turned around and looked up at the hill to see a dozen members of the Blue Ridge Militia emerge from the trees and begin to walk across the field toward them, securing the scene. "Sorry it took so long, fellas, but the Apache wasn't easy to come by on such short notice."

Quentin hugged the man and said, "Brian, you have no idea how good it is to see you guys."

"I'll bet," he replied. "Sorry it took so long. We had a lot of details to get worked out, and our resources were scattered across the region. We had to pull it all together to make this happen. We're not set up for full-scale assaults. We've just been the eyes and ears until now."

"No problem, man. Is that the Apache from the Morrisville guard base you were talking about?"

"Yep," Brian replied. "It took some wheeling and dealing, but this bird and its crew are gonna be helping us out around here for a little while."

Quentin looked up, saw the Apache circle once more, and then it headed off in the direction of the farmhouse. "Where are they going now?"

"They're gonna clean the rest of the mess at the farmhouse and provide cover while we look for casualties and other survivors. Let's get you guys out of here, and we can go over the rest of the details later. We'll take care of everything here."

Chapter 37: Friendships through Fire

Evan opened his eyes and stretched, looking around the tent, hoping it wasn't just a dream. Jason was already up and going over some of the maps he had gotten from the militia guys when they arrived. Evan and Jason had accompanied Quentin to a mobile militia base at an undisclosed location, deep in the Blue Ridge Mountains. They had been there for two days and received medical attention, food, lodging, boots, and clothing. They also spent many hours being debriefed on what they had seen and learned along the way. Evan and Jason kept the AK-74s they had recovered during the escape and ensuing battle. They planned on holding on to them as reminders of what still might come their way, as well as tools to make their way home to their families as soon as they were healed up and ready to go.

"Nice to see you up, old man," Jason said as Evan sat up on his cot.

"Man, it feels good to get a good night's sleep after all we've gone through."

"Yeah, it does. How are your feet?"

Looking under the bandage wrap on his feet, Evan replied, "I may never ballroom dance again, but these ol' feet will always be ready to get me home. Some loose-fitting boots and a bunch of gauze, and I'll be fine. You got everything figured out over there?"

"Like you said, good enough. We need to get moving. If Nate and Ed, or even Charlie and Jimmy didn't make it back, we'll need to get hot on their trail tracking them down. We can't relax yet."

"Agreed," replied Evan as he joined Jason in looking at the chart.

As Evan and Jason sat in their tent, going over their plans, they heard Quentin say, "Knock knock," from outside the door.

"Come on in, man," Jason replied.

"How are you boys feeling?"

"Good enough," replied Evan.

"Good enough for what?"

"Good enough to be getting on our way soon."

Quentin scratched his chin and said, "Are you sure I can't talk you two into staying on with us? Kyle has decided to join us. Watching you two in action, I take it this wasn't your first rodeo, and we could definitely use guys that work well together, like yourselves. You clearly see the need."

"We've been through some... stuff... that's for sure," Evan replied. "And we do see the need, but we've got families and children back home. We also need to get back there to make sure the others from our group made it back safely. We started out with six; we sent two back early to help a young girl we stumbled across along the way. The other two were captured with us, and we haven't seen them since. Once we get home, if all of them haven't made it back, we'll be back out here to find them, and we will look you up for sure. But even if you don't see us back out here, rest assured, we will be keeping up the fight back in our neck of the woods. If you guys find yourselves in East Tennessee in a bind, or you just need a place to stay and resupply, send word to Del Rio, and we'll come running with everything we've got."

The End

To be continued in – The New Homefront, Volume 4

A Note from the Author

I just wanted to personally thank each and every one of you who have purchased and read *The New Homefront* series. These three books have been a labor of love and a great experience for me both personally and professionally. As I continue to develop the story and characters, I try to put in place the feelings and experiences that the average American might have in such a situation. I feel that although this exact scenario is merely one of myriad things that could happen to our great society, we all need to have the mindset that nothing in this world is certain, and nothing is guaranteed. Having the proper mindset during the onset of a world-changing situation, could mean the difference between our survival and our demise.

I would also like to personally thank everyone that has provided me with support and encouragement along the way, as well as the readers of Volumes 1 and 2 that provided online reviews and email feedback, which I used to help improve the reader's experience and the quality of Volume 3. Please follow me on Facebook at www.facebook.com/homefrontbooks and Twitter at @stevencbird. If you have specific questions or feedback, please send me an email to scbird@homefrontbooks.com.

Respectfully,

Steven C. Bird

Made in the USA
Middletown, DE
12 May 2016